Praise for the authors of
WHAT DREAMS MAY COME

Sherrilyn Kenyon

"A grand dame of the paranormal." —*Publishers Weekly*

"A wild, wicked delight . . . No one does sexy, tormented heroes better—or more inventively—than Sherrilyn Kenyon." —Nicole Jordan, bestselling author of *Ecstasy*

Rebecca York

"York delivers an exciting and suspenseful romance with paranormal themes that she gets just right . . . a howling good read." —*Booklist*

"A true master of intrigue." —*Rave Reviews*

"[Her] books deliver what they promise: excitement, mystery, romance." —*The Washington Post Book World*

Robin D. Owens

"Owens writes the kind of futuristic romance we've all been waiting to read . . . She provides a wonderful, gripping mix of passion, exotic futuristic settings, and edgy suspense. If you've been waiting for someone to do futuristic romance right, you're in luck, Robin D. Owens is the author for you." —Jayne Ann Krentz

"[Will] sweep readers into an unforgettable adventure with every delicious word, every breath, every beat of their hearts." —Deb Stover

What Dreams May Come

Sherrilyn Kenyon

Rebecca York   Robin D. Owens

BERKLEY SENSATION, NEW YORK

THE BERKLEY PUBLISHING GROUP
Published by the Penguin Group
Penguin Group (USA) Inc.
375 Hudson Street, New York, New York 10014, USA
Penguin Group (Canada), 90 Eglinton Avenue East, Suite 700, Toronto, Ontario M4P 2Y3, Canada
(a division of Pearson Penguin Canada Inc.)
Penguin Books Ltd., 80 Strand, London WC2R 0RL, England
Penguin Group Ireland, 25 St. Stephen's Green, Dublin 2, Ireland (a division of Penguin Books Ltd.)
Penguin Group (Australia), 250 Camberwell Road, Camberwell, Victoria 3124, Australia
(a division of Pearson Australia Group Pty. Ltd.)
Penguin Books India Pvt. Ltd., 11 Community Centre, Panchsheel Park, New Delhi—110 017, India
Penguin Group (NZ), Cnr. Airborne and Rosedale Roads, Albany, Auckland 1310, New Zealand
(a division of Pearson New Zealand Ltd.)
Penguin Books (South Africa) (Pty.) Ltd., 24 Sturdee Avenue, Rosebank, Johannesburg 2196,
South Africa

Penguin Books Ltd., Registered Offices: 80 Strand, London WC2R 0RL, England

This is a work of fiction. Names, characters, places, and incidents either are the product of the authors'
imagination or are used fictitiously, and any resemblance to actual persons, living or dead, business establishments, events, or locales is entirely coincidental. The publisher does not have any control over and
does not assume any responsibility for author or third-party websites or their content.

WHAT DREAMS MAY COME

A Berkley Sensation Book / published by arrangement with the authors

PRINTING HISTORY
Berkley Sensation trade paperback edition / July 2005
Berkley Sensation mass-market edition / July 2006

ISBN: 0-425-21085-5

BERKLEY SENSATION®
Berkley Sensation Books are published by The Berkley Publishing Group,
a division of Penguin Group (USA) Inc.,
375 Hudson Street, New York, New York 10014.
BERKLEY SENSATION is a registered trademark of Penguin Group (USA) Inc.
The "B" design is a trademark belonging to Penguin Group (USA) Inc.

PRINTED IN THE UNITED STATES OF AMERICA

10   9   8   7   6   5   4   3   2   1

Contents

Knightly Dreams

Sherrilyn Kenyon

One

"Well," Taryn Edwards said into her cell phone as she stood beside the road, watching the steady Dallas traffic pass by her broken-down car, "I would throw myself under the nearest bus, but considering my luck today, I'm sure it would break down less than a millimeter from me and just ruin my clothes. . . . Probably break my watch, too."

"You wear a Timex."

She snorted. "Trust me, today not even my Timex could take a licking and keep on ticking. Give me a Tonka truck and I'll squash it with my ink pen."

Janine's laughter echoed through the static. "Taryn, is it really *that* bad?"

Holding her cell phone in a tight grip, Taryn looked at her stalled-out Firebird, which was the prettiest, most expensive lawn ornament she'd ever purchased.

Of all the rotten luck, especially since all she wanted to do was get home and drown her woes in gallons of Ben & Jerry's Phish Food. "Considering the fact that I'm stuck out in this wretched heat wearing high heels with a black car that currently wouldn't go downhill with a hurricane pushing it, I'd say yes."

Janine laughed again. "Do you need me to come pick you up?"

"No. I appreciate the thought, but I have to wait on the tow truck, which seems to be the only thing moving slower than my DOA Firebird."

"Jeez," Janine said. "You are in a pissy mood."

That's because I just caught my boyfriend in his office with his secretary showing her a position I'm sure would qualify them for the Kama Sutra Hall of Fame. . . .

Pain sliced through Taryn's heart as she remembered the sight of them going at it on his desk. Unable to breathe for a moment, she wanted desperately to tell Janine the whole story, but the last thing she needed was to cry on the side of the road. Her dignity was all she had left, and she had no intention of giving Rob that last piece of her.

"Taryn, why don't we . . ."

All of a sudden the phone, much like her car, went dead. "Janine?"

Nothing.

Taryn tried to redial the number, but the static was so severe, she couldn't hear anything.

"Great," she mumbled, turning the phone off and glancing at the shopping center across the street. It would be a bit of a hike through screaming traffic, but at least it had a grocery store where she could grab something cold to drink and a few shops she could browse in to pass the time until the tow truck could get here.

And with any luck, a car or truck might plow into her and put her out of her misery.

Dodging traffic, she made her way over to the shopping center. Damn, she actually arrived without bodily injury. It really wasn't her day.

Disgusted by that, she headed for the grocery store, but as she drew near the entrance for it, she happened to see the small bookstore next door.

Taryn paused and frowned at the cozy-looking place. When had they opened that? She couldn't recall ever seeing it here before.

She stared up at the hand-painted sign: DAYDREAMS AND RAINBOWS.

How odd.

Well, thank God for small favors. A good book would cure her woes tonight almost as much as Ben & Jerry.

Heading inside the cheery store lined with bookshelves, she saw an elderly woman straightening the books on the wall to her right. There was something about the old woman that appeared youthful, almost sprite-like as she came off her ladder to greet Taryn. The woman moved with surprising agility. Her platinum gray hair was pulled back into a tight bun, and she wore a pair of faded blue jeans and a pink summer sweater.

The store smelled like musty old books, and there was a small café in a corner on the far left where a pot of coffee percolated.

"Welcome," the woman said, her brown eyes bright with friendship. "I'll bet you're looking for something to read."

For the first time that afternoon, Taryn smiled. "You must be psychic."

The woman laughed as she closed the distance between them. "Not really. You are in a bookstore, after all." She winked as she came to rest in front of Taryn. "So, what's your pleasure? Thrillers, science fiction . . ." The older woman tapped her chin as she studied Taryn. "No. *Romance.* You look like you need a good romance to read."

Taryn wrinkled her nose at the very thought. She'd given up reading romance novels a long time ago. She had buried that naive Cinderella-wanting-Prince-Charming part of herself in the closet along with her Barbie dolls, and other childish fantasies and beliefs. "To be honest, I don't read those."

The woman looked offended. "Why not?"

"One man, one woman. Happily-ever-after. Forever and ever . . . baloney."

The woman shook her head at her. "My name's Esther," she said, extending her hand.

"Taryn," she said as she shook a hand that felt like warm velvet in her palm.

Esther gave her a probing stare. "Now, tell me about this man who stole that dream from you."

Taryn had never been the kind of person to confide in anyone much, least of all a perfect stranger, and yet before she knew it, her entire history with Rob Carpenter came pouring out of her right down to the grittiest of details.

"It was horrible!" she said, taking a tissue from Esther to dab at her eyes as she continued to tell her the whole miserable event. "I believed in that snake and he lied to me."

Esther led her to a small table in the café area and made her a cup of coffee.

"So you see," Taryn said before she blew her nose, "he told me that I was the only woman for him. That he would love no one else. And then the next thing I knew, he was calling me by the wrong name when he answered the phone. Good giveaway, you know?" She sighed. "I should have known then, but I stupidly believed his lies and now . . ."

Again, she saw Rob and his secretary on the desk, their clothes scattered on the floor around them.

Taryn fisted her hand in her hair as pain, embarrassment, and grief assailed her anew. "How could I have been so stupid? How could he be so damned clichéd?"

Esther patted her hand. "It's all right, love, and I am so sorry, but you shouldn't base your opinion of all men on the actions of one thoughtless ass."

Taryn smiled at that, even though her heart was broken. "He *was* an ass."

"Of course he was. You're a beautiful young woman with your entire life before you. The last thing you need is to be so jaded. What you need is a good old-fashioned hero."

Taryn sighed dreamily at the thought as that buried part of her reared its ugly head. Whether she wanted to admit it or not, there was that tiny, infinitesimal part of her that still believed in fairy tales. At least, it wanted to. "Some knight in shining armor, come to sweep me off my feet. It does sound nice, doesn't it?"

"Yes, it does."

She watched while Esther got up and went to the shelves on her left. After a minute Esther came back with a book in her hand. "You need a champion, my dear, and I know just the man. Sparhawk the Brave, the fourth Earl of Ravensmoor."

Taryn studied the purple paperback where a handsome, bare-chested man with a sword grinned roguishly at her. The wind swept at his ebony hair, and his honest eyes were a deep, vibrant green. A wicked green that was tinged with a look of esoteric knowledge and intelligence, and they bore the glint of a man who knew his way around a woman's body. A man who would take his time and make sure he did the job right.

Oh, yeah, he was a major hottie.

His smile was devilish and there was something captivating about him. His arms bulged with strength and power, and he wore a gold, wolf-tipped torc that deepened the perfect tan of his skin.

He was striking and gorgeous, and the woman in her responded automatically to such overt masculinity. It might only be a drawing, but it was a damn good drawing. The kind that made a woman wish for one minute that she could find such perfection in the flesh.

At least for a night or two.

The title, *Knightly Dreams,* swept across the cover in gold foil, but the name of the author appeared to have been worn off.

Oddly enough there was no blurb on the back and she didn't recognize the publisher. *"Ma Souhait?"*

"They're an old publisher," Esther said. "Been around since before I was born."

"Really?"

"Oh, yes. You'll like it, trust me." Esther looked out the windows to where Taryn's Firebird was waiting. "Your tow truck is here. You'd better run."

Taryn pulled her wallet out.

Esther waved her hand at her. "Oh, pooh, dear, after the day you've had, consider it a gift."

"Are you sure?"

"Absolutely." Esther walked her to the door. "Good luck to you and Sparhawk. And remember, sometimes our dreams appear where and when we least expect it. Sometimes, just sometimes, you can even find them waiting in your own bed when you open your eyes."

Taryn arched a brow at the odd comment, but then Esther was quite a wonderfully eccentric character. "Thank you, Esther."

With Sparhawk in her hand, Taryn headed across the parking lot, then crossed the street and told the driver where to take her car.

Later that night, after she'd had a good cry over Rob, a pint of Phish Food, and a long geld-the-useless-bastard conversation with Janine, Taryn pulled out her book and decided to give Sparhawk a try.

And reading this book will help you how?

It was stupid, she knew that, and yet she couldn't seem to help herself from wanting to read the book and get Rob-the-Prickless-Bastard off her mind before she fell asleep.

She skimmed the first paragraph. .

The Earl of Ravensmoor was a hero like no other. Tall, powerful, and magnetic, he had wind-swept jet hair and a ruggedly handsome face that was neither pretty nor feminine. He was all male.

Rumor said he'd killed over a thousand men in battle, and as he walked through the crowded hall of bejeweled nobles with one masterful hand on his gilded sword hilt, his arrogant swagger bespoke of a man whose very presence had devastated over a thousand women. . . .

Taryn smiled at the image. Oh yeah, he definitely sounded like someone who could get Rob Dickhead off her mind.

She sighed as she read more about the wandering, rogue champion and his quest to claim his fair, if somewhat insipid, maiden. It was a pity they didn't make guys like this in modern-day America.

"Sparhawk," she whispered, smiling slightly, "I wish for two seconds that you were real."

Closing the book, Taryn laid it on her nightstand, turned out the light, and settled down to sleep. But as she lay there, all she could see was the last image she'd read of the hero.

A knight in armor on the back of his huge white stallion, riding into the forest to seek out the village enchantress . . .

Sparhawk dismounted halfway through the forest, his heart pounding in expectation. The brush was so thick, he knew from this point on he'd have to travel afoot.

Not that he minded. He would traverse the very fires of hell to escape that which he was sworn to.

Life with Alinor.

A shiver of revulsion went down his spine. He had to find some way to escape his fate, and if the town gossips were to be believed, the old witch in the woods should have some miracle that could save him.

He picked his way through the dense underbrush. No one ever ventured this deeply into the forest. No one except the Hag. This was her home and it kept her safe from any who would see her harmed.

As he walked, he felt an eerie presence. Almost as if the trees themselves were watching him.

But he feared not at all. Not this man who had stared down the heathens in Outremer. This man who had built his wealth on the strength of his sword arm and sweat of his brow. There was no ghoul or demon inhabiting these woods that was more dangerous than he.

Indeed, it was said that the devil himself was terrified of Sparhawk.

He walked forward until at last he found the earthen hut draped with twisted vines. The only sign of life from within was the flicker of a large, tallow candle.

More determined than before, Sparhawk knocked upon the vine-encrusted door. "Witch?" he called. "I mean you no harm. I come seeking your guidance and help."

After a brief pause the door slowly creaked open to reveal an old woman with long, silvery-gray hair. Her old brown eyes glowed with the vigor of a much younger soul, and her long gray hair fell loose about her frail shoulders.

"Milord," she greeted, opening the door to allow him entrance. "Come and be seated and tell me of this matter that has you venturing into my realm."

Sparhawk did as she bade him. He followed her into the small, cramped hut and took the seat she indicated by the window. He sat there for a few minutes to collect his thoughts. 'Twas the first time he'd told anyone of his problems with Alinor, and once he started to speak, all the sordid details came pouring out.

"So, you see," he said gently as the old woman handed him a strange black and bitter concoction she'd brewed by the fire. "'Tis not my duty I find offensive so much as milady's presence. I would give aught I own to have a lady who . . ." Sparhawk didn't finish the sentence. He couldn't.

What he wished for was something more fable than reality. No one married for love in this day and age.

No one.

Not that he knew anything of love anyway. He who had never known a kind touch. Never known what it felt like to be welcomed. He'd spent the whole of his life alone and aching.

His parents had died when he was scarce more than a babe, and he had been cast off first to his uncle, who despised his very presence, then squired to a man who thought nothing of him at all.

While other boys looked forward to trips home to their families, he had been left to muck out the stables and fetch for his lordly knight. He'd spent his holidays in a corner of the hall watching the families around him celebrating their gifts while he had nothing at all to call his own.

As a man, he'd carved out his destiny from the point of his sword and found plenty of women eager for his titles, wealth, and body, but none of them were ever eager for his heart. He'd found them all selfish and vain.

All he'd ever wanted was to see one face, either fair or foul, to light up when he entered a room. To find a pair of open arms to greet him when he returned and a pair of eyes to weep for him when he was gone.

But it was a foolish wish and well he knew it.

"I want out of this story," he said at last. "I cannot marry Alinor and live here with her another moment. I have seen my ending and it is a pale one indeed. Please, I beg you, tell me how to change this."

The old woman touched him lightly on the arm. "I can help you, milord."

"Can you?" he asked, noting the lack of enthusiasm in his voice. He doubted if even the saints above could aid him through this plight. But he hoped. He always had hope.

She nodded. "I shall send you to a world of many miracles. A world where anything is possible . . . A place where your ending isn't yet set."

Sparhawk held his breath. Dare he even hope for such? "At what cost?"

She smiled gently. "There is no cost, milord. What I do, I do for love."

"For love?"

"Aye. I know I am not to meddle, but every so often—it's rare mind you—but every once in a while there are special cases that call for special measures. And you, good Sparhawk, are just such a case. Have no fear, I won't see you suffer through this anymore."

Sparhawk offered her a smile. The villagers were wrong about this woman. She wasn't a witch. She was an angel.

"Have you a name that I may know so that I can say a prayer of thanks for you?"

She smiled kindly at him. "Aye. They call me Esther."

"Then I owe you much more than I can every repay, good Esther."

"But," she said, a note of warning in her voice, "what I give you is only a chance. My powers, such as they are, are limited. I can give you no more than seven days to work your miracle. If you cannot find love within that time, then you must return here and marry Alinor."

His stomach turned with the thought of it. Still, the woman before him offered him a chance, and the good Lord knew he had been given far worse odds than that and returned victorious.

"Then I shall work this miracle," he breathed. "No matter what it takes."

"Then drink, milord," she said, lifting his hand that held the cup. "And remember, sometimes our dreams appear where and when we least expect it. Sometimes, just sometimes, you can even find them waiting in your bed when you open your eyes."

Two

Sparhawk came awake with a start. His head pounded
from a severe ache as if he'd drunk far too much mead
the night before. By the light of the early morning sun,
he would judge the day to be just starting. The faint but-
ter rays spilled from the unshuttered window across the
wooden floor and onto the bed wherein he lay.

'Twas a bed he knew not at all.

Immensely large, with a light yellow blanket, the bed
easily accommodated his full six-foot-four height. As
well as that of the woman lying beside him.

Arching his brow, he studied her beautiful brown hair
that barely swept past her shoulders. It was thick with
strands of russet and honey laced liberally through the
darkness. She was not Alinor, but a new heroine for him
to pursue.

His lips curling into a smile, he felt a stab of desire

lance through his middle. What treasure was this to be found in this bed?

And truly she was a treasure, all warm and soft as she slumbered. Her long lashes resting gently on her cheeks, her rosy lips parted.

He reached out to touch the silken curls of her hair. The soft strands wrapped about his fingers, firing his blood instantly.

Who was she? And how had he happened into her bed?

He frowned as he struggled to recall what had happened. The last thing he could remember was leaving the witch's hut and coming face-to-face with a most angry Alinor.

Alinor.

He flinched at her name. He was supposed to marry her in a handful of days, and yet the very sound of her voice grated on his ears. Even though she was without a doubt the most beautiful woman on earth, the image of her face and form turned his stomach.

Cease! She is to be your lady-wife and you will honor her.

Aye, he would. Even if it be the death of him.

And quite frankly, he might one day cast himself off the nearest mountainside to be rid of her. It was quite an intriguing possibility.

But not nearly as intriguing as this stranger at his side.

This stranger with the small pixie face and dark brows that arched above eyes closed in sweet slumber. He slid his thumb over her rosy cheek that was softer than the king's down and touched the gentle petals of her lips.

She lacked the great beauty of Alinor, and yet something about her drew his notice anyway, letting him know that even as he lay here, his story was changing. He thanked the Lord for that. Finally he'd found something new.

And she was a fetching morsel. Her looks were earthy and sweet, not perfect and sharp like Alinor's. Before he could stop himself, he pulled back the blanket to better study her. And as his gaze roamed her partially clothed body, heat surged through him, straight to his groin, which ached with want of her.

By her clothes he would guess her to be a tavern maid of some sort, though the color and style of her garment was unlike anything he had ever seen before.

The short gown barely trailed past her hips and betrayed a pair of stunningly smooth and shapely legs. Legs he desperately wanted to sample with his lips. Legs he ached to feel wrapped around his hips as he made love to her slowly and completely until they were both well spent and fully sated.

Sucking in his breath in appreciation, he ran his palm down her outer thigh. His body grew even harder in response as the woman sighed in her sleep and shifted dreamily.

His heart stopped as the gown rose higher, betraying a tiny, thin covering that concealed the moist, female part of her.

Just who was this temptress?

Was she the one the old witch had told him of?

She must be. Only that would account for his presence here in this very strange place.

And as he watched her respond to his touch, he knew he wanted nothing more of Alinor and her mewling ways. He wanted this woman by his side with a ferocity that was as stunning as it was demanding.

Her and her lush, full curves so unlike Alinor's thin, frail frame. This woman's body was made to comfort a man on a cold winter's night. Aye, her high breasts would spill freely over his palms and her thighs were made for cradling a man's hips as he sank himself deep inside her body.

Hungry and aching, he slid his hand back up the curve of her thigh to the hem of the short, dark blue gown.

Taryn sighed from her hot dream of a hero larger than life. Of a man who controlled the world around him and made no apologies.

All night long she'd been dreaming of the handsome, dark stranger who had flashing green eyes and strong arms to hold her. He had whispered to her in a deep, evocative voice. Tormented her with images of his life and with a need to make his life better.

Sparhawk the Brave.

What a stupid name and yet . . .

Somehow it suited the hero of the story.

Even now in her dreams she could see his handsome face from the book's cover, feel his warm hand sliding down her outer thigh, then up the front of her leg. Her body rolling into his caress, urging him on as a fire and fever consumed her.

She held her breath as that hand moved to her waist, then higher. Over the curve of her stomach and up to her . . .

Her eyes flew open as someone touched her breast.

Screaming, Taryn jumped out of bed to see a tall man dressed in medieval clothing staring at her with one arched, arrogant brow.

"Who the hell are you!" she demanded, realizing too late she had jumped to the wrong side of the bed.

He was between her and the door.

Dear God, help her!

But he didn't make a move toward her. He merely watched her from the bed with a look that could only be called patience. His silver chain-mail suit shimmered in the light, and he wore a white surcoat that held a red crescent moon and a stag.

He looked just like . . .

Her head swam at the implication. It couldn't be. *It just could not be.*

"I am the Earl of Ravensmoor. And you are?"

"Totally freaking out," she said.

"'Tis a most peculiar name, milady. Are you by chance Welsh?"

Taryn struggled to catch her breath as she stared at the gorgeous man on her bed who talked with a deep, evocative English accent. A man who looked entirely too much like the hero on the cover of her book.

He even wore the same gold torc around his neck. . . .

What the hell was going on here?

In that moment she half expected to hear the theme from *The Twilight Zone* start playing and for Rod Serling to begin his spiel about dimensions.

"How did you get into my house?" she asked.

It was only then he moved from the bed. Like some languid, graceful predator coming out of a crouch, he approached her. His muscles literally rippled with movement as his mail suit rasped slightly with his steps. A wickedly warm smile toyed at the edges of his handsome lips as he tilted her chin to where he could stare down into her eyes.

The power of him overwhelmed her. He was massive and tall, and so incredibly gorgeous that all she really wanted to do was take a bite out of him. The manly scent of sandalwood and leather invaded her head, making her breathless and warm.

His fingers stayed against her jaw, raising chills over her as she looked into eyes so incredibly green they barely seemed real. Eyes that hypnotized her with the danger and intelligence they revealed about the man who possessed them.

He was being gentle with her, but there was no doubt he could be lethal. No doubt he had the strength to do with her as he pleased.

And yet he made no other move to touch her. He merely stared at her with a leashed hunger that burned her from the inside out.

When he spoke, the deep possessiveness of his voice actually sent a shiver through her. "In truth, milady, I know not. I only know that I am here to win you."

Win me? She frowned at his strange choice of words. "Win me how?"

"With whatever it takes."

Oh, yeah, this was weird. Had she hit her head on something? Was she still dreaming? Maybe she had a fever that was causing delusions. Early dementia? Taryn bit her lip as she tried to sort through this to come up with a plausible explanation for why this gorgeous piece of anachronistic male flesh was in her house and not trying to rape her.

Maybe this was just some hallucination brought on by too much stress and too much caffeine.

But the hand on her face felt too real and the man before her too commanding to be imagined.

"Look, Mr. Freaky Man, I don't know how you got in here, but you need to leave or I'm calling the cops."

"Cops?"

"Police. Bobbies. You know, *the law*."

He frowned at that. "I am the law, milady. I answer to no one save myself."

Oh, this was so *not* good.

He dipped his head down until his dark whiskers scraped her cheek, and he whispered in her ear. "Never fear me, little one," he breathed huskily. "You are my heroine and I have no intention of harming you. Ever."

"Then what do you intend to do?"

He pulled back and gave her a devilish grin. "I intend to woo you. To make you head over heels in love with me by week's end."

Nervous laughter bubbled up through her. This was just too bizarre for words.

"You don't believe me?" he asked with an arrogant look.

"Buddy, I don't know what to believe." She really didn't. "How did you get into my house anyway?"

He shrugged. "One moment I was in front of my . . ." His eyes turned sharp with anger as he hesitated. He cleared his throat. "I blinked and here I was."

"You blinked like Jeannie, right?"

"Jeannie?"

"Never mind."

He moved his fingers down her jaw, then laced them through her hair. And when he dipped his head toward hers, she quickly stepped out of his embrace and moved to the door. Halfway there, she stumbled to a standstill as her gaze caught the book on her nightstand.

Her dark knight with the sword was gone, and in his place was a blond guy holding a bouquet of flowers.

Nuh-uh!

Disbelief ran through her. It couldn't be. It just could not be. . . .

"Sparhawk?"

He cocked his head at her. "You know my name?"

"Okay," she said slowly. "I'm on drugs." It didn't really matter to her that she had never once taken any, but there seemed no other logical explanation. Esther must have slipped her a mickey in her coffee. Though why it had taken seventeen hours for it to work, she didn't know.

There just had to be some sane, logical reason why the stupidly named Sparhawk the Brave, Earl of Ravens-moor was here in his armor and she was losing her mind.

But there really wasn't one.

I need to call Esther.

If anyone knew what was going on, it would surely be her. After picking up the phone and dialing for information, Taryn quickly learned there was no listing for the store.

And honestly, it wasn't really a surprise. Somewhere deep in the back of her mind, she had figured as much.

Still, she felt the need to find out whatever she could. "Tell you what, I'm going to get dressed real fast and you and I are going to take a trip."

"Where?"

"To a little bookstore."

He frowned at her. "What is a bookstore?"

She rubbed her temple. "I guess they didn't have those in the Middle Ages, did they?"

"Middle Ages? Lady, you use very strange words."

She gave another nervous laugh. "Yeah, okay, let me not tarry," she said, using words she hoped he'd understand better. "I shall dress forthwith and hasten myself back to thee or thou or whatever it is."

If anything his frown increased, and as she headed for the bathroom, she could have sworn she heard him say, "She's a strange demoiselle, but a highly amusing one."

Sparhawk ventured from the room as he waited for Lady Totally Freaking Out to return. The witch had not been jesting when she said this world would be filled with strange marvels. There were plants inside containers that held no water or soil. Strange furniture covered in dark green fabric. Nothing in this woman's dwelling appeared even remotely familiar to him.

What was this place the witch had sent him to? Was it another planet perhaps? A world of sorcerers?

Perhaps he should fear for his immortal soul, but then, given the thought of returning to Alinor, even something that threatened his eternity had to be better than her cloying smile and lackluster wit.

As he poked at the plant that had a strange, unnatural texture to it, he felt a presence behind him. Turning his head, he froze. His new lady wore a strange short-sleeved tunic and a pair of breeches that had been shorn off high on her thighs. The sight of those long legs made him think of how soft her skin had felt in his palm and of how much better it would taste under his tongue.

He trailed his gaze over her lush curves to her face, where her pink cheeks told him his stare made her uncomfortable. He smiled at the knowledge.

Taryn couldn't move as she watched Sparhawk watch her. The man was so incredibly hot. His green eyes filled with heat and carnal knowledge. She knew what he was thinking, and quite honestly, she was thinking it, too. Imagine having *that* naked and spread out on her bed . . . over her body.

Yeah, boy!

He filled out that armor in the way she was sure medieval smiths had meant for it to be worn. His broad shoulders were thrown back with pride, and he bore the presence of a man confident in himself.

The man in him devastated the woman in her.

And it was then she realized she couldn't really take him into public wearing medieval armor. Not unless they were going to a Ren Faire. People might begin to ask questions she couldn't even begin to answer, and the last thing she needed was for this to turn into some bad low-budget B movie with the two of them ending up in a lab somewhere.

Or worse, an asylum.

While she stared, he crossed the room to stand before her. "Tell me, milady, where is your guardian?"

She frowned. "You mean my parents?"

"I mean whoever is responsible for your future."

"That would be me."

A puzzled look crossed his handsome features until they melted into one of amusement. "Truly? You answer only unto yourself?"

"Just like you."

He smiled at that, and before she realized what he intended, he captured her lips with his.

Taryn tensed for a moment, and started to step back, but his arms quickly surrounded her, drawing her closer to his heat as he opened her mouth and ravished it. There was no other word for the complete possession he took.

She'd been kissed plenty of times in her life, but never like this. Never with such heated intensity. His tongue coaxed hers, his lips demanding.

And the smell of him . . .

So manly. So warm. So sexual.

Rising up on her tiptoes, she moaned from the feel of him, wanting to draw him in deeper. To taste more of this incredible male.

Sparhawk growled at the passion in her caress as she wrapped her arms about him. She clung to him and met his kiss with a hunger that surprised him. Aye, she was a wild one. One who would bed him well, and he in turn would never leave her wanting more. Never leave until she was completely spent and satisfied.

In that moment he knew she was the one he would take as his own. He would never go back to Alinor.

Never.

He cupped her face in his hands and reluctantly pulled back. She kept her eyes closed as if savoring the moment.

He smiled.

When she opened her large, doe-like eyes and stared up at him, he felt a strange surge through him. It was raw and aching and it demanded her in a way that stunned him.

"That was nice," she said breathlessly.

He laughed. 'Twas the first time any woman had said that to him.

Taryn tried to regain her equilibrium, but it wasn't easy. Not when all she really wanted to do was step back into his arms and have her most wicked way with him. Worse was the little tiny voice in the back of her mind that kept saying having sex with a character from a romance novel didn't count anyway. Right?

She could do anything she wanted to with him, and no one would ever know. . . .

Oh, yeah, that could be fun.

"Okay, Spar . . ." She paused on his name. *Sparhawk* just sounded too ludicrous for words when spoken out loud.

What had the writer been thinking?

Oh, do me, great big Sparhawk. You the man. Taryn laughed in spite of herself. Nope, that name did not work in reality.

"What would you like me to call you?" she asked.

He cocked an arrogant brow at her. "You may call me Earl."

Taryn bit back another laugh. Yeah, right. That was probably the only thing worse than Sparhawk. And for some unholy reason the Dixie Chicks song *Goodbye Earl* started going through her head.

Oh, good grief!

"Okay, look, your majesty or grace or whatever, Earl and Sparhawk aren't going to cut it for the moment, okay?"

Somehow Sparhawk managed to look ever more regal and arched. "I beg your pardon? This from a woman called Totally Freaking Out?"

This was rapidly disintegrating into even more chaos and bizarreness. "My name isn't Totally Freaking Out. It's Taryn. Taryn Edwards."

He seemed to relax a bit. "Lady Taryn?"

"No, just Taryn."

"Very well, Taryn. You may call me Sparhawk."

Taryn bit her lip as she winced. "You know, big guy, I just can't really do that."

"Then call me milord," he said, totally missing her point.

Taryn took a deep breath. "Let me explain my world to you. If I call you milord and you call me milady, people are going to lock both of us up."

"In the stocks?"

"Sure. Um, so I need a name I can call you that won't make anyone look at us strangely." *Or make me laugh out loud every time I use it.*

"Since this is your world, mi—" He broke off his words as she cocked a brow. "Taryn. Tell me, what name should I use?"

Taryn stared at him for several minutes as she ran over the possibilities. He was too incredible to be something simple like Tom or Ken or Robert. He needed a more studly name.

Finally she settled on just shortening it. "How about just Hawk?"

Still a little ridiculous, but better.

He nodded. "Very well, Taryn. For you, I shall be known as Hawk."

A strange flutter shot through her at his words. *For you.* No doubt he had meant nothing special by them; still they warmed her.

"Now we have to do something about those clothes."

"You would change my name and my clothing, milady. Is there nothing about me you find acceptable?"

A hurt look flashed across his eyes so fast that she thought she might have imagined it. And it was then she remembered what she had read about him in the book. . . .

Alinor's words made his old wounds bleed anew.

He had cut his teeth on criticism and had long ago ceased holding any tolerance for it. No one needed to point out his shortcomings to him, for he knew each fault he possessed quite intimately as it had been pointed out with crystal clarity in his youth, under the violent tutelage of his lord.

If this was really the Sparhawk character come to life, then he would have had the same past as the Sparhawk in the book.

Her heart lurched at the thought. The man in the book had borne solitude and suffering the whole of his life. It was his pain that had kept her up late reading about him, her need to see him happy that had her turning page after page as she hoped Alinor would get a clue and realize what a great guy she had.

Taryn paused at the thought.

No, it's not real. He's not real. Sparhawk is a book knight. He can't come to life.

And yet . . .

"What happened to your parents?" she asked.

His eyes turned dull. "My mother died birthing my stillborn brother, and my father died of grief a few months later."

"Had you been worth anything, boy, your father wouldn't have damned himself to the devil by taking his own life to be rid of you. . . ."

Taryn flinched as she remembered the words Sparhawk's uncle had said when they delivered the frightened boy to his door. Barely eight, Sparhawk had dared to argue at his unfair treatment, and his uncle had struck him so hard, the cut from the man's ring had left a scar.

A scar on his left cheek, right below his eye.

A scar that would probably look just like the faint one Hawk had on his left cheek.

Her heart stopped.

"You were sent to live with your uncle when you were eight?" she asked, hoping he would deny it.

"How did you know that?"

Taryn felt ill. Taking deep breaths, she sat on the arm of her dark blue sofa. "Oh, boy," she breathed.

•

Her head swam from the possibilities. How could this be real? How could he have gotten into her world? How?

Hawk moved toward her, taking her arm. "Are you all right, Taryn? You look faint."

In all honesty, she felt faint. "I'm fine," she said, staring at the long tapered fingers grasping her arm. Fingers that were as flesh and bone as the man at her side.

"We need to see Esther." Oh, yeah, they really did. She had to have some real answers.

"Esther? The witch?"

"Pardon?"

"The witch who sent me here. Her name was Esther. Do you know of her?"

Taryn's eyes widened. "Little gray-haired woman with brown eyes?"

"Aye."

"*She* sent you here?"

He nodded.

Oh, that figured. "Did she happen to say why you were sent here?"

"I asked for it. I wanted a way to escape my impending doom with Alinor, and she told me that I would find myself in a miraculous world, which I have. But I don't know the script here, only that you are my heroine and that I should make you fall in love with me."

Oh . . . good . . . grief. "Why would you ask such a thing? Your world didn't seem so bad."

By the look on his face, she could tell he disagreed. "I have my reasons, milady. There are many unpleasantries at home that I would soonest avoid."

She could understand that. She had her own unpleasantries she'd like to avoid. Taking a deep, fortifying breath, she forced herself up and returned to the issue that had started it all. His clothes.

She had some of Rob's sweats that she'd borrowed one night when she had accidentally spilled Coke all over herself at his house. Though Rob wasn't nearly as large as Hawk, the sweats should stretch enough to at least be decent.

Ten minutes later after she'd given them to Hawk, she recanted that idea as Hawk came out of the bedroom wearing navy sweats that hugged a rump so prime she was amazed the USDA hadn't stamped it. And her XXL T-shirt was pulled taut over a chest so well-toned she could hire him out for a muscle magazine ad.

Worse, those sweats rode low on his lean hips, showing his six-pack of abs off to perfection.

Oh, mama, she wanted a bite of that.

And in that moment she wanted to thank the unknown author of his book. The woman was a goddess! And her taste in men should be applauded until the cows came home and tap-danced on the front lawn.

Sparhawk paused as he caught the heated stare of Taryn's large brown eyes. She never so much as blinked as she sized him up. He smiled from the knowledge.

Lust he could work with. It was indifference that would spell the end to his plans.

"Are my clothes appropriate?" he asked.

She nodded, blinked, then met his gaze. "What was that?"

He laughed. "I asked if my clothing was now acceptable to you."

"Mmm-hmmm," she said, the noise carrying her approval. "All we need are tennis shoes and we're in business."

He didn't ask. In truth, he feared the answer. Tennis shoes sounded almost painful. "I have my boots."

She shook her head. "No offense, chain-mail footwear and sweats just don't go together well."

"I'll take your word for it."

Taryn decided he was dressed enough to take to the bookstore anyway. Grabbing her keys from the kitchen counter, she led the way out of the house and showed him to her car in the driveway.

He walked toward it with a frown on his face. A frown that deepened considerably as another car drove by and he watched it with fear and curiosity warring on his face. "How do these things move with no horses?"

"They have engines which probably makes no sense whatsoever to you."

"'Tis one term I understand, milady. We had engines in my world as well."

"Really?"

"Aye, but nothing like this." He ran his hand over the top of her car as if marveling at it.

She smiled at the enthused look on his face, and something inside told her he was going to love riding in her rental car.

A wildly appreciative look came over his face as he took a seat on the passenger side and she started it.

Once they pulled out of the drive and started down the street, his eyes glowed like a child seeing the ocean for the very first time.

"'Tis like wings," he said, watching the scenery fly past. "This is incredible!"

"It's all right. Not as fast as my Firebird, though."

His eyes lit up even more. "You ride on a bird that flies faster than fire?"

"Not exactly. It's a car like this one, only cooler and faster." At least on the days when it ran. Laughing, she drove to the interstate and headed toward where she'd been yesterday.

Half an hour later they stood outside the vacant store where Esther's bookstore had been the day before. The windows were covered, and it looked as if nothing had been there for at least a year. There was no sign, no books. Nothing.

"This can't be," she said under her breath.

"What is it?"

"Yesterday the store was here."

He gave her a puzzled stare. "Are you in error?"

She shook her head. "No, I swear. I sat in there just yesterday and drank coffee while I talked to Esther, who said her book would help me. . . ."

It was unbelievable.

"So what does this mean?" Hawk asked.

Taryn shook her head. "I guess it means I need to teach you to read modern English. 'Cause, buddy, it looks like you're stuck here."

Sparhawk saw the disbelief in her eyes, and it was on the tip of his tongue to correct her. But he didn't.

She seemed too eager for him to leave. As had most people of his acquaintance. Mayhap if he could convince her to spend time with him, she could come to care for him, at least somewhat.

But then why would she when even your own kind can't tolerate you?

He squelched that voice. Surely the witch wouldn't have sent him here unless she believed it were possible to make this strange woman crave him in this story.

Holding on to that thought, he took Taryn's hand from the door and held it in his. "Tell me, milady, would being stuck with me be so terribly bad?"

Taryn wanted to say yes, but she couldn't. "I don't know, Hawk. I know nothing about you other than what I've read in my book."

"And I know nothing of you, my lady Taryn, other than you seem a decent and kind woman."

"Yeah." So decent and kind that her boyfriend tossed her over for a cheap thrill in his office. "C'mon, we need to get you some more clothes and some shoes."

She took him across the busy road to TJ Maxx so that they could start to outfit him. It was actually kind of fun since Hawk had no idea what was fashionable and what wasn't. He wore whatever she told him to, and hon, he looked damned good in jeans. When he came out of the dressing room, one woman actually walked into a rack of ties because she couldn't stop staring at him.

Not that Taryn blamed her. She was feeling rather giddy herself. Hawk didn't seem to notice the stir he was causing with other women. He only seemed to see her, which was really nice for a change.

"Do these fit correctly?" he asked.

Taryn bit her lip as she nodded impishly. "Oh, yeah, babe, those fit the way God and Calvin meant for jeans to fit a man."

"Calvin?"

"It's just an expression." She reached up to unbutton his collar so that the long-sleeved dark green shirt wouldn't choke him. The color of it made his eyes even more vibrant. Made his skin more tan, delectable.

It was all she could do not to shove him into the dressing room and rip those clothes off him for her viewing and fondling pleasure.

Really, no guy should be this hot and tempting.

Taryn sent him back in to undress while she went to pick out underwear and socks. When he returned to her, he was again dressed in his sweats with the clothes held in his arms.

Once they had those bought, Taryn took him to a sports store for shoes.

"You have the biggest feet," she said as they measured them. He really was a fourteen. "Good grief, they're earth pads."

"Are you mocking me?"

"Nope," she said with a grin. "Trust me, in my world those are a vital asset."

"How so?"

"Well, women equate foot size to . . ." She dropped her gaze to an area of his body that she had been curious about for hours now.

His eyes widened as he caught her meaning. "Milady!"

"I know, I'm wicked, but I can't help myself. Have you seen yourself in a mirror?"

He smiled at her as he rose to pull her toward him. He dipped his head down so that he could whisper in her ear. "Anytime my Lady Wicked wishes to appease her curiosity, I am a most willing supplicant." Those words sent a shiver over her as did the sensation of his hot breath against her neck.

Taryn closed her eyes as she inhaled the scent of him. It really was all she could do not to pull him flush to her body and kiss the daylights out of him.

"Don't tempt me," she said quietly. "We need to find earth-pad covers."

But before she could escape, he did place a very quick, very powerful kiss to her lips. Taryn melted. "You are too good to be true."

But then he wasn't. Not really.

Was he?

She pulled back with a frown. "How did you get here, Hawk?"

He let his fingers linger in her hair as he smiled down at her. "I asked the old witch for a miracle that would keep me from Alinor's clutches, and the witch sent me to you."

"How, though?"

"I know not. One moment I was there with Alinor screaming at me, and the next I awoke in your bed."

"Can you get home again?"

Sparhawk hesitated. If he didn't make Lady Taryn fall in love with him, the witch had said he would be forced back into his own story. That was the last thing he wanted. He'd had enough of Alinor all these past years. Truly, he would rather be dead than forced to woo her one more time.

"Nay," he lied, unwilling to think of his life in his own book. "I was sent here for you, Taryn. You needed a hero and I am here to be him."

On her face he saw the joy and the pain his words wrought.

"Do you not want me with you? Is there another hero you would prefer?"

She sighed. "It's not that exactly. I just don't know what to do with a man from the Middle Ages. I mean, it's not like you can work a job or anything. There's not much opportunity for a knight in shining armor in twenty-first-century America."

"Then you do want me to return to my book?"

She looked confused. "No . . . Yes . . . I don't know. I'm just not sure what I should be doing with you."

"What is it you want to do with me?"

Taryn swallowed at his question. The images in her mind were hot and wicked and wholly inappropriate while she was standing in a public place. "I don't know, Hawk," she answered truthfully.

"Then pretend that I am only here for seven days. Pretend that at week's end you will never have to see me again. That I would just go back whence I came. What would you do with me then?"

She smiled wistfully at that. "I'm not sure."

"Give me seven days of your time, Lady Taryn. Just seven. Then I swear to you that if you no longer wish for me to be near you, I shall vanish from you forever and return to my book to marry Alinor."

Taryn bit her lip at the wonderful idea. A hot boy-friend for seven days who wouldn't break her heart. Esther had been right; it was just what the doctor ordered. "All right, then. Seven days."

Moving away from him, she went to buy his shoes, then led him out of the store, to her car, and then back to her house.

It was so odd to have him with her after what had just happened with Rob, and yet there was some part of her that really enjoyed his company. Hawk doted on her in a way no man ever had.

He stayed by her side the entire afternoon and he was actually helping her cook dinner even though he didn't really have a clue about how to do the simplest thing. In fact, the electric can opener had completely mystified him.

At first he had thought it was possessed and had tried to kill it with her serving spoon. Finally she had convinced him that it was a good thing and had showed him how to use it.

She frowned as she tried to get the lid off her jar of spaghetti sauce.

"Here, my lady, allow me."

She handed it to Hawk, who immediately whisked it open.

"Thanks," she said, taking it back. So there was something he was really good at.

Hawk inclined his head before he went to the stove to examine the burners. "There's no fire and yet 'tis hot."

"It's electricity."

He turned his frown to her. "Electricity?"

Taryn tried to explain the concept, then realized she didn't really understand it herself. "It's magic," she said at last. "Cool magic."

"Hot magic more like," he said, replacing the pot. "You have a most remarkable world here in your book, Lady Taryn."

"This isn't a book. This is reality."

He looked puzzled by that. "Nay, milady. I am a character and you are a character. Our world is a book that is being written by another even as we speak. Our every action and every word is being carefully scripted."

"No," she said, trying to explain it to him. She went to her bookcase and pulled out a paperback. "These are books and this is reality. We're not in a book. We're in my house."

"Are you sure, Taryn? How do you know this isn't a book and that we're not just puppets being led about by someone else's whims?"

"Because I am a real, flesh-and-blood person. No one controls me. I control myself."

"And if you asked me that, I would say the same, so how do you know it is true?"

He had a very weird point that made her horribly uncomfortable. "Let's not do this, okay? I'm starting to feel like those people in *The Twilight Zone* who were trapped in the giant kid's toy town for his amusement." She shivered, then stopped. "If this is a book, then how is it everything here is crisp and clear? All the colors are vivid and the world is never ending."

"'Tis the same in my book."

That surprised her. She would have thought everything would be sketchy and vague. "Really?"

"Aye. There is nothing different in terms of tactical or sensory experience. Only the setting has changed."

Oh, that was just creepy.

He offered her a kind smile. "But I have to say that I much prefer your world to mine."

"Why is that?"

His green eyes burned her with their intensity. "Because you are in it."

She melted at those words. Damn, the man could be unreasonably charming at times. What was it about him that made her want him so? Was that magic, too?

She tried to imagine what it would be like to have a real-life modern-day Hawk. Would he be so enamored of her? Would she be so enamored of him? It was hard to know for sure.

Perhaps all of this was because he was a hero and not a real man. But then, what was *real*? Wasn't real something that could make her feel emotions? Wasn't it something she could see, taste, touch, smell, and hear? If that were true, then Hawk was every bit as real as Rob had been.

And that thought actually terrified her.

As soon as dinner was ready, she served him a plate of spaghetti, then took it to the dining room so that they could eat. Something that proved easier said than done. Hawk had no concept of how to eat with a fork.

He stared at it as if it were some alien creature.

"Don't you have forks?" she asked him.

"Nay, milady. I've never seen anything like this before."

"Oh." She took it from him and showed him how to wrap the angel hair pasta around the tines. He tried to lift it to his mouth, but it slid off the fork, into his lap.

Taryn forced herself not to laugh at him as she reached to pick it up, but the minute she touched him, she knew she'd made a mistake. As her hand brushed up against his body, she realized he was completely hard. His eyes flamed as he sucked his breath in sharply between his teeth.

Clearing his throat, he shot to his feet and moved

away from her. The spaghetti landed with a splat on her floor. "Forgive me, milady," he said as he stooped to clean it up. "I didn't mean to offend you."

"Offend me how?"

"With my, um . . . my untoward condition. I realize that you are a lady of proper virtue, and I apologize if I caused you any discomfort."

The only thing that caused her discomfort was his embarrassment. "It's okay, really," she said, helping him clean the floor. "I'm not offended."

He paused to look at her. "Nay?"

She shook her head. "I'm actually flattered."

Those green eyes turned dark, probing. "Are you?"

"Aye," she said, using his own language. She moved closer to him until they were almost touching. She could see the longing on his face. See the need he had for her. She felt it, too. It was hot and wicked. Demanding. And all it wanted was to taste this man in front of her.

Sparhawk wasn't prepared for her kiss. He growled at the taste of her as his body hardened even more. All day long his groin had been aching for her. It was all he could do not to force himself upon her, but he would never do such a thing. She was his heroine and as such deserved nothing but his utmost respect and admiration.

His head spun at the sweetness of her mouth and the scent of her hair that invaded his head. She clutched him to her as she ran her hands over his back, making him ache even more.

And then she did the most unexpected thing of all. She dipped her hand down into the waistband of his breeches. Sparhawk hissed as he felt her hot hand against his bare flesh. Chills ran the length of his body as her hand moved slowly over his hip to his waist.

"Taryn." He breathed her name like a prayer.

She kissed him deeply, sweeping her tongue against his as her fingers brushed against his hard cock. He clenched his hands in her hair and groaned as she touched him for the first time. Every part of his body shivered in bittersweet need.

Taryn's head swam at the feel of him in her hand. Her knight was a large man, and she melted at the thought of having him inside her. She brushed her fingers lower to the base of his shaft so that she could cup him in her hand. He growled deep in his throat as she gave a light squeeze.

Laughing in excitement of pleasing him, she nipped at his prickly chin. She'd never been the kind of woman who slept with a guy she just met, and yet she felt as if she knew him intimately. And in a weird way, she did. She knew more about his life from what she'd read than she'd ever known about Rob. More to the point, she knew the truth about Hawk, whereas Rob had filled her with lies.

Sparhawk couldn't think straight with her hand on him. In all his life he'd never had a woman so eager to bed him. Could it be his newfound lady might actually have a tenderness in her heart where he was concerned?

Dare he even hope it?

It was all he'd ever dreamed of. All he'd ever wanted. In all the battles he'd fought and in all the women he'd met, it was the thought of finding the one true heart who could love him that kept him going through his life.

She pulled her hand away before she whisked his shirt off over his head. "I know we shouldn't do this, Hawk," she whispered. "But I want you too much to just throw myself in a cold shower."

"I am yours to do with as you please."

She smiled at that. "Then come, milord champion, and let me please us both."

She stood up first and started for her bedchambers. Sparhawk took two long strides before he scooped her up in his arms and carried her to the bed.

Taryn laughed at his enthusiasm. It felt so good to be this desired. She couldn't remember any man ever being this excited to be with her. And definitely not a man who looked as fine as this one.

He placed her carefully on the bed before he joined her there. He gathered her into his arms and kissed her soundly.

She moaned at the taste and feel of all that delectable weight pressing against her. His entire body was on top of hers, and she reveled at the exquisiteness of it. His every muscle rippled under her hands. Desire burned through her, pooling itself into a deep thrumming need at the center of her body.

He pulled back to stare down at her as he slowly, carefully unbuttoned her shirt. He spread the fabric open, then frowned at the sight of her bra.

"What is this?" he asked, tracing the cup of it with his fingers.

"A bra." She showed him how to unsnap it from the front.

His eyes glowed as soon as she was exposed to him. "You are beautiful," he moaned, cupping her breast in his hand.

Taryn's entire body sizzled as he dipped his head to suckle her taut nipple. His mouth was hot and magical. His breath was scorching against her skin. Desire spread through her like liquid fire that wanted more and more of his touch.

She ran her hand down his hard back so that she could feel his muscles flex as he moved.

He was incredible.

Sparhawk took his time tasting the sweet morsel of her flesh. He nipped at her swollen peak before he pulled back to rub it gently with his whiskers. She shivered underneath him. He smiled in satisfaction, delighting in the way she reacted to his touch.

Taryn cradled him with her body. It was so good to have a man hold her again.

She trembled as he pulled her pants from her, then kissed his way up her body, all the way to her lips. She'd been right yesterday when she first saw his picture. He did know his way around a woman's body. This man had some serious skills.

Wanting to explore more of his talents, she peeled his jeans off his body so that she could feel every inch of that lush, masculine body against hers. His legs were dappled with dark hairs that tickled her skin.

Her heart pounded. She'd been hurt so badly in the past that a part of her couldn't help but wonder if Hawk would hurt her as well. But how could he?

Maybe all of this really was just some bizarre dream.

Maybe a bus had hit her after all and she was lying in a coma and this was her mind's way of holding on to life.

Or maybe he was real and she could find some way to keep him.

It was that last thought that was most appealing to her.

Sparhawk gently placed his body between her thighs. Closing his eyes, he savored the feel of her body beneath his. Of her crisp hairs teasing at his stomach.

She smiled up at him as she reached down between their bodies to find him. He held his breath as she closed her hand around him, then guided his cock, inch by slow inch, deep inside her.

He moaned at the sleek, wet heat of her body. No woman had ever sheathed him better. Gathering her into his arms, he held her close to his chest as he started moving against her.

Taryn moaned as pleasure tore through her as he started thrusting against her hips. Every stroke echoed through her body, filling and teasing her. It was the most incredible sensation she had ever known.

If she didn't know better, she'd swear he loved her. He held her like some precious object. His every stroke soothed and thrilled her. It reached that deep-seated ache that wanted only to have him fill her and ease it.

Taryn arched her back as her body exploded into pleasure.

Sparhawk growled as she came beneath him. She cried out, clutching at him. The sound of her pleasure drove him over the edge as he, too, found his own paradise.

He collapsed on top of her, letting the softness of her body soothe his. 'Twas the most miraculous feeling he'd ever known. He felt connected to her. A part of her.

It didn't make sense.

She sighed contentedly as she ran her hands over his back. "That was incredible."

"Aye, it was."

She laughed and then kissed him. Sparhawk nuzzled her neck so that he could inhale the sweetness of her scent. It was enough to almost make him grow hard again. He licked her tender skin, marveling at the texture of it. "I don't ever want to leave this bed, my lady Taryn."

"Me either," she said before she gave a light laugh. "But if we don't, it could get ugly after a few days. We'd shrivel up from lack of water."

"I can think of no better way to go."

"That makes two of us."

Sparhawk rolled to his side, then pulled her against him. She lay herself over him like a blanket and traced circles on his chest.

"Thank you, Lady Taryn."

"For what?"

"For making me feel like this."

Taryn smiled at that. No man had ever given her thanks for making love to him, and she found that she liked it. A lot. "My pleasure, Hawk. Anytime you need to feel this way again, just give a whistle."

He grinned at that, then whistled low.

She laughed again. "You are evil."

"Nay, my lady. I am only in awe of you."

Taryn crawled even more on top of him so that she could feel the whole length of his body under hers. If she could have one wish, it would be to stay like this forever. But she knew in her heart that they couldn't.

Sooner or later they would have to leave this bed.

And sooner or later they would have to part company. No doubt forever. She winced at the thought, but in her heart she knew it was true. She didn't know what "magic" had brought him here; however, this couldn't last. He was a character from a book. He could never be hers to keep and whatever had brought him here would most likely return him to his world.

Yet even the mere thought of it made her want to scream out in denial and injustice. How weird. She barely knew him and already she wanted to keep him.

If only she could . . .

Three

❧

The next four days were the best of Taryn's life. Hawk stayed at her house during the day while she worked, and every night when she came home, he was there with something special for her. One night he'd raided her rosebushes out back and had the entire house covered in roses and candles lit for her. It looked like something out of a movie. Or better yet, a dream.

He'd even learned to work the stove, and though his cooking left much to be desired, it was so sweet of him to try that she didn't even mind eating burned bread. In fact, she was developing a taste for "blackened" chicken and steak.

But more than that, she was developing a taste for whipped-cream-basted Hawk as they spent their nights naked and in her bed. There was nothing she loved more than lying in his arms while she explored every inch of him. He was funny and supportive, which for a man who had been a barbaric knight said something.

"Are all knights so gentle?" she'd asked him the night before.

"I know not, Taryn, since I don't make it my habit to lie abed with other knights."

She'd laughed at that while he stroked her hair.

"But to be honest, there is only so much battle a man can take. I think all of us crave a quieter life with a tender touch."

Taryn closed her eyes as he kissed her until her knees were weak from it. There was pure magic in his touch. Magic in his kiss. She pulled back to stare down at him while she straddled his hips. She had a sneaking suspicion that she was starting to fall in love with this man.

How could that be? How could she be in love with a character from a book? And yet all she could think of was him. The sound of his voice, the curve of his jaw, the masculine beauty of his face. He haunted her day and night. Called to her every time she left him. All she could think about at work was getting home to spend time with him alone.

It was spooky just how much of herself she had already given him and they had just met. He cupped her face in his hands. Taryn turned her face into his palm so that she could taste the salty-sweet flesh as she slowly lowered herself onto him.

Hawk groaned as she took him in all the way to his hilt. Smiling up at her, he arched his back as she started to move against him.

"I love being inside you, Lady Taryn."

She had to admit she liked feeling him so deep inside her. There was something special about this connection to him. He lowered his hands to her breasts, where he gently cupped her as he lifted his hips to drive himself even deeper inside her.

Taryn rode him slow and easy, reveling in the sensation of his thick fullness.

Sparhawk closed his eyes as he let her take complete control of their pleasure. He didn't know what it was about this woman, but she touched him in ways no one ever had before. In her arms he felt loved. Cared for. He lived only for the sight of her face, the touch of her hand. The thought of living without her . . .

He would rather be dead than even contemplate it. How could such a thing be possible?

He ran his hand over her taut nipples, letting them caress his palm. She hissed in response to his touch. Wanting to please her even more, he trailed his hand slowly from her breast, down the curve of her stomach, down to the moist dark curls at the juncture of her thighs.

His gaze locked with hers, he sank his thumb deep into the folds of her body to find her sensitive nub. She cried out in pleasure as he gently stroked her. Even better, she quickened her strokes against him, pulling him in deeper and deeper.

Taryn couldn't think with his hand on her. All she could do was feel him, his strokes, the depth of him inside her. She wanted satisfaction, and when she got it, she screamed in pleasure.

Her heart pounding, she fell forward, over him.

Sparhawk rolled with her in his arms, their bodies

still joined until he was on top of her. Her body continued to spasm around his. He drove himself in deep and quickened his strokes so that he could elongate her orgasm. She kissed him fiercely, her tongue spiking against his as she clawed at his back.

Delighted with her reaction, he thrust himself into her over and over again until his own body found its release. He growled in pleasure. She wrapped her body around his and held him close as they lay in the sweaty aftermath of their play.

Taryn drew a ragged breath as she waited for her body to calm. This was her favorite part of the night. The time after they were both spent and all she could hear was the sound of his breathing. Skin to skin, heartbeat to heartbeat. There was nothing else like it in the world.

With the smell of her champion enchanting her, she let the sound of his heartbeat lull her into sleep.

She woke in the morning, late for work. Sparhawk was still asleep. Unwilling to wake him, she took a minute to ogle the gorgeous backside that was completely bare. His dark tawny skin was a perfect contrast to her cream sheets. She smiled at the sight of his black hair tousled and the whiskers that darkened his cheeks.

"Do me, Sparhawk," she said under her breath with a short laugh.

It took every ounce of her self-control not to fondle him awake and have a quickie before she left. But she was already late. Pouting, she forced herself into the bathroom to get ready.

But the memory of him in her bed and the feel of his body against hers kept her company all day at work. And it had her rushing home to find him dressed in a dark blue shirt and jeans, waiting for her.

Tonight, they were going out. She'd gotten the idea the day before from one of her coworkers whose daughter had just had a birthday. It was something she was sure Hawk would enjoy . . . dinner at Medieval Times.

She greeted him with a quick kiss, then herded him out to the car so that they would get there in plenty of time.

"I do not understand the rush," Hawk said as he paused outside the car.

By the disappointed look on his face, she could tell what he was thinking. "We can't spend every second in the bedroom, babe."

"Why not?"

She laughed at him. "Are you sure you weren't in an erotic novel?"

He frowned at that. "What is that?"

"A book where they do nothing but have sex all the way through it."

His green eyes sparkled at that. "There is such a thing? Methinks I should have had another conversation with Esther and made my demands more clear. I feel I may have chosen poorly with our story."

Taryn rolled her eyes at him. "I keep telling you, this is not a story. You're a real man now."

"But I was real before."

Oh, he was never going to get it. To him the real world was every bit as real as his fictional one. And every time he insisted his world was real, she heard her mother's voice in her head. *"Put down the book and join the real world. There's more to life than words on a page, and I'm sick of watching you waste your time on such asinine things."*

As a girl, she'd been like Hawk and had believed that those places and people were as real as the ones around her. But her mother had finally worn her down, and over time Taryn had read less and less as she followed her mother's advice.

But the truth was, she enjoyed being with Hawk more than she had ever enjoyed anything else. If Hawk was right and this was a book, then she didn't want reality. She only wanted this man who was climbing into her Firebird.

Taryn got in and headed out of the driveway.

By the time they reached the "castle," she was practically giddy in expectation of Hawk's reaction to the restaurant. She'd always thought of the place as kind of cheesy, but after Rachel had talked about it and Taryn had seen the Web site, she knew she had to bring Hawk to it. She hoped he would feel at home here.

Once they were parked in the lot, Hawk looked suspiciously at the building that was fashioned to resemble a medieval castle, complete with banners hanging outside.

"What is this place?" he asked.

"It's a restaurant modeled on your time. I think you'll like it."

He didn't say much as she took his hand to lead him inside, but she could tell by his face that he was completely baffled by it. As they waited for the arena to be opened for seating, she took him to the gift shop, where he gravitated toward the wooden swords and shields.

"Bring back fond memories?" she asked. One of the things she'd learned about him was that his "memories" from the book were as real to him as her own past was to her. There really was no difference between fantasy and reality to Hawk.

He nodded. "We practiced with such when I was a squire." But it was the toy trebuchets that held his interest most.

"Would you like one?"

He shook his head. "Nay. I have seen more than my share of them."

She could see by the sadness in his eyes that it brought back unhappy memories. "You've spent much of your time at war, haven't you?"

"Aye. Too much. When I was younger, I never thought there could be anything better than the glory of battle."

"And now?"

His gaze met hers and the heat in those beautiful green eyes set her on fire. "Now I would much rather coax a smile from your face."

She laid her hand against his cheek before she gave him a quick kiss to tide them both over until later.

Wrapping her arm around his, she led him toward the arena and made sure to get them a seat right up front so that he could see the show in all its glory.

"What is this?" he asked as he looked around the staged medieval tournament field.

"While we eat, they're going to reenact knights fighting and practicing."

When their server came up in wench's garb, Hawk did a double take.

"This is all very strange," he said to her once they were alone again. "Familiar and yet not."

Taryn smiled and waited until the knights appeared. Hawk sat forward, his eyes alight with bemused interest.

She was actually thrilled to watch him. It reminded her of a child experiencing his first trip to the circus. "So what do you think?"

He gave her a smug look. "They are most skilled, but I could defeat them."

She laughed at his arrogance, not doubting his abilities in the least.

Taryn was enjoying the show immensely until something went terribly wrong during one of their fight scenes. One of the special effects was a blast of fire that shot too close to one of the horses. The red knight's horse threw its rider and began to run wildly about, shrieking and spooking the other horses. As the red knight stood up, the horse charged him, then dodged before it made contact to run at the barrier wall. The crowd started screaming, which only added to the chaos as the horse reared too close to the wall. Its hooves came dangerously close to the metal barrier.

The red knight tried to catch his horse, only to have it rush at him and trample him.

Taryn cringed. "I think he's hurt. Bad."

Before she realized what was happening, Hawk vaulted over the side of the arena and ran toward the panicking horse. Taryn came to her feet, terrified of what he was about to do.

The horse pawed at him while the staff shouted for him to get back into the stands. Hawk didn't listen. He dodged the horse's flailing hooves and in a move that was poetic and beautiful, he whirled himself into the saddle.

Taryn watched in awe as he took the reins and then carefully brought the animal back under control while the other knights ran to the red knight to make sure he was okay.

Hawk slid from the back of the horse and patted it gently while talking to it in a slow and calm voice.

A man in a black T-shirt and jeans, who must be the horse's trainer, came out to take the horse away. He said something to Hawk before Hawk inclined his head.

"Our champion!" the king said from his dais, indicating Hawk with a grand extension of his hand. "Truly, he is a marvel. We thank thee, gracious knight."

Hawk turned toward the king and placed his right fist to his left shoulder before he bowed regally. "'Tis an honor to be of service, Your Majesty," he said in a tone that sounded as if he enjoyed playing along with them. Then he ran at the wall and did a flip over it to land just before Taryn.

"Wow," she said, amazed by his ability. "Most impressive."

He shrugged. "Thank you, but it's more impressive in a full suit of armor." He winked at her.

Taryn laughed while the staff cleared the arena and then picked up the show where it had left off.

A few minutes later the man in black came up to them. "Hey," he said, taking the vacant seat next to

Taryn. "I just wanted to say thanks for what you did. This was Goliath's first show, and I hate that he got spooked."

"I am just glad that I was able to help," Hawk said.

"You're English?"

"Aye."

The man smiled as he extended his hand to Hawk. "I'm Danny Fairfield."

He shook his hand. "Hawk."

Danny laughed. "So do you do reenactments?"

"All the time," Taryn said. "He can joust with the best of them."

"Really?" Danny looked extremely interested in that tidbit.

"I've trained many a man and squire for battle."

"Well, hey, anytime you want to audition for a position here, just give me a call. We're always on the lookout for new talent."

"Thank you," Hawk said.

Danny got up and paused between them. "By the way, dinner's on us tonight."

"Cool," Taryn said. "We appreciate it."

Danny inclined his head and left them alone. But as he walked away, Taryn's mind whirled.

Hawk could get a job. . . .

"Is something wrong, Taryn?"

She shook her head at Hawk. "No. I was just thinking that we might have found something you are more than qualified to do."

"Is this a good thing?"

"Oh, yeah," she said excitedly. "It means if you were to stay here that you would have a job."

"Do you want me to stay?" he asked with a note of hope in his tone.

Taryn stared at him for a full heartbeat. How could she not want this man to become a permanent part of her world? "Yeah, I think I do."

Sparhawk's heart pounded at that. It was the first time Taryn had said anything about him staying longer than his seven days. It was a good sign. A very good one.

But she still said nothing about love, and there were only three more days before he returned to Alinor. It was the last thing he wanted. These last few days with Taryn had been wonderful. Magical. What would he do without her?

In truth, he didn't want to know.

They didn't speak much during the rest of the meal and once it was over, they returned to Taryn's house.

As they entered the living room, something odd started to happen. Hawk's skin turned grayish.

He looked as if he were completely ill. "What is happening?" he asked.

"I don't know." Taryn helped him toward her couch. He was writhing as if he were in pain. She put her hand on his brow to feel a severe fever. "Baby, are you okay?"

Holding his stomach as if something were rupturing, he grimaced and cursed.

Suddenly her hand passed right through him. "Hawk?"

He looked at her with panic in his eyes. It was as if he were fading out of existence.

"Hawk?"

The next thing she knew, he was gone. There wasn't even a scrap of fabric left behind.

"No!" Taryn screamed as she found herself completely alone in her living room. "You said we had seven days."

Come back to me.

The words whispered through her head as if Sparhawk had said them.

"How?" she asked out loud.

There was no answer. None. He was gone now. Taryn sat there in stunned disbelief as pain washed over her. How could he be gone like this?

Sparhawk jolted awake to find himself back in his own bed. It was early light by the looks of it. Rolling over on the large hand-carved mahogany bed, he found himself face-to-face with Alinor, who stared at him as if she wanted to run him through with his sword.

"Good," she said, narrowing her gaze on him. "You're back, milord."

"There is nothing good about this," he grumbled, getting up. He had to find the witch and return to Taryn. He hadn't had enough time with her.

Alinor blocked his way to the door. "Where is it you go?"

"'Tis none of your business. Now stand aside."

She lifted her chin defiantly as she held her arms out. "Nay! I most certainly will not. Nor will you leave this castle again. You are my hero, Sparhawk. Mine. You don't belong in that other story with that other woman. Taryn. What sort of name is that anyway? 'Tis a man's name and yet you would sooner be with her than me? I will not allow such."

Sparhawk went cold at her words. "How do you know about Taryn?"

She stamped her foot at him. "Because you cheated!" She threw a book at him.

"Ow!" Sparhawk said as he picked it up. It was the original book of his story, only now it had Alinor's name listed as the author. "What did you do?"

"Me?" She snorted at him. "You're the one who changed it first. I was minding my own business, doing what I was supposed to be doing when you decided to go off and change our lives. Well, I'm not having it. I was supposed to be the damsel you grew to love and you are supposed to be my champion, so now I have created a new master book."

He couldn't breathe as her words sank in. If she had created her own version of their lives, there was nothing he could do to alter it. God help him if she really were the author. "Where is the master book?"

She gave him an arrogant, taunting smile. "Someplace *you* can't find it. But don't worry, I'm writing the story now and we're going to be just fine, you and I. We're going to have lots of children and castles all over Christendom. We'll be the envy of everyone."

It was a nightmare even to contemplate. "I do not love you, Alinor. I love Taryn."

She shrieked at him. "You are going to love me, Sparhawk! You're *my* hero! I know you're resisting it right now because that's what heroes do. But you will settle into this role just as soon as I finish shopping for my wedding clothes. You just wait here and be thoughtful for a bit while I attend my role like a good character."

Sparhawk gaped as she spun about and left the room. Taking three steps, he opened the heavy wooden door. "I will not stay here, Alinor!" he shouted out the door after her.

She paused halfway down to the hall to look back at him with smug satisfaction beaming on her beautiful face. "Oh, yes, you will. I wrote the old witch out of the book entirely, so even if you go into the woods, all you'll find now is a creek that goes nowhere."

Sparhawk slammed the door, then opened it again immediately. He wasn't about to take her word for what was happening. He wasn't going to blithely submit to this storyline. He was Sparhawk the Brave. The king's champion. No one was going to take charge of his life without a fight.

Sprinting through the castle, he ran out to the stable to find his horse waiting for him. He saddled his stallion, then headed back toward the witch's hut.

Only this time, just as Alinor had predicted, there was nothing there but a creek, with large overgrown trees surrounding it. No sign of the hut or witch existed anywhere.

"Damn you, Alinor!" he shouted at the sky above. "I love Taryn."

But there was no one to hear him. Taryn was gone and now it was his fate to marry Alinor again. Heartsick and weary, he wheeled his horse about and headed back to the castle.

Tears gathered in his eyes, but he refused to let them fall. There had to be some way out of this. Some way to reach Taryn again. He couldn't give up, not on his lady.

By the time he reached the castle's gate, he'd decided on a new course of action. He had to find Alinor's master copy of the book. If he did, then there was a chance he could change it as Alinor had done, so that he could return to Taryn and her story.

If not, then he was doomed to stay here forever.

Taryn sat on her bed with voices speaking in her head. She swore she could hear Sparhawk's deep baritone and another woman she'd never met before. The voice was high pitched and whiny. Shrill. It went through her head like shattering glass.

Alinor?

It was eerie what was going on in her head. She could see Sparhawk searching the castle in her mind like a movie. She could feel his despair and his pain as he ached for her and sought his book. Every thought, every emotion he felt, was in her, too. It was as if she was experiencing it with him.

"I'm completely losing my mind."

"No, dear, you're not."

Taryn turned sharply at the old voice behind her. It was Esther. "What are you doing in my house?"

Esther sighed as she came farther into the room to sit beside her. "I'm breaking all kinds of rules . . . again. I'm not supposed to be here, but then I wasn't supposed to be there in the store, either, when your car broke down, but I had no choice. I still don't. I have to make this right before it's too late."

"Make what right?"

Esther smiled at her. "Your happy ending."

Taryn rubbed her head as a severe pain started in her right temple. This was it. She had lost her mind. There was nothing more to be done about it. Maybe she should call the psycho ward now.

"You're not crazy," Esther said quietly. "Please don't even think it. We lose enough of you to that as it is."

"Enough of who you?"

"Writers," Esther said simply. "For some reason, a lot of you reject what you hear and see in your heads. If you go too long ignoring it, it builds up and then you do all sorts of weird things. Mumble to yourself. Nightmares. Daydreams. Total anarchy and chaos. Before you know it, the writer is either sitting in a corner feverishly humming to his- or herself or on Prozac." She hesitated. "You're not on Prozac, are you?"

No, but she was beginning to think she ought to be.

Taryn frowned at her and completely disregarded everything she was saying. "How did you get into my house anyway?"

"The front door. You left it unlocked."

No, she hadn't. However, she wasn't about to argue. "How did you know where I lived?"

"I know where all good writers live."

The ache increased. "I'm not a writer," Taryn insisted. "I've never been one."

Esther patted her hand in an extremely patronizing manner. "That's what Hemingway said, too, when I sent him *A Farewell to Arms,* and then look at what he went on to do."

Okay, they were both nuts. But insanity aside, there

was only one matter that was weighing heavily on her. "Can you get me back to Sparhawk?"

Esther sighed heavily. "No."

Tears welled in Taryn's eyes as she heard the last word she needed to. She didn't even want to think about not seeing him again.

Esther leaned forward and spoke in a low tone. "But *you* can."

Taryn swallowed as hope began to swell inside her. "What do you mean I can? If I could, don't you think I'd be there?"

"Hon, you already are. Why do you think you can hear him in your head right now?"

"Because I've gone insane."

Esther laughed and shook her head. "No, sweetie. You hear him because *you're* a writer."

Here we go again.

"I don't have time—"

"Remember a few weeks ago, when you had that strange dream about a man lost in the woods?" Esther asked, interrupting her denial.

Taryn snapped her mouth shut. That dream had haunted her for days as she tried to figure out what it meant. She hadn't told a soul about it. Not even Janice.

"How do you know about that?" she asked the old woman.

Esther shrugged as if it were nothing unusual. "I'm the one who sent that dream to you. I'm the repository for romance novels."

"The what?"

"Repository," Esther said in a patient voice. "There

are several dozen of us and we are the keepers of books written and those yet to be written."

Taryn was about to reach for the phone to call the cops when her room suddenly changed from her bedroom to what appeared to be a giant library.

Her heart hammering, she looked about at the glistening shelves that were covered with thousands and thousands of leather-bound books as far as her eyes could see. It was the most incredible thing she'd ever heard of. "I have totally snapped a wheel."

"No, dear. I knew you wouldn't believe it unless you saw it yourself." Esther, who was now dressed in a glowing red robe, walked down a row of shelves, dragging her finger lovingly along the edge of the carved wood. It was obvious the old woman loved every volume in the room.

"Where is this place?" Taryn asked.

"Let's just say it's 'other.' There's no place like it on Earth . . . exactly."

Esther walked over to the shelf on her right and swept her hand across the spines that held no author name whatsoever. "These are all the books that have yet to be written. Each one is a very special creation, and I am one of the overseers who is charged with making sure that the people who live inside the books get to the writer who can birth them properly." She pinned Taryn with a dark stare. "You were destined to be a writer, Taryn, but you have gone astray. Do you remember when you were a girl and you wrote all the time about all the people who talked to you whenever you closed your eyes?"

"Yeah," she said defensively, "and my mother told me

to get my head out of the clouds and focus on what was important."

Esther sighed. "I hate it when that happens. We lose so many wonderful stories that way. 'Be practical. Stop listening to the characters who only want to live.' It's why we have people like Sparhawk, and it's why we end up losing them, too. Such a tragedy, really."

Taryn frowned at her words. "What do you mean, losing them, too?"

Esther indicated a steel vaulted door that was on the wall behind Taryn. "That is the Valley of Lost Souls. It's where we send the books whose characters have revolted."

"Revolted?"

She nodded. "You see the characters for the books that haven't yet been written are in a holding pattern while they wait for their stories to be finished. We, the repositories, send out an idea, usually the first chapter or a snippet from later in the book, to the writer. It plays over and over again in the writer's head until the writer is forced to sit down to write it. If the writer fails to follow the idea and commit it to paper, then the characters can get caught in a loop where they relive the same scenes over and over again, sometimes with only minor changes until they essentially go mad from the monotony. Then they can get a little cranky and revolt against the writer and us."

Esther shivered as if the very mention of it horrified her. "So whenever we sense that is happening, we pull the characters out of that writer's mind, then send them on to another writer where the process repeats until someone finally pens the story of their lives."

Taryn stared at all the volumes of "unwritten" books. "I don't understand. Where do all these ideas come from?"

Esther shrugged as she glanced over the infinity of books. "They are gifts from the universe to mankind. Honestly, we don't know where they come from. They just appear on the shelves, and we are charged with bringing them to life. It's kind of like a child being born. Where does his or her soul come from? Some call it God, others fate, whatever you believe or want to call it, it sends the books to us. Our personal theory is that a baby's soul and a character's soul are born from the same place. Some are destined to be living, breathing people in the flesh, and the others are living, breathing people on paper."

Esther picked up a book off the shelf closest to her and handed it to Taryn.

Just like the copy of *Knightly Dreams* Esther had given her in the store, there was no author listed. The cover showed a dark-haired Regency rake holding on to a scantily clad blond woman. "This book has been sent out over and over again these last few years. The first writer decided she didn't want to do romances and went on to write mysteries instead. The next one was all excited to write it until she got married. Another one got all the way to the middle of the book before she got rejected one time too many and decided she couldn't take the rejections anymore. She quit and burned what she'd written. The last writer we sent it to finished the first three chapters, but has since become distracted by a rumor that no one wants to read historical romances anymore. So she has set the book aside to write something she thinks is more marketable."

Esther sighed as if her heart were broken. "All we have now are the first three chapters and they repeat over and over again. The characters are in London, in the Regency period, where they attend the same party and speak the same lines ad nauseam. Miles is a rake, but he, like Sparhawk is tired of listening to Henrietta rant about her season and her boorish uncle out to steal her inheritance. If the writer doesn't return soon, then I shall have to send this off to another to write before we lose the characters completely."

"Lose them how?"

Esther took the book back and held it lovingly in her arms. "They essentially start writing the story themselves and refuse to take orders from a writer. If we have a strong enough writer who loves them, then she can save them. If there is no writer, then they can no longer be corralled and the story falls apart. You have medieval knights abducting Regency governesses, dogs sleeping with chickens. Chaos. Total chaos. The story is then lost for all time, and we are forced to place the book in that room." She indicated the vault again. "It's truly tragic. The greatest book of all time is in there now because the author who was destined to write it thought he was losing his mind when he started hearing the characters talking to him. He's now on Prozac, living in an isolated cabin in Montana."

Taryn was still confused by all of this. "Are you telling me that Sparhawk isn't real?"

"Oh, no," she said sincerely. "They're *all* real. All of them. Just like you or I, only they live in their own world that is apart from ours. I allowed Sparhawk to cross over from his world into yours in a more tangible form so that he could win you. I knew that if you didn't fall absolutely head over heels in love with him that you wouldn't save him, and if he had to go back on the shelf one more time, he would rebel and take over his book so that no one would ever be able to finish it. Now it appears that Alinor has rebelled instead of him and threatened the whole thing."

Esther handed her a copy of *Knightly Dreams*. Sparhawk was again on the cover, just as he'd been originally. Only now the author's name read Alinor de Blakely.

Taryn ran her hand over the embossed letters. "How can she do this?"

"Alinor has found the original copy and has taken it over. She wanted Sparhawk back and so she has written his return." Esther opened the book to show her the parts that now held her name on the pages.

Taryn's heart stilled as she saw her life laid out in ink. It was horrifying. "This can't be."

"Yes, hon, it can and it is." Esther turned to the last page of the book, where it showed Alinor marrying Sparhawk.

Taryn's heart sank. The book was over and she wasn't mentioned at the end.

"Don't despair," Esther said quickly. "Notice there is room on the page and if you turn to the last page of the book, it's completely blank."

"Most books are like that."

"Yes, but not all. Those with no blank pages are the ones that are completely finished. There is nothing more to be done with them. But books like this one, where they have blank pages, can still be added to."

A glimmer of hope went through Taryn. "What exactly are you saying?"

Esther handed her a pen that appeared out of thin air. "I'm saying that you can alter Alinor's book and make it your own. We are all the authors of our own lives, Taryn. We make the rules of our world, and we are the ones who decide which road to take. It's all up to you and you alone. This story ends the way you want it to. But only if you have the courage and the imagination to see it through."

It sounded too good to be true. Too easy. "But it won't be a published book."

Esther held her hand out to indicate all the books around them. "Only a small percentage of all books written ever get published, dearest. Many more stay in the hearts, minds, and closets of their authors forever after they are committed to paper. They are there solely for the author's pleasure and benefit alone. But more importantly, they are there for the characters because until they are on paper, the characters aren't truly alive. Every author owes it to her people to birth them as best as he or she can."

Esther urged her toward a table that also appeared out of thin air. "Sparhawk the Brave is in desperate need of a champion of his own. Someone who can save him from certain death and torment. Otherwise he will spend eternity with Alinor lost in the vault."

Taryn knew from the short time they had been together just how much Sparhawk hated the thought of being stuck with Alinor. Esther was right. It would kill him.

If what she said could be believed, then Taryn was his only hope. . . .

Esther gave her a hopeful look. "So what's it to be, Taryn?"

four

✥

Taryn was still confused even after Esther had dropped her back into her home. Then again, who wouldn't be confused being dropped in and out of places? She still wasn't completely sure she wasn't in the middle of some psychotic episode. Her entire concept of reality was completely altered now. Maybe she *was* in a book.

Maybe nothing was real.

No, she thought as she pinched herself for the eighth time. She was real. This was her house. Her life. And there for a time, Hawk had shared it all with her.

Now, as she lay on her bed with the paperback that had Sparhawk on the cover, her mind drifted through the last few days—something that was easy to do since everything they had shared was there in black-and-white. Everything. Every time they had made love, every

meal, every line. It even had her in the library or whatever that place had been.

It was so odd to see her name on the pages, to read in
the book what the two of them had done.

But even scarier than the passages with her in them
were the ones where she was off in her own world and
Hawk was in his. Alone. Those were horrible scenes
with Hawk being wounded and tortured for no apparent
reason. Perhaps it was Alinor's way of getting back at
him for his having escaped in the first place.

She didn't know. All she knew was that she didn't
want him to suffer any more than she wanted to face the
rest of her life without him. He'd been wonderful.

God help her, but he really had been her hero and she
wanted him back.

"I have to save him," she whispered as she read one
particularly painful page where he was gored by a wild
boar in the woods while saving Alinor from pygmy
bandits. . . . Pygmy bandits? Ay! If Alinor really was
writing this, she had lost her mind completely.

Taryn sat up with the book. "Okay, let's pretend that
I'm not hallucinating and that everything Esther has told
me is the truth. . . ."

Then she could save him. She laughed in spite of herself. This had to be the most ludicrous thing she'd ever
done. But what the heck? What did she really have to
lose?

"Either I'll get him back or they'll lock me up," she
said under her breath as she grabbed the pen. "Okay, Esther. Here goes nothing."

Closing her eyes, Taryn conjured up a picture of

Sparhawk in her mind as he was on page 342 in the book, just after his return to his world.

He should be alone, sitting at the table with his head in his hands. The chapter ended there, but there was blank space at the end of the paragraph. . . .

Taryn opened her heart and listened carefully until she could see and hear Hawk clearly. Her chest tight in fear of failing, she started writing. . . .

Sparhawk sat in his hall, completely bereft of hope. Alinor had hidden the master book so well that he had no idea where it might be. There was no way back to Taryn. No way to get out of this so long as Alinor had control of their story.

Damn her for this! How could she be so selfish? But then, that was what had caused him to want to escape her clutches to begin with.

"I miss you, Lady Taryn," he breathed.

"I missed you, too."

Sparhawk shot to his feet as he heard the tender voice behind him. It couldn't be, and yet as he turned, he saw his lady there, watching him with a guarded expression. Her smile was gentle as she looked up at him.

"Wow," she said, looking around his hall. "It really worked."

He couldn't believe what he was seeing. Was it possible? "How is it that you are here?"

Taryn held the book up in her hand, and this time the author's name on the cover was hers. "I'm making some changes in how the story goes."

He frowned. "What?"

She drew near him. "Esther said that I was supposed to be the writer of your book, so here I am . . . writing for the first time since I was a kid. It's actually kind of fun. Did you know Alinor is off shopping?"

"'Tis what she told me."

"Yeah, but she has tacky taste in jewelry," Taryn said as she made a note in the book. "But that's okay. The jeweler is about to look a lot like my ex-boyfriend. In fact, I'm thinking Rob really should end up with Alinor. She's demanding and beastly. They should be quite happy together, especially after I give Rob some very choice moles in awkward locations." She wagged her brows at him.

Hawk shook his head at her. "And what about me?"

Taryn sat down at the table where he'd been and started writing. One minute they were in his castle, and in the next they were back at her house, naked in her bed.

Hawk frowned at her. "I don't understand this."

"Neither do I. At least not exactly. But that's okay. Esther said that I was the author of my own life, so I am going to make sure that . . ." Taryn paused as a bad thought struck her. "Wait. I'm being extremely selfish here. I didn't even ask you what you wanted."

Fear gripped her as she realized that for all she knew, Hawk wanted to return to the Middle Ages and be with someone else.

His gaze hooded, he looked rather hesitant. "Do you want the truth?"

Be careful what you ask for; you just might get it. . . .

Her mother's favorite phrase went through her as panic swelled in her heart. *C'mon, Taryn, you're a big girl. You can handle whatever he says.*

As a character, Hawk had never had any say in his life. The least she could do was give him a choice in this. "Yeah," she said quietly. "I want the truth."

He reached out to brush the hair back from her face. "What I want . . ."

She waited for him to speak as he continued to play in her hair. "Is . . . ?" she prompted.

"You," he said before he pulled her into a sizzling kiss.

Taryn groaned at the taste of her medieval knight. Hawk was everything she had ever dreamed of. Everything she'd ever wanted. She nipped at his lips before she pulled back. "Okay, then, we shall have a big wedding. . . . "

Sparhawk watched as she started writing lines in her book. Every time she got to the bottom of the page, she turned it over and a new blank page appeared magically at the end of the book so that she could continue onward with her writing.

He tried to read what she was writing, but couldn't understand it. "What are you putting there, Taryn?"

"I am making you independently wealthy, 'cause we know that all good heroes are, and I'm making sure that Alinor's copy of the book is spontaneously combusting into flames."

"Can you do that?"

She smiled at him. "Baby, I'm the writer. According to Esther, I can do anything I want to."

"And so what do you wish to do now?"

Taryn bit her lip as she raked a hungry gaze over his naked body. "Right now I wish to spend the rest of my day making love to you."

She kissed him on his cheek, then scribbled a few more words.

"What are you saying now?" he asked.

She smiled at him. "I'm writing that we go on to live happily ever after."

And then Taryn made sure to do the one thing that Alinor had forgotten to do. It was the one thing to make sure that no one added any more pages to her future or altered her life with Sparhawk.

She wrote the three most powerful words on the planet. "I love you."

"Do you?" Hawk asked her.

Taryn paused as she realized that she had spoken those words out loud. "Yes, Sparhawk the Brave. I do."

"Good," he whispered, nuzzling her neck as his whiskers gently scraped her skin. "Because I love you, too."

Her heart melted at his words. And then she quickly added the other two most powerful words on earth . . . The End.

Shattered Dreams

Rebecca York

Ruth Glick writing as Rebecca York

One

꧁꧂

Miranda Grove had known all along that she must choose between hell and purgatory. No matter what happened, she wanted to get past the pain of the hard landing.

Grim-faced, she walked to the front door of her small wood-and-stone house high in the hills above Monterey, California.

In the five years she'd lived here, she often stopped to admire the breathtaking panorama that swept to the sparkling blue ocean miles below. Today she barely noticed her surroundings.

"Damn you," she muttered, tears blurring her vision. Swiping them away, she climbed into her blue pickup and started toward the city where she had grown up.

"Why are you making me do this?" she raged into the empty truck cab.

Since she was alone, no one answered, and the silence sent her pain and anger boiling higher. In her mind, she began going over the speech she was planning to deliver. She would ask questions. Demand answers. And she could hear the angry responses snapping through her brain cells like a whiplash.

Her attention was so focused on the confrontation ahead that several minutes passed before she realized a vehicle was behind her, coming up on her bumper. Fast.

Lord, she didn't need the kids up the hill playing games. Not today. Speeding up, she tried to get away.

Caleb Mancuso swiped his black hair back from his forehead as he examined the life-sized figure of a woman he was bringing to life out of Carrara marble.

She was sitting with her legs drawn up and her delicate hands clasped around her calves. Her head rested on her knees, concealing her face. But he knew her features by heart. Her large green eyes, her beautifully shaped lips, her small nose. Though the face was hidden, her hair flowed out behind her in all its glory. Rendered in marble, it was light in color. In reality, it was a dark waterfall.

He picked up his hammer and chisel, weighing them in his hands. The woman's body language spoke to something deep within him. She looked caught in the grip of despair, hugging herself for comfort.

Probably he'd made up that part—projecting his own pain onto the statue, when the woman herself was doing just fine without him.

• • •

Miranda's attention zinged back to her own vehicle as the SUV grazed her bumper with a thunk of metal on metal, shoving her toward the shoulder—and she knew that either her obnoxious neighbors had taken fun past acceptable limits, or someone was trying to kill her.

She was a good driver, thanks to her father, hard-as-nails Colonel Frederick Grove. He'd made sure of that— just the way he had insisted she know so many other skills he considered essential—like shooting and martial arts. But her beloved blue truck was old. With another hit from the SUV, she could be in serious trouble.

Mouth dry as sawdust, hands gripping the wheel, she pressed on the accelerator, trying to get away, but the SUV bashed her bumper again, shaking the truck, the sound screeching inside her head.

With her teeth clamped together, she fought to keep from flying off the road and into space. But she could barely control the vehicle now. Fear clogged her throat as she felt a front tire skid on gravel. Somehow she wrenched herself back to safety.

Caleb had just set the chisel against the statue's left hand when he felt a jolt like a flash of lightning crackling through his head. He cried out, as much from surprise as from the stab of pain.

The figure in front of him and the walls of his workshop vanished as though they had never existed.

To his astonishment, he found himself sitting behind

the wheel of an old but well-cared for pickup truck, hurtling down a hill.

"Jesus!"

Hands clenched on the wheel, he fought to keep the tires on the blacktop.

He had no time to think about how he had gotten from his studio into the truck. All he knew was that he had to keep the vehicle on the road, or he would die.

An engine roared behind him. Metal screeched on metal, and the truck shook. At the next curve, despite his efforts to prevent it, he left the pavement, went airborne, then landed with bone-jarring impact before plunging down a heart-stopping incline.

Suddenly Caleb was back in his workroom, gasping for air, his head spinning, his mouth dry as marble chips.

His hammer and chisel slipped from his hands, landing with a thud on the concrete floor. Swaying forward, he grabbed the statue's arm to keep himself from falling.

For a space of time, he had lost his identity. Now he was back in his own body, but he knew his consciousness had leaped into another person's mind.

It hadn't happened to him in years. No—nothing like that had *ever* happened. Nothing that real. That vivid. That terrifying.

Dragging in a deep breath, he struggled to regain control of himself. But fear still clogged his throat. Not fear for himself. He'd recognized the interior of the truck. It was Miranda's truck. And now that he had a moment to think clearly, he knew that the hands he'd seen on the wheel hadn't been his. They had been *her* delicate hands—the same ones he'd been sculpting.

Another man might have dismissed the whole incident as some kind of feverish delusion. But not Caleb Mancuso. Not the son and nephew of Gypsy fortune-tellers. Not the grandson of a talented faith healer.

He knew in his gut that it had been real. And cold dread twisted inside him. The crash had flung him back into his workshop. But what about Miranda? In a truck that was too old to have an air bag.

He had to get back there and make sure she was all right! Now. But he hadn't tried using psychic mumbo jumbo in years. No, not mumbo jumbo. It was real. Too real. Which was why he had struggled to shut it out of his life. He'd succeeded by brute force. And he didn't know how to claw his way back to the accident scene.

"Miranda," he murmured. "Miranda, let me find you. Let me find you the way I always could."

When the plea fell into a vast, chilling void, he couldn't hold back a surge of panic. Ruthlessly he tamped down the fear and reached out for the intimate mental link he had thought was broken long ago. He felt like he was in a pitch-dark room searching for the door with only his sense of touch.

He wanted to roar in frustration. Instead he ordered himself to calm down—to let the old skills come back. He couldn't describe what he was doing. But he felt a sense of connection gathering as he opened his heart and mind. Opened himself to the pain of loss.

When he let his guard down far enough, it happened again. Somewhere deep in his consciousness, images flickered. And he was *there*, although it wasn't the same.

He wasn't behind the wheel. He was standing on the road—up the hill from the blue truck.

It had traveled down a steep incline and ended up crumpled against a tree trunk. Miranda was in the driver's seat, slumped over the wheel, her upper body eerily like the statue he had been sculpting.

He couldn't move. He could only stare in horrible fascination at the picture before him.

Heart pounding, he started picking his way down the hill, sliding when he couldn't keep his footing. Again the scene flickered. He tried to hang on, tried to claw his fingers around a rock sticking out of the ground. But it slipped from his grasp, leaving him back in his workshop again and sick with fear and frustration.

Years ago he'd told himself he was better off without Miranda Grove. But that hadn't stopped him from secretly keeping tabs on her—not with psychic abilities but with real-world facts. He knew she owned an outfitter business and led wilderness expeditions all over the western states. And he knew the location of her isolated house. The accident scene looked like it was up there in the hills above the city. And if she was on a road that few people used, who was going to call for help?

Sprinting down the flagstone path from his studio, he leaped through the kitchen door and snatched up the receiver of the wall phone.

But as he began to dial 911, he stopped and slammed down the receiver before he got to the last number.

The police and fire departments recorded these calls and checked them for location. What was he going to say, "I had a psychic vision of a location twenty miles away. Send an ambulance."

When it dawned on him that he had another alternative, he ran to the bedroom and grabbed the prepaid cell phone that he'd bought recently. The dispatcher might record the call, but they wouldn't know where he was.

Quickly he turned on the phone and punched in the digits.

"What is your emergency?"

"I want to report a vehicular accident."

"What is the location?"

"The Old Logging Road. About halfway up the mountain. It looks like a pickup truck went off the blacktop and crashed against a tree. I can see somebody in it."

"Can you give a more specific location?"

He thought back over the scene, praying he had the details right. "About five miles from the turnoff to San Miguel. Right after the trees start. Hurry. The driver isn't moving."

Knowing that there was no more information he could logically give, he cut the transmission and set down the phone, then pressed his hands against the kitchen counter to keep them from shaking.

He wanted to jump into his car and drive to the Old Logging Road. He wanted to make sure the EMTs arrived on the scene. But his home and studio were on the coast, and Miranda's house was in the mountains. It would take him almost an hour to get to her—given the back roads he'd have to travel. Too long to do Miranda any good.

Pacing the length of the kitchen, he tried to bring his mind back to the accident scene.

But it had moved beyond his reach now, as though

somebody or something was deliberately keeping him away.

He ached to dismiss the whole episode as a psychotic break. But he knew it was real. Knew it in his mind and in the icy tendrils gripping his gut.

On a surge of frustration, he walked into the bedroom and stood staring at the dresser, clenching and unclenching his fists. Finally he pulled open the top drawer and took out the small box where he'd put Miranda's opal ring. The ring she had given back to him.

As he held it in his hand, he felt long-denied emotions clamoring for release. Anger. Sadness. Frustration. Ruthlessly he choked them off. He hadn't dragged out the ring to torture himself. He needed to use it—to strengthen the connection to Miranda.

Long ago his grandpa Arthur had taught him to sit quietly with an object that belonged to someone else and open his thoughts to that person's mind. Could he still do it?

Fighting the tightness in his chest, he carried the ring to his leather recliner and tried to get comfortable, despite his tension.

With his eyes closed, he let his mind drift, clenching his hand around the circle of hard metal and the small opal cradled in the delicate gold setting.

As he thought of Miranda—of days and hours they had shared— the metal grew hot in his hand. He remembered the first time he'd met her—when he was ten and she was nine. Her mother had come for a psychic reading, and he'd been left in charge of the little girl. At first they'd been shy with each other. But over those first few weeks, they'd gotten to be friends. He smiled as he remembered their secret rockbound hideout in the woods. It had been their fort, their pioneer camp, their bomb shelter, their spaceship.

They'd gathered underbrush to use for beds and poked sticks through cracks in the rocks and fired at the enemies surrounding them. And they'd brought chips and soft drinks and candy bars for provisions.

Against his will, another memory grabbed him. He was sixteen, and she was fifteen. He'd been living with Grandpa Arthur for the past few months, and the moment he and Miranda had seen each other again, they'd headed straight for their wilderness hideout, both of them nervous and both of them apparently with their minds on the same thing. Because when they stepped inside the circle of rock, the atmosphere grew thick with adolescent sexuality. When he'd turned toward her, she'd burrowed into the circle of his arms and lifted her head for his kiss.

Even now he remembered every detail of the scene. The tall trees above them. The feeling of heat traveling over his skin as he looked at her. The nervous flush on her cheeks. And the wonderful pressure of her lips against his, the marvel of her young body cleaving to his.

Adolescent Caleb Mancuso was instantly hard as a hockey stick—and embarrassed about it. So he had broken off the kiss and told her they were too old to be sneaking off alone. But they had done it again. And again.

Years ago he had been so close to her that he could sometimes read her thoughts. Then a half hour ago he'd been inside her head. Because she needed him. She still did!

"Let me come back to you," he whispered, opening his mind and praying that he could reach her again.

But now it felt as if she was putting up barriers, the way she'd done eight years ago.

"Stop it," he pleaded. "Let me help you."

It felt as if he were trying to push his way through a thick rubber wall.

Teeth gritted, he rammed his shoulder against the strange, virtual surface, fighting the fear that making the connection would be impossible.

Two

❧

You crashed in that truck. Then you saw the accident scene. Go back there now, Caleb ordered himself.

On a deep breath, he pushed harder against the imaginary wall. He knew the thick rubber palisade was a metaphor—a way for him to deal with something that defied human description.

Even as the thought skittered through his brain, he felt just the barest amount of give in the barrier and redoubled his efforts.

Somehow, he battered his way through the obstruction, and found himself back on the Old Logging Road. Only this time he saw the flashing lights of an ambulance and a police car.

Thank God. They are here. The dispatcher had believed him. Or someone else had reported the accident.

It didn't matter which. He was just grateful that help had arrived.

As he watched, two paramedics carried a stretcher up the steep incline. Miranda was lying on it, her eyes closed and her head bloody. Above her a bag of IV fluid dangled on a metal pole.

Quickly the rescue workers slid the stretcher into the open doors of the ambulance.

Without warning, just as it had before, the mental picture snapped off, like a door slamming in his face, leaving him sitting in his chair, gasping, his T-shirt clinging damply to his chest. They were taking her to the hospital. He had done what he needed to do.

He could stop worrying about her now, he told himself— wanting it to be true.

Miranda floated on a strange feeling of detachment. The ambulance door clanked open, and she was wheeled down the hall into a large room with bright lights. She knew she was in the hospital. She knew people were gathered around her, transferring her from the gurney to a table.

She could hear them talking. Someone called out her blood pressure—100 over 60. Someone else stuck a needle in her limp arm, drawing blood. Other hands exchanged the fluid dripping into her arm for a fresh bag, then began washing the blood from her dark hair.

One of the nurses cut off her plaid shirt and jeans. From the chatter around her, she knew they were getting her ready for a CAT scan.

It was odd to be aware of all that when she lay on the table with her eyes closed. But she could observe the scene because her mind wasn't in her body. Instead, she hovered far above the table, looking down on herself, watching a doctor and nurses work over her.

She should go back to her body. That was where she wanted to be. As she started to descend from her high perch, something pushed at her shoulder, stopping her. It felt like a giant hand holding her back.

She tried to shove against it, but she didn't have the strength. Then the hospital scene flickered and went black.

Terror grabbed her by the throat. She could feel nothing, hear nothing, taste nothing. She was nowhere.

She tried to scream, but there was no air to pull into her lungs. Desperately, she grabbed for something, anything. She thought of the trick she sometimes used to calm herself—thinking of a lovely, familiar place. A picture of her favorite campground leaped into her mind, and as soon as the scene came to her, she sighed her relief. She reached for that image, caught it in a tight embrace, and felt solid ground beneath her feet again. Gratefully she dragged in a deep breath of pine-scented air, then looked up at the sun slanting through the trees. It was late afternoon, and the scent of pine perfumed the air.

She glanced down at her plaid shirt and jeans. Hadn't somebody cut . . .

No. She shied away from that thought. Raising her head, she looked toward the bright reds, blues, and yellows of camping tents that beckoned her forward.

Thank God! She had been frightened and confused for a few minutes. Now she knew where she was—at a camping site she loved. She had led many wilderness expeditions here. Probably the rest of the group was waiting for her. And they'd be really happy to see her.

Her brow wrinkled. The rest of the group? Were others with her? She hoped so, because then she wouldn't be so alone.

Her mind made another leap. Maybe when she got to the campsite, she'd find Caleb. He'd been here—hadn't he? She remembered sensing him with her.

Where had he gone?

Suddenly her head was throbbing. What would Caleb be doing out in the woods with her? She hadn't seen him in a long time. Not since the awful day she'd sent him away.

He was no longer part of her life, she told herself firmly. But she'd kept up with his career. She was so proud of him. She'd gone to galleries and public buildings and parks where his huge metal or stone sculptures were displayed. She'd seen him in a documentary on television about talented young artists. She'd read articles about him. And she had collected pictures of some of his major works.

"Caleb?" she said aloud.

He didn't answer. Should she be expecting him? A few minutes ago she'd thought he was here.

She tried to make her thoughts come clear, but her head hurt too much. The pain made it hard to think, hard to see, hard to breathe. She'd go back to camp, take some headache medication, and lie down. The others would leave her alone, but Caleb would crawl into her tent with her and hold her in his arms.

More than hold. A shiver of sensation went through her as she imagined being close to him again, kissing him, touching him. The hardest thing she'd ever done was walk away from him. She'd thought it was over between them—forever. But she sensed that he was back— even though she hadn't seen him yet.

She smiled to herself and let her thoughts drift, calling up wonderful images from the past. His hands and lips on her body had been magic, setting her senses on fire.

She had missed him. So much.

An aching longing pierced her. She needed him with her. She needed all the things she had denied them both. Quickly she set out toward the camp.

Need and reality warred within Caleb.

He ached to go to Miranda. Even if she was unconscious, he wanted to be close to her. He'd stop pacing the living room and start to pick up the phone so he could find out what hospital she'd been taken to. Then he'd tell himself not to be a damn fool—and to stay home.

But someone had run her off the road. Someone who *wanted* to hurt her? Would they try again?

Panic surged through him. Struggling to hold his hands steady, he started calling the hospitals in Monterey. The second one he reached, Monterey-Carmel General, had a patient named Miranda Grove. She was in intensive care, her condition was guarded, and he knew that he had to go to her. Whether she wanted him there or not.

Preparing to camp out in the parking lot if necessary, he threw some clothing and toilet articles into an overnight bag. As he was about to walk out the door, the phone rang, and he muttered a curse.

He didn't want to stop and answer, but he sensed the call would be important.

So he want back to the kitchen and snatched up the receiver.

"Hello?"

"Caleb. I'm glad I reached you."

It was his aunt Edith, and his mind conjured up a picture of a sixty-year-old woman with dyed red hair, wearing an emerald green dress, three or four sparkling necklaces, half a dozen rings, and a fringed shawl. When she and his mother had worked as fortune-tellers, they had both dressed flamboyantly as part of their image. Somehow Aunt Edith had always managed to look a bit more outrageous.

He hadn't spoken to her in weeks. This evening the tone of her voice made him instantly alert. "Aunt Edith, is there something wrong? Is it my mom?"

"Loretta is fine, living it up in that retirement community she loves so much. I'm calling about something else. Don't go up to Monterey."

"How did you know I was?" Anger made his voice gruff, because he wondered if she had been eavesdropping on his thoughts.

To his relief, she gave him a plausible reason for her call. "I saw on the evening news that Miranda Grove had been in a one-truck accident. And I knew that if you found out about it, you'd go flying to her like a moth to a flame."

"I wouldn't put it that way."

"Stay away from the Grove family."

"Are you giving me your professional opinion?"

"I'm retired. I'm speaking as your aunt—as someone who cares about you. It's our fault you met that girl. I'm sorry about that. Don't let her hurt you again."

"Did Mom put you up to calling?" he asked.

His aunt made a frustrated noise. "What does it matter whose idea it was?"

"Well, I'm old enough to make my own decisions. I'll talk to you later," he said, his voice firm.

She tried to hold him on the phone. "Caleb, don't hang up. . . ."

Before she could finish the sentence, he put down the receiver, picked up his carry bag again, and strode out of the house.

Frederick Grove's slate blue eyes had turned dark. He had gone past angry to enraged, but somehow he kept himself from picking up tables and chairs and dashing them against the wall. He needed information. And he needed to talk to his daughter, because he had a lot of questions to ask her.

Every time someone in a white coat walked out of the intensive care unit, his head jerked to the right in expectation of some news.

Finally Dr. Donovan, the neurological consultant, came out, looked around, and focused on him.

Striding forward, Frederick demanded, "What can

you tell me about my daughter? I mean besides what the doc fed me in the emergency room?"

The dumb shit repeated what Frederick already knew. "There are no internal injuries, and she escaped without broken bones. We stitched the cut on her forehead. We've done skull X-rays and a CAT scan. At this time, there is no bleeding inside the brain. No swelling. And she's breathing on her own."

"I want to talk to her."

The doctor's expression became more serious. "Unfortunately, she's still unconscious."

"Why?"

"It could be a reaction to trauma."

"What the hell does that mean?"

"She needs time to recover from the head injury," the doctor said slowly.

Frederick didn't like the sound of that. "In other words, you don't know squat," he guessed, his tone accusing.

"Since there is no obvious reason for her failure to wake up, we're hoping for a full recovery." He smiled reassuringly. "When you're dealing with the brain, sometimes it's impossible to predict how fast a patient will recover."

"I want to see her."

"You can have ten minutes with her every hour."

"Ten minutes!"

"I'm sorry. As soon as we transfer her to a room on the neurological floor, you can spend more time with her."

The doctor retreated behind the door again. Frederick was thinking about marching into the unit after him, when he felt someone's gaze drilling into his back. Turning on his heel, he saw a man staring at him, a man with dark hair, angry dark eyes, broad shoulders, and the muscles of a day laborer.

"Caleb Mancuso. What the hell are you doing here?" Frederick challenged.

The big-deal sculptor shoved his large hands into the pockets of his jeans. "I found out Miranda was in an accident. I came to see her."

"You can't. She's unconscious," Frederick answered.

"Why?"

Because he was in a hospital, Frederick kept his language relatively mild. "They don't effing know!" he snapped, then was immediately sorry that he'd given away any insight into his own fears.

Mancuso shifted his weight from one foot to the other. "I'm sorry to hear it," he said.

"Yeah, well, we don't need you here."

"Do you know anyone who would want to hurt Miranda?"

"No!"

Mancuso opened his mouth, then closed it again. After several charged seconds, he backed away.

Frederick breathed out a sigh, hoping he had seen the last of the low-life son of a Gypsy fortune-teller. Yet he couldn't help focusing on one of the questions the guy had asked.

Do you know anyone who would want to hurt Miranda?

• • •

Caleb had learned to pick his fights. He wanted to punch out Colonel Grove. But getting them both thrown out of the hospital wasn't going to help Miranda.

Instead, he went in search of the hospital chapel room. He'd gone there before to pray—when his mother had been rushed to M-C General for intestinal surgery. Once again he slipped inside, thankful that he had the place to himself.

Dropping onto a hard wooden pew, he sat staring at the stained-glass window above a small altar. He remembered thinking on his previous visit that the window was magnificent, a symphony of color and pattern, with no obvious picture from religion or nature. Today the artwork barely registered. He was too worried about Miranda. Her father said she was unconscious, and the doctors didn't know why. That confirmed the information Caleb had gotten from the front desk. As he'd rushed upstairs, he'd hoped against hope that she'd improved.

The expression on the colonel's face had informed him otherwise. Miranda's father was scared shitless. So he couldn't have been the one to try and force her off the road! Right?

Caleb couldn't be sure. But he did know that as he'd driven to the hospital, one scene kept coming back to him over and over. Miranda out in the wilderness, in a place where she felt safe.

Where did the mind go when a person was unconscious? Was she dreaming? And what if the dream stayed fixed in one setting? Like an alternate reality.

Had her sleeping mind taken her into a secret forest setting where she knew her way around, where she felt sheltered from the pain of the real world? Had she gone there on purpose—to heal herself?

Or was she stuck there against her will?

Either way, could he make direct contact with her there? Like when she'd been driving the truck. Or could he only watch her—the way he had done after the crash?

Fear turned his skin icy. Fear that she would never wake up—unless he went into her mind and brought her back to the world.

Was that pure, male arrogance on his part?

No. Deep in his heart he sensed that she was in trouble. Bad trouble.

Without realizing what he was doing, he reached into his pocket and wrapped his hand around the opal ring. It was warm from the contact with his body. Almost like a living thing.

He pulled it out, flattening his palm and looking at the lights sparkling in the blue-white stone. And he was snared by an achingly sharp memory. His most vivid sexual encounter—even if it was hardly his most mature experience.

He was seventeen and home for Christmas vacation from the Academy of Art in San Francisco.

He was back with Miranda at their fortress. And he was gripped by all the tender, urgent, arousing feelings that swamped him every time he thought of her.

Only now they were together again, and she was staring at him with eyes so large and green that he thought he might drown in them.

"You've changed," she murmured.

"No."

"Yes." She gulped. "Did you sleep with other girls while you were away at that fancy art school?"

He felt his cheeks heat, thought of lying. Instead, he managed to say, "Yes."

"So the things we did together . . . won't satisfy you anymore."

"Of course they will," he answered automatically. He'd been hoping they could go farther—if she wanted it as much as he did. Now he made an instant revision.

Ignoring the quick assurance, she asked, "You think I'm . . . old-fashioned, don't you?"

"I think you were raised with strict morals. So was I, believe it or not, even if my mom does tell fortunes for a living."

Moral values or not, the ache she set off inside him was intolerable. So he folded her close, pressing her body against his.

He kissed her, stroked his hands up and down her ribs, feeling her shiver of reaction.

"I want to . . . be with you. But I promise we won't go any farther than we already have."

"Girls at school talk about boys who get carried away and force you to do it."

"Have I ever forced you into anything?"

"No," she admitted in a small voice.

"Well, nothing has changed. If I do anything you don't like, just tell me to stop, and I will."

She answered with a shaky laugh. "The problem is . . . I like what you do . . . too much. And we're . . . out here alone. Private."

"Yeah, but I would never do anything to hurt you," he murmured, then stepped away from her and picked up the blanket he'd brought, spreading it out on the bed of brush that he'd already gathered.

"Let's sit and talk," he said and sat down like he was sure she was going to join him.

She did—but she left a foot of space between them. Instead of reaching for her, he made himself start a conversation—about school, his hopes for the future, and what she'd been doing since he left. And as the words buzzed in his brain, he maneuvered her back into his arms, where he could touch her and kiss her.

When the pressure inside himself reached boiling point, he slid his hand under her top, stroking the silky skin of her back, then unhooked her bra and pushed it out of the way.

They both sighed as he took her wonderful breasts in his hands, and he marveled again at the contrast between their soft weight and the hardened tips.

"Can I take off your top?" he asked, then waited with his pulse pounding in his ears for her consent.

When she gave a little nod, he slowly pushed the top up, then helped her discard it.

The sight of the dappled sunlight shimmering on her breasts took his breath away.

"Lord, you are so beautiful," he whispered, then pulled off his own shirt and took her in his arms, moving her breasts against his naked chest, overcome with desire for her.

With a needy sound low in his throat, he angled his head so that he could kiss her deeply. And she opened her lips, giving him her trust.

"Miranda, I would never do anything to hurt you," he said again. "Never."

The hitch in her breath told him she was still nervous. Holding his own needs in check, he kissed the line of her jaw, the side of her neck, the hollow at the base of her throat.

His head was spinning—with desire and with all the words of love he wasn't free to say. But he could show her what he felt.

They had gone pretty far together. But he knew this was different. Because he was sexually experienced now. He had wanted to find out if other women had the same effect on him. He had enjoyed the experiences, although nothing else had come close to what he felt with Miranda. Still, he understood exactly what he was doing with each touch, each kiss.

Slowly he lifted his hand again, drawing circles around her swollen nipples before catching them between his thumbs and fingers, squeezing slightly, wringing a small sob from her.

"That's so good," she breathed.

"Would you do the same thing for me?" he asked.

This was something new. Something he hoped would make her feel more comfortable.

Her eyes focused on his chest, at the sprinkling of hair that hadn't yet thickened out and at his small, flat nipples.

Raising her hand, she stroked him, smiling when his breath caught. He had thought her touch would be merely pleasant. It was much, much more.

"In case you can't tell, this is making me dizzy," he whispered.

"Me, too."

"Then maybe we should lie down."

A small shadow crossed her face.

"Unless you don't trust me," he said, looking up at her as he stretched out on the blanket.

Heart-stopping seconds passed before she eased to his side, closing her eyes as she pressed her head against his shoulder.

He let out a deep sigh as he cradled her in his arms, relieved to have brought her this far. Yet he forced himself to keep the pace slow, kissing her and caressing her before he opened the snap at the top of her jeans. Watching her face, he slowly lowered the zipper, then reached into the opening, slipping his hand into her panties, pressing his palm against the springy hair at the top of her legs before sliding his fingers lower to dip into her silky folds.

She was aroused, her sex slick and swollen for him. He wanted to make her come then, just to watch pleasure shimmer through her.

He longed to strip off her jeans and his, too. But they had never been completely naked together, so he left her half dressed while he kissed her face, her lips, the beautiful column of her neck as he stroked her most sensitive flesh. At first she lay still. But when she arched into his touch, he brought his lips to her ear, telling her he wanted her to feel all the pleasure her body could give her.

She tensed when he slipped his finger inside her. He kissed her as he let her adjust to the feel of that intimate caress before he stroked up to her clit and down again, watching sweet ecstasy gather on her face.

He caressed her breasts at the same time, knowing the sensations would reinforce each other, building her arousal, loving her response to him.

"Caleb, Caleb," she cried out, her hips rising and falling as he brought her higher and higher.

She sobbed his name as she came, clinging to him. He felt aftershocks shudder through her body, then she lay quiet and boneless in his arms.

"That was beautiful," he murmured. When he brushed his lips against her cheek, her eyes came slowly open.

His own need was like a raging forest fire eating its way through his brain and body. Somehow he kept his voice even as he asked, "Would you do that for me?"

As he spoke, he took her hand and carried it to his middle, pressing her fingers against the hot, rigid shaft straining behind the fly of his jeans.

She had made him come before, and he suspected she felt as if she was doing something wrong. To prove he wasn't going to force her into anything, he lay with his eyes half closed and his arms at his sides, watching her through a screen of lashes.

With hands that weren't quite steady she unzipped his pants. Tugging down the waistband of his shorts, she freed him from the knit fabric, her gaze fixed on his distended, reddened flesh.

When she wrapped her hand around his cock, he sighed out his thanks. He had showed her what he liked. She did that now, quickly—probably to get it over with. Her hand tight around him, her arm pumping. He was so aroused that it didn't take much effort on her part to make his body jerk and semen spurt in an arc into the air. When he could breathe again, he reached for her, rocking her against him as he told her how much he loved everything they had done together.

"Oh, yes," she answered, kissing his cheek, his jaw, his lips. Arousing them both. And this time before he made her come, he got her jeans off.

Over the vacation they came back to their hideout to make love four or five times. Maybe he was even secretly thinking he could get her to take the ultimate step. Hell, they had come this far. Why not the rest of the way?

But the last time she met him in their secret place, it was to tell him that she had been thinking about their relationship. It wasn't going anywhere. They couldn't see each other again, and he must take back the ring he had given her.

The shock and pain of her words hit him again like rocks falling out of the sky and landing on his head and shoulder.

He squeezed his eyes closed, fighting his own sadness and frustration. Trying to break into her private world was useless, because she didn't want him in her life. That episode in the truck had just been a fluke. He didn't have the skill to forge a real connection with her, anyway.

Anger and frustration threatened to swallow him whole. Then he sat up straighter. She might not want him with her, but he was going there anyway. And he was going to bring her back to this world.

He put the ring back into his pocket for safekeeping. But he kept it in his fist as he closed his eyes, blotting out all distractions, turning his consciousness inward.

When he had centered himself, he reached outward—
toward Miranda. Not the girl he had loved and lost. But
the woman.

He whispered her name. Then realized there was no
point in speaking aloud. Instead he shouted inside his
own head. *Miranda? Where are you Miranda? Help me
find you. Let me into your mind.*

He had no guidelines for what he was doing. Nobody
had ever taught him the Vulcan mind meld. He was making the rules up as he went along. If he'd tried to explain
the process to anyone else, they probably would have
sent for the guys with the butterfly nets. Still, he kept
reaching out, striving to make contact with her. On the
road he'd known where to find her. Now he didn't even
know where to look. But he kept calling to her, and he
thought he was moving in the right direction when he felt
himself crashing up against the mental barrier he had en-
countered before.

Miranda?

She didn't answer. But he sensed her, somewhere beyond his grasp. On the other side of a high wall, like a
princess locked in a castle.

Frustration boiled inside him. *Miranda, let me in!* he
shouted in his mind, not even sure that she was the one
barring his entrance.

Still, desperation kept him butting his head and
shoulder against the enormous barrier that loomed in
front of him. He knew how to attack it. Sort of.

Finally, as he had before, he crashed through and
came roaring to a stop, swaying on his feet, flailing his
arms to keep from falling.

A moment ago he had been sitting in the hospital chapel. As far as he knew, his body was still sitting there.

But his consciousness was somewhere else. Or was his body really in this place? It certainly felt like he was here, in the woodsy scene he had imagined, with pine needles under his feet and the scent of the forest around him. It didn't feel imaginary. On the contrary, it had the crystal clarity of reality.

Although he had arrived at the hospital in the evening, in this place, it looked like late afternoon. And if he had to guess where he'd landed, he'd say he was in the wilds of Northern California. Which made the time difference impossible—unless he'd battered his way through some kind of temporal distortion.

He chewed on that thought as he walked toward the sound of rushing water and came to a river flowing fast over stones and boulders.

As far as he could see, he was the only person in this world—wherever it was. When he listened for sounds of life, all he could hear was the roar of the river in back of him.

So, had he outsmarted himself? Had he sent himself crashing into his own dream?

Cupping his hands around his mouth, he lifted his head and pitched his voice above the torrent. "Miranda?"

When she didn't answer, he spoke more loudly, struggling to keep fear or anger out of his voice. "Miranda, answer me."

Long seconds ticked by. Finally he heard a crunching

in the underbrush and let out the breath he'd been holding.

She'd come to him!

But when he whirled in anticipation, the look of relief on his face froze.

Miranda wasn't there. Instead he found himself facing a large angry-looking grizzly bear.

Three

❧

Bits of outdoor lore raced through his mind. As a kid, he'd belonged to a boys' club where the big events each year were weekend camping trips. One of the leaders had warned them about bears. He knew they could climb, so going up a tree would do him no good.

Then he realized that real-world facts might not apply. This was a dream—Miranda's or his. And the bear might be able to fly, for all he knew.

Still, his best option was to act like this was reality. As the bear lumbered toward him, he took an involuntary step back, then realized the river blocked his escape.

With strangely cool detachment, he considered what to do now. Maybe the dream would work to his advantage. Maybe he could affect the outcome.

Again he pitched his voice above the roaring of the river. "Go away, bear!" he shouted. "Leave me alone. Vanish!" He accompanied that last order with a wave of his hands like a magician working a spell.

Instead of backing off or turning into a white rabbit, the bear sped forward.

So much for his magic powers in this place. He risked a glance behind him. Maybe he could escape by plunging into the river. But he knew it would be icy cold this far north—and he had seen it was fast moving. If the bear could kill him, so could the frigid water. And if he ran along the shore, the animal would eventually catch up.

Determination gleamed in the animal's eyes, as though it was being directed by a human intelligence, Caleb thought. The beast bore down on him like a monster in a horror movie. Picking up half a dozen egg-sized rocks from the riverbank, he lobbed them at the massive brown body, scoring several direct hits.

His arms were strong from his work, and he knew the shots had hurt. The brute growled, but it didn't change course.

This was just a dream, Caleb told himself again. He could escape any time he wanted. All he had to do was wake up.

But that didn't seem to be an option. Not when he felt like some outside force was holding him here.

Dropping his remaining supply of missiles, he snatched up a dead branch lying on the ground and swung it in front of him as the bear charged.

He scored a direct hit on the animal's snout, and it roared in pain, then slashed at him with one enormous paw, its razor-sharp claws ripping through the fabric of his leather jacket and digging into his skin.

He was so focused on the animal that a loud crack from somewhere nearby barely registered.

The bear's body jerked. Again he heard the sharp sound and watched as the monster toppled sideways, landing with a thud on the ground. It took several seconds for his brain to switch gears, but finally he realized that someone had shot the animal—and saved his life.

Looking up, he saw Miranda, dressed in a plaid shirt and jeans, standing with a rifle stock against her shoulder, the weapon pointed in his direction. Her expression still registered a mixture of terror and resolve.

"That was a pretty risky shot," he said in a deadpan voice.

"I didn't know what else to do." Her eyes fixed on the shredded shoulder of his jacket. "Caleb, oh Lord, Caleb. Are you all right?"

"Yes." Now that the emergency was over, he felt a stab of hot pain, but he ignored the sensation. Feeling strangely light-headed, he started forward. As he reached Miranda, he had the sense to take the weapon out of her hands and set it on the ground.

Somewhere in his mind he remembered that he had forced his way into this place with her. It wasn't reality. It was a dream. Yet it had a sharp, heart-stopping clarity.

And he knew that if Miranda hadn't shot the bear, he would be lying torn and bleeding on the riverbank.

"Thank you for saving my life," he murmured as he looked down at her.

At the accident scene, she'd been pale and unconscious. In this place a healthy glow colored her cheeks.

In wonder, he studied her. The last time he had been close to her in real life, she'd been only sixteen. Now she was an adult. She'd filled out in all the right places. And maturity had given her face a more distinctive look.

Once more, she was gazing at him with the soft look that had warmed his blood.

Every warning he had given himself about being vulnerable to her again flew out of his mind. With a deep sigh of satisfaction, he folded her close and felt the remarkable strength of her grip as she clasped his body to hers.

A low, inviting sound eased out of her, a sound that melted his heart. She tipped her head up, her expression sweet and dreamy. "I was hoping I'd find you here," she murmured. "Everybody else is gone. And I thought you'd be gone, too. But now I've found you."

He swallowed painfully. "Yes."

"Did I make a wish, and you appeared?" she asked, sounding bemused.

"Did you wish for me?" he whispered.

"Yes."

He clasped her tighter, then as he processed what she had said earlier, he felt a knot form in his stomach. "Who else were you expecting?" he asked quickly.

"My clients—from the wilderness expedition. But I went back to our camp, and it was empty." Panic flashed in her voice. "They've disappeared. And I'm worried."

He wanted to tell her none of this was real. Not the woods. Not her missing clients. He wanted to explain that she'd made them up to give the dream a familiar context. But now that he was here, with her, he wasn't sure if that was the right thing to say. Telling her she'd taken herself off to never-never land might send her into a tailspin.

"Don't worry," he said soothingly. "Everything's okay. I came to bring you home."

She stepped away from him and gazed into his eyes, her tone firm. "I don't leave people stranded in the woods. I'm responsible for their welfare. I need to find where they went." Her words were determined, but as she spoke, her face registered uncertainty, then fear.

Her emotions tore at him. He wanted to soothe away all her hurts. But he suspected there was nothing he could say that would make any sense.

Which left him with one option—the option he had been secretly thinking of all along.

Swiftly, before he could stop himself, he gathered her close and lowered his mouth to hers.

As his lips touched hers, she sighed his name. And for this moment out of time, he knew with unswerving certainty that she had missed him as much as he had missed her.

Or was he lying to himself, because that was what he wanted to believe? Wanted it so much.

He had to know. He had to separate lies from truth. So he silently asked her to deepen the kiss, his tongue playing along the seam of her lips. At the slight pressure, she opened for him, and he swept inside like a conqueror, stroking the tender inside of her lips, the serrated line of her teeth and beyond.

Her eager hands crept upward to clasp the back of his head, holding him in place as her fingers winnowed through his dark hair.

He was instantly so aroused that he could barely think. He shifted his own hands, gliding them up and down her ribs, then cupping her bottom, gathering her in.

She could have jerked away. Instead, she clung to him.

They were both breathing hard when he dragged his mouth away from hers to gulp in air.

"Caleb. Oh Lord, Caleb. It's been so long."

"Yes."

She slipped her hands under his leather jacket, spreading the front apart then sliding her fingers up and down his chest, sending fire through his blood.

"Yes," he growled again between small kisses. He wanted to go on and on, kissing her, touching her, making love with her. He longed to claim the prize she had never allowed him to take.

But he hadn't come here for his own gratification.

When she swayed on her feet, he caught her in his arms, then looked around. Locating a fallen log twenty feet up the riverbank, he carried her there and sat down, holding her in his lap.

She moved her head against his shoulder, then looked up at him, her eyes questioning.

He was still aroused. And when she shifted her hips against his rigid cock, he held back a groan. "Jesus! Don't."

She went very still, studying his face with those remarkable eyes of hers. "Are you going to make love with me? I mean with you inside me—the way we never did it before."

It took every drop of strength he possessed to answer, "Later."

She looked uncertain, and for the first time since he'd taken her in his arms, he realized that later might be only a pipe dream.

The selfish part of him whispered seductively in his mind, *Take what you can get—while you can.* He wanted her. So badly. Years ago she'd ripped his world to shreds and walked away from him.

But she wasn't acting like the girl who had broken his heart. She had melted in his arms. And now he was sure he could undress her and do anything he wanted to her.

Back in the real world a visitor walked into M-C General Hospital and inquired about Miranda Grove like a concerned friend or relative anxious to pay her a visit.

Too bad visits were restricted, because Miss Grove was still in intensive care.

That was bad news. The rooms in intensive care had glass walls, and the patients were hooked up to a bunch of monitors. All the nurses had to do was glance at a computer screen and press a switch, and they'd see who was in the patient's room. So barging in there was a bad move.

Of course, there were ways around that. Ways of taking care of the hospital staff. But anything like that was risky.

Too bad little Miss Grove hadn't died in the crash. She knew too much. But she was still in fragile condition. Still unconscious. Nobody would think anything of it if she took a turn for the worse.

So the best thing to do was hang around and wait for the right moment to finish the job.

• • •

Caleb teetered on the edge of temptation. Two things pulled him back from the sensual trap. His fear for Miranda. And his resolve not to take advantage of her at her most vulnerable.

"You look . . . wonderful. You feel wonderful," she said, stroking her hand over his muscular shoulder.

"So do you." *At least here,* he added in his mind.

"I came to bring you home." He repeated what he'd said earlier, hearing the raspy sound of his voice.

"I don't need to go home!" She looked around. "I mean, I can't. Not until I make sure everyone is safe. That bear . . . could have hurt you. He could have hurt the others. . . ."

Her voice trailed off, and he heard her uncertainty. She was giving him reasons why she had to stay, but she didn't sound like she believed them.

He soothed his hands over her shoulders, knowing he had to drag her back to reality—before she got sucked any further into this fantasy.

He was still trying to figure out his strategy when she suddenly asked a question.

"Remember when we used to meet at our secret place? That circle of rocks we called our fortress?" she asked.

"God, yes," he breathed. He had let himself travel back to that place, let himself experience again the hot, intimate things they had done there.

"We used to talk. You said you were going to be a force in the art world."

Talk. The talking had just been a side issue, maybe because he was a guy, and a guy was as likely to think with his cock as his brain. "That was pretentious of me," he muttered.

"But you made it. You're a famous sculptor. You did what you said you would."

"And you're running a wilderness expedition company. You're good at it."

"I like it. But it's not what I planned. We were going to get married and have two kids—a boy and a girl," she said wistfully. "Why didn't we?"

His gaze sharpened. "You know why!"

"I forgot," she said in a small voice.

Forgot. The single worst event of his life, and she had wiped it out of her mind.

He wondered what she saw in his face when she said, "There's something wrong with me, isn't there? I mean stuff is all confused in my mind. I feel like I can't think straight." She pressed her fingers against her temple, then whispered, "Am I losing my mind?"

"Of course not," he answered automatically.

Her fingers moved to his shoulders and clamped down hard enough to make him wince—as her troubled green eyes searched his face. "Caleb, don't lie to me."

He swallowed as he thought about what to say. Finally, because he couldn't come up with a better plan, he simply plunged in. "Miranda, this place isn't real. You made it up. Really, you're in the hospital. In a coma. You need to wake up. That's why I'm here."

"No!" Terror washed over her features. With surprising strength, she wrenched away from. "No," she said again, then turned and ran.

Her headlong flight caught him by surprise, but that didn't stop him from jumping up and going after her.

She knew her way around this patch of forest. And he didn't. She dodged past trees and boulders, but he kept her in sight as she ran into a clearing, past a cold camp-fire and a group of tents, then farther into the woods.

"Miranda!" he shouted. "Miranda, stop."

four

❧❧❧

Caleb pounded after Miranda. She slipped on wet pine needles, then scrambled up—which gave him the seconds he needed to catch her.

When he tried to hold her, she fought him, her movements jerky and disorganized. The way she'd described her thoughts.

He easily ducked under her defenses and grabbed her, wrapping his arms around her and holding tight.

"Let me go!" she shouted, sounding as if she was fighting panic as much as she was fighting him.

"Not until you listen to me," he growled.

She went still as a statue. Then, to his dismay, all the starch went out of her. Sagging against him, she started to cry—great wracking sobs that shook her whole body. Leaning back against a boulder, he held on to her, his voice low and soothing as he stroked her and rocked her.

He could feel her trying to get control of herself. And finally she calmed in his arms.

"I'm sorry I frightened you," he murmured.

She made a hitching sound.

"But you have to listen to me," he added.

She nodded against his shoulder.

This time he kept his voice level and reasonable as he suggested, "Let's take this step by step. Okay?"

"Okay," she agreed in a small voice.

"Do you remember driving in your truck?" he asked gently. "From your house—down toward town."

She answered with a small nod.

"Then what do you remember?" he asked.

This time she answered with a gasp.

"What?"

"He drove up close and rammed my back bumper!"

"Who?" he pressed.

"Someone. I said 'he,'" she mused. "But really, I don't even know if it was a man. I couldn't see him. The sun was hitting his windshield."

He'd felt the impact. "Who would want to hurt you?"

"I don't know! Maybe it was the kids up the hill—playing games."

It hadn't felt like a game to him. But he didn't think she could answer his question. So he focused on what else she might be able to remember.

"What happened after that?"

She tensed in his arms, and he was afraid she might bolt again. But she stayed where she was, tipping her face toward his, her eyes large and round. "He ran me off the road. I . . . I went down the hill." She gasped and he felt her terror, because he had been there with her. In her mind.

"There was a tree in front of me. I must have hit it." She stared at him, panic gripping her features. "What happened to me? Am I dead?"

"No!"

"Then what?"

He held her firmly by the shoulders, feeling her fine bones. "I told you. You're in the hospital, unconscious."

"How did you find out?"

"I . . . I saw your truck piled up against that tree," he said, because the part before that was too hard to explain.

"You were there?" she whispered.

He sighed, wondering if she would believe him. "No. I saw it in . . . my mind."

Fear bloomed in her eyes. "Like fortune-telling? Like your mother? And your aunt?" she asked in a barely audible voice.

"Yeah, like that. Sort of."

"No!"

He tried to reassure her. "It's all right. I wouldn't eavesdrop on you."

"I'm not worried about that. My father . . ."

"What about him?" he asked sharply.

"I . . . I remember . . . He didn't like what your mother and aunt told my mom."

"About his affairs?"

She made a strangled sound. "You knew about that?"

"I heard my mom and my aunt talking—after they thought I was in bed. They were afraid of the colonel and they were arguing about whether to tell your mother." He swallowed. "I guess they did, because she left him, didn't she?"

"That's not why!"

"Then what?"

She turned her head away.

"Miranda, you can't just say something like that— then clam up!"

"Caleb, don't ask me any more questions."

"Why not?"

"It's dangerous."

Before he could get her to explain what she meant, the world shook around him.

At first he thought she was fighting him again—until he saw the look of stark terror on her face.

"What?" she whispered. "What's happening?"

A wind sprang up, whipping her hair around her face.

"I don't know," he answered, but he felt his grip on reality slipping. This reality. The dream reality.

He reached for her, but somehow she was beyond his grasp. Not in distance. Her body had turned to mist in his arms. And when she said something else, he could see her lips moving, but he couldn't hear the words above the roaring in his ears.

Then he was speeding away from her, not on his own feet but as though he were on an open railroad car, racing down a track.

"Miranda!" he called out.

He saw her lips form words. "Caleb, be careful."

She screamed something else to him. But he couldn't catch the words. And billowing fog shrouded his vision, blurring his sight of her. The vapor poured down on him, wiping out the forest scene.

All at once he was somewhere else. Sitting on a hard bench, feeling sick and disoriented.

"Are you all right, young man? Are you all right?"

His eyes blinked open and he found himself staring into the wrinkled face of a gray-haired woman.

"What happened to Miranda?" he asked stupidly.

"I don't know. But you were sitting there, looking like you were in a trance. With your eyes open and your jaw slack."

"Charming," he managed, then sat up straighter. He was back in the hospital chapel. Alone, except for the old woman.

Lurching to his feet, he had to steady himself against the back of the pew when he wavered on unsteady legs. The back of the stained-glass window had been illuminated with floodlights when he came into the chapel. Now he could tell he was seeing daylight.

When he looked at his watch, he couldn't believe the time. It had seemed like he was in the dream with Miranda for less than an hour. But out here in the real world, half a day had passed.

He raised his eyes to the old woman. "Sorry I alarmed you."

"Not just me. The man and the woman."

"Huh? What man and woman?"

"They had to leave. They asked me to wake you." She shook her head. "But I didn't do it."

He struggled to take all that in. "You didn't wake me up?" he asked stupidly.

"No. It could have been dangerous. What if you'd been having a seizure?" she asked.

He didn't bother to tell her that if he'd been having a seizure, he doubted she would have had any effect on him.

The important point was that he'd been yanked out of the dream—by something. Not her, apparently.

He started to turn away, then saw she was staring at his jacket sleeve.

"Your arm!" she wheezed.

Her words brought a stab of pain—pain that had been there all along, under the surface. He looked at his left arm and saw the tattered jacket. Blood had oozed through and dried on the dark leather.

He stared at the bloody patches. Gingerly he pulled his arm through the sleeve. Below the jacket, his shirt was shredded—and so was his skin.

"Young man, what happened to you?" the woman asked.

"I was attacked by a bear," he answered, still trying to come to grips with what he saw.

She sucked in a startled breath. "Where?"

Where, indeed?

It had been in Miranda's dream. And contrary to all logic, he could see the marks on his arm—in the real world.

A lightning bolt of fear shot through him. Not for himself. For Miranda. If he could be hurt in that place—so could she.

What dangers, besides wild animals, waited for her there?

And what had jerked him awake? Some disturbance in her dream? Was her medical condition worse? Or was she awake?

Frederick Grove had never learned how to sit around and wait. He was a man of action. Now anger made his blood pressure throb in his temple as he leaned over his daughter, shaking her by the shoulders. She was still in intensive care, and they were keeping him out of her cubicle most of the time—like her father wasn't entitled to see her.

He'd had to sit in the waiting room and jump up like a trained monkey when they allowed him to come in here and stare into her pale face.

She had one of those air tubes sticking in her nose. And an IV drip in her arm. Stitches in her head. And she was attached to a bunch of monitors.

She'd already had all the standard tests. The doctor had said that if she didn't wake up soon, they were going to do an MRI. And another CAT scan, with contrast, whatever that meant.

So far, she was just lying there like a lump. "You can't do this!" he shouted. "You have to wake up and tell me what happened to you. You're a good driver. You wouldn't have a goddamn one-car accident. So what the hell happened? Who did this to you? That son of a Gypsy—pretending to be all concerned when he was probably up to his ears in this?"

When Miranda didn't answer, he gave her another shake.

Her eyes stayed closed, and her only response was a moan. She seemed to sink further into unconsciousness—making him madder than he had been a few minutes ago.

"You can't get away with this," he told her. "Stop burying your head in the sand like an ostrich."

He was sure he could get through to her—given enough time. And given the fact that she was malingering. At least that was the way he saw it. The doctor didn't know why she wouldn't wake up. But he did. She was hiding in there. And he wasn't going to allow it!

As he reached for Miranda again, a hand closed over his shoulder.

"Sir. Stop that, sir."

He looked up to see one of the nurses staring at him in horror.

They had caught him. They could call the security guards if he didn't do what they wanted. So he stepped away from Miranda and stalked out of the unit.

Caleb came pounding up the stairs to the intensive care unit, praying that Miranda had regained consciousness.

"Is she awake?" he gasped when he saw her father.

"No."

The colonel's eyes shifted away, and Caleb felt a spurt of fear. Lord, had the fool been acting true to form. Had he tried to wake her up? Was that what had happened to tear the fabric of the dream?

He warned himself not to jump to conclusions. Yet now that his sixth sense was operating on overdrive, he thought he wasn't off the mark.

Forcing himself to speak in a low, calm voice, he said, "Let me talk to her. She might respond to me. I've heard that when people are in a coma, sometimes they can hear what people are saying to them."

Colonel Grove laughed in his face. "You must be kidding. She gave you the boot eight years ago. If she's going to respond to anyone, it will be to me. To her father. So get the hell back where you belong—that fancy art studio of yours."

The urge to land a punch in the middle of the man's thin lips was overwhelming. It took every ounce of control Caleb possessed to back away. Once again, he reminded himself that if he got into a fight with the colonel, they'd both get thrown out of the hospital. And neither one of them would know when Miranda woke up.

That was the only thing stopping him from physical violence. But he sure as hell wasn't going to follow Colonel Grove's directions. He was going to stay right here in M-C General. Close to Miranda.

Slipping his hand into his pocket, he wrapped his fist around the opal ring. It helped to center him, and he clung to it as though it could make a difference in his destiny as he walked away from the intensive care unit.

As he passed the elevator, he saw a man get off. A man with a hard face and salt-and-pepper hair in a buzz cut. He noticed the guy because he looked like an ex-army officer. A friend of Colonel Grove's? Come to lend support?

Turning, Caleb watched to see where the guy was going. But when he walked on past the unit, Caleb switched his attention back to his main objective—communicating with Miranda.

• • •

As Frederick stood in the waiting room looking out the window, he heard the sound of footsteps behind him. That son of a Gypsy was back!

Whirling, he prepared to lunge across the room. He changed his stance when he saw his business partner, Dustin Auger, standing in the doorway.

Carefully he studied the other man's face. "It's about time you got here," he muttered.

His partner spread his hands in a conciliatory gesture. "Sorry. You know I was in San Francisco receiving that shipment of Chinese porcelain."

"Porcelain vases. Yeah." He wanted to ask some questions—like about what else had arrived. He wanted to ask more pointed questions about where Dustin had been for the past thirty-six hours. Instead, he simply said, "I left a message on your cell phone."

"Sorry," Dustin said again. "The battery went out. I couldn't pick up my messages until I got home." He looked over Frederick's shoulder toward the door to the intensive care unit. "You said Miranda had an auto accident."

"Yes."

"I just saw that big celebrity sculptor guy. What's he doing here?"

"Sticking his honker in where it doesn't belong."

Dustin nodded, his eyes probing. "You look pretty wrung out. Why don't you go get something to eat. I'll stay here, in case they have some new information on Miranda."

"Maybe later. I'm not hungry now," he answered. There was something about the tone of Dustin's voice that made his nerves prickle. Not just his voice. Their business had been running smoothly for a while, but he was coming back to the conclusion that trusting Dustin Auger was a mistake.

"It won't do her any good for you to sit here if she's unconscious," his partner said.

"I'm doing it for me," Frederick snapped. "When she wakes up, I want to know about it."

"I'll sit with you for a while," Dustin offered.

As she pressed her shoulders against a tree trunk, Miranda felt as though she were holding on to her sanity by her fingernails.

She'd thought she'd lost a group of tourists. After talking to Caleb, she was pretty sure there had never been anyone in this woodsy prison but her—until Caleb had somehow battered his way into her dream.

She'd accepted his word on that—too late. Because he'd vanished as quickly as he'd appeared.

She pressed more tightly against the tree bark. Bending her legs, she clasped them in her arms and lowered her head to her knees.

Although the hard surface behind her felt reassuring, her heart was still pounding like a tom-tom inside her chest. Caleb had forced her to remember the accident in her truck. He'd said she was in a coma. She didn't want to believe it.

But she had no choice. Because now she remembered the shock and terror of trying to steer while another driver bashed at her bumper.

Somebody had driven her off the road. She knew that much, even if she didn't know who it was.

Panic threatened to swallow her whole, and she struggled to fight it off—and to think calmly. Her memory was flaky. Maybe from the accident.

Where had she been going?

She couldn't remember! Still, she was pretty sure that she'd been on an important mission.

Her jaw clenched. If she could wake up, maybe she could figure it out. Or maybe she didn't want to. Maybe she was staying here because she was afraid to go back to the real world.

Her head started to ache again, and she pressed her temple against her knees. It didn't feel like she wanted to hide. She wanted to wake up. She had to wake up!

Raising her head, she shouted, "Let me out!"

Her voice reverberated through the empty woods. She looked at the sunlight filtering through the branches over her head, and her breath caught. It was late afternoon. It had been late afternoon ever since she'd arrived here. The time never changed, she thought with a shiver.

Feeling exposed and vulnerable, she struggled to stay calm, even when fear clogged her throat.

She could go back to the campsite. That was where she'd picked up the rifle earlier. It had been lying on the ground. But she hadn't looked in any of the tents.

Maybe there was something else she could use there. A jacket to keep her warm. And another gun. She'd feel safer with a gun in her hand.

"Stop drifting back to that way of thinking," she said aloud, speaking to the trees and the sky. "Caleb told you the truth about this place. You're trapped in a dream. No, a nightmare. And you'll never be safe here. You need to wake up."

She sent her thoughts out—searching for the door to reality. Instead she sensed a wall, wrapping around the forest. And when she mentally shoved against it, she could make no headway.

All at once she remembered that her cell phone was in her pocket. Pulling it out, she pressed the End button. The screen lit, and she felt a spurt of hope. But when she tried to make a call, the roaming symbol came on, telling her there was no connection. Apparently she wasn't going to be able to call out of this place.

Had she walled herself in here? And now she was caught in her own trap? Or had someone else locked her in?

As Caleb descended in the elevator, he wondered what he was going to do now. He couldn't go back to the chapel because the mystery couple who had found him there once could do it again. But there must be lounges and waiting rooms all over the hospital. Maybe he could find one in an out-of-the way location—where he could sit quietly and get into Miranda's dream again.

That was his plan. But as he stepped out of the elevator, a wave of dizziness assaulted him. He hadn't eaten since yesterday morning. And he'd been here all night.

In the hallway a sign caught his eye, giving directions to the public parts of the hospital, including the cafeteria. He was in agony to get back to Miranda. But he knew the demands of his own body. He couldn't keep going without fuel. And he might do her more harm than good in his present condition.

Maybe he'd better stuff a sandwich into his mouth.

In the cafeteria he grabbed a turkey sandwich and a carton of milk and started eating while he was still waiting in the line at the cash register.

Miranda stopped at the edge of the camp.

"It looks so familiar," she said aloud, because the sound of her own voice helped fill the empty landscape. "But now I remember why."

A month ago she had led a group of computer executives on an expedition into a wilderness area near Eureka.

The trip had been a company team-building exercise. She'd been responsible for the woodcraft and safety on the trip. She'd taught the middle-aged executives how to pitch two-man tents, cook all their food over the campfire, and build an outdoor shower and latrine. She'd also led them on rock-climbing expeditions.

Unfortunately, an acne-scarred jerk named Buck Holden from the company personnel office had been in charge of the psychological aspects of the group experience.

He'd corralled her into late-night planning sessions when she would have preferred getting the sleep she needed. And while they'd had the camp to themselves, he'd made a pass at her.

She'd tried to be firm and professional when she'd said that she didn't want a personal relationship.

But Buck had taken the rejection personally. And his behavior toward her had strained the atmosphere in the camp.

She'd come out of the experience feeling emotionally bruised, and she'd turned down another corporate assignment.

As she stood at the edge of the clearing, a sound made her head whip to the right. One of the tents rocked gently. Then, inside, she saw the shadow of a man—a man holding a knife in the air.

"Buck?" she called out.

He didn't answer, and her whole body tensed. Was it Buck doing this? Had he figured out a way to get back at her? Had he run her off the road?

Or was it the other way around? She'd been thinking about Buck Holden. Did that mean she had dragged him into this dream?

While she was wrapping her head around the possibility, the shadow on the tent wall changed. She had thought it was a man—holding a knife. But now she saw a bear with its jaw open.

She blinked, rooted in place as the image changed to a woman.

Her pulse pounded as she stared at the tent.

"This isn't reality," she whispered. "This is a dream." But her next thought was hardly comforting. If this was a dream, then anything could happen.

Her eyes fixed on the tent, she took a step back—then another. Once she was out of the clearing, she started running. At first she was running away from the camp. Then she realized she was going in the other direction— coming back again.

Stopping abruptly, she got her bearings, then carefully started away from camp once more. But the same thing happened. Again she was heading back to the

clearing. A scream of terror bubbled in her throat.
Somehow she held it back.

Caleb had finished half the small meal by the time he
started looking for a place to set down his tray. But it
was lunchtime, and most of the tables were occupied.

Balancing the tray on a trash can cover, he chugged
the carton of milk and gobbled another bite of the
sandwich. He was thinking that he might as well finish
eating standing up when a flash of color caught his eye.

His gaze zoomed to two women sitting at the other
side of the room. One had dyed red hair, a bright shawl,
and a purple patterned dress. The other had a similar
outfit. But her dress was blue, and she'd let gray creep
into her brown hair. They were leaning toward each
other, deep in conversation.

He blinked as he stared at his aunt and his mother,
feeling the hairs on the back of his neck prickle.

His aunt and his mother! That was no coincidence.

five

Caleb crossed the room rapidly and set his tray down on the table with a clunk.

Two heads jerked up, their expressions a mixture of concern and wariness.

His aunt stood. His mother looked from her to Caleb.

"Edith, don't leave."

His aunt shook her head. "I think the two of you need to talk," she said stiffly, then turned and walked away.

He and his mother were left staring at each other, as if they were the only two people in the room full of humanity. Silently he took the vacant seat.

"Caleb, I'm so glad you found us," she said. Her gaze flicked to his jacket sleeve, and she gasped. "What happened to you?"

"It's just torn. I'm fine," he snapped. "Tell me what you're doing here."

"Aunt Edith thought I should come with her."

"Why?"

His mother gave one of her shrugs, and he wanted to reach across the table and shake her.

"What did Aunt Edith say?" he pressed.

Loretta Mancuso straightened her shoulders. "She thinks you're making a mistake sticking your nose in where it doesn't belong."

He glared at her. "You'd better explain that."

When she looked down at her hands, he asked, "Did Miranda's mother leave her father because you told her about the colonel's affairs?"

Her head came up, and she looked over her shoulder, then back at him. "What makes you think that?"

"What am I supposed to think?" he asked in a gritty voice. "You won't give me any information. And neither will . . . the Iron Colonel."

"Is that what you call him?"

"Sometimes."

"Stay away from him. And stay away from his daughter."

"Why? Give me a reason!"

His mother sighed. "All right. We did tell Hilda that her husband was having . . . affairs. She said she could deal with that."

"Then why did she leave him?"

She struggled through a silent debate, then lowered her voice. "We also found out he was engaged in . . . il-legal business practices."

"Like what?"

His mother kept her gaze steady. "Drug smuggling."

He felt like he'd been socked in the stomach. "You're

kidding. How could the straight-arrow colonel get involved in that?"

"His import business was in trouble, and he needed a source of cash. I guess he rationalized it somehow. You know—who cares if a bunch of filthy lower-class people get hooked on drugs.

"We told Hilda, and she was going to confront him. But you know how he is. He hates anyone to challenge his authority."

"Yeah," Caleb muttered.

"Hilda went home. And we never saw her again."

He fought to rearrange his thinking. About Mrs. Grove—and about Miranda.

His mother reached across the table and covered his hand with hers. "Caleb, I never talk about your father."

"We're talking about Colonel and Mrs. Grove. Don't change the subject!"

"I have to. I want you to understand something else. You thought your dad left me. Really, he had no choice. He was sent to prison, and when he got out I was relieved that he stayed away from us."

Caleb was stunned. "Why didn't you tell me any of that?"

"I wanted to protect you. I want to protect you now."

He stared into her anxious face. She was telling him things he'd never known—never considered.

"Where is my father today?" he asked.

"He was a heavy smoker. He died of lung cancer when you were in middle school."

Caleb took that in, then asked, "And that's why you were so upset when you caught me smoking with some of my friends?"

"Yes," she murmured.

"And Dad was the reason you were so strict with me," he said, letting the theory take form. In a way, he'd known that all along, but the confirmation was important.

"Yes. I was terrified that his genes would be more important than the upbringing I gave you."

He felt like he'd been stabbed in the stomach with his own chisel. His upbringing hadn't exactly been conventional. How could it be—when your mom and live-in aunt supported themselves as fortune-tellers. But his mother had been strict with her only child. She'd even sent him to live with his grandfather one summer when she didn't like the company he was keeping. And now he understood that better.

They were sitting in the hospital where Miranda lay unconscious, and he was learning things about himself and his family that he had never known. It was too much all at once. He barely remembered his father. Would he have visited him in prison if he'd known where to find him? He wasn't sure. And his mother had never given him that chance.

At the same time he was caught by a sense of urgency. Not about himself, but about Miranda. As he sat here in this crowded cafeteria, he was sure that she needed him, and he had to reach her again.

"I feel better now that I've told you," his mother said, pulling his thoughts back to the hospital cafeteria.

He shifted in his seat. "Yeah."

"Do you forgive me?" she asked anxiously.

"I understand you better," he answered. His mother had revealed long-buried family secrets. "I need to think about how I feel," he answered honestly.

His mother's face crumpled, and he couldn't help feeling torn. "Mom, this is a lot for me to digest. And I need to worry about Miranda now," he said gently.

"What can you do for her?"

He gave her a steady look. "I can help her wake up."

Her eyes went round. "You mean . . . use your talent?"

"Yes." He started to say he had already been inside Miranda's coma dream, then decided to hold that information back. "We'll talk later," he said instead.

"Edith said you might try something like that. Please, think about the consequences."

"I am."

Her eyes went back to his jacket. "You could get hurt. I think you already got hurt. Making contact with an unconscious person is risky."

"You've done it?" he asked, switching the focus back to her.

She shifted in her seat. "I'm not that talented."

"Then how do you know?"

"Edith . . . said."

Edith again. He wanted to ask his mother if she could think for herself. Instead he repeated his offer to talk later, then stood up.

He knew now that she had delayed him from getting back to Miranda. Maybe she had done it on purpose. Maybe that was why she'd suddenly started talking about his father.

As he walked away from the table, terror gripped him. He felt like the world was shifting under him. Like he had one foot on Planet Earth, and one foot in outer space.

He reached for the door, moved to the side of the hall, and stood with his eyes closed, picturing Miranda.

"I'm coming. Hold on. I'm coming," he whispered.

He imagined her running through the woods. He didn't know if that was real—or if he was just giving rein to his own overactive imagination.

Fists clenching and unclenching at his sides, he strode up the hall, his gaze darting to the left and right, as he searched for some place he could be alone. When he reached an exterior exit, he stopped abruptly.

Now that he knew his mother and his aunt were looking for him in the hospital, maybe the safest place to do this was his car. Outside, he trotted around the building to the visitor lot.

Fear made his heart pound inside his chest. The need to break through into Miranda's world was like a terrible pressure building inside him. But he had learned caution—the hard way. So he took the time to glance around the parking area. He didn't see anyone obviously watching him. He hoped he'd have privacy.

In the backseat he pulled off his ruined jacket and shirt and looked at his arm. The claw marks were fading fast—faster than if he'd gotten them in the real world, he thought. After inspecting the wound, he pulled a sweatshirt from his overnight bag and put it on.

Once he'd changed, he brought out the large cardboard covering that he sometimes put across the front window to keep the sun from blasting the car. On the front was a large picture of sunglasses. On the back, facing him, was a wavy blue-and-green pattern that he'd always thought was relaxing.

After wedging the screen into the window, he slipped behind the wheel, then pushed back his seat so he could stretch out his legs. With the sunscreen and the tinted windows, the atmosphere in the car was dim and restful.

His mother had warned him this could be dangerous. Too bad. He was going into Miranda's mind—using the quickest route he could. Leaning his seat back, he stared at the blue-and-green pattern in front of him, imagining blue sky and green trees.

A peaceful outdoor scene. But he could feel tension stringing his nerves tight. His tension. And maybe Miranda's.

As he stared at the blue-and-green screen, he reached into his pocket, finding the ring, closing it into his fist as he sent his thoughts toward the swirling colors. Instantly he felt a little closer to Miranda.

"Let me in, sweetheart," he murmured. "Whatever is wrong, I'll help you deal with it," he promised, hearing the rough quality of his own voice.

When she didn't answer, his heart started pounding harder.

The design wavered in front of his eyes, and he let them go unfocused, turning the pattern into a green and blue blur.

He felt himself slipping into the colors. It was a strange sensation—as though he were losing himself. His first panicked impulse was to pull back. But he focused on Miranda. She needed him. And the eddy of bright hues was the way to forge a link to her private world.

He wasn't certain how he knew that. But he was sure it was true.

As he stared at the sunscreen, he felt himself rushing forward again, the way he had the first time he had entered her dream.

But he found out quickly that it still wasn't going to be easy.

With a groan of mingled pain and protest, he slammed into the familiar rubber wall. This time, he felt the breath whoosh out of his lungs, and he had to struggle to keep his eyes on the blue-and-green pattern.

Now he was sure that something—or someone—was deliberately holding him back. His mother? His aunt? Both of them? Maybe together they had the power.

"Leave me alone!" he growled, sending the words out in a burst of mental energy. The effort drained him, and his body sagged against the seat.

But with his mind, he kept pressing ahead in his silent quest. If he hadn't wanted it so badly, he knew it would have been impossible.

He kept up the pressure, feeling his muscles and his mind go weak as he fought the force that seemed determined to defeat him.

And finally, finally, with a silent shout of triumph, he pushed into the green-and-blue design.

Only that didn't signal his success. The pattern had changed to a sticky mass, and he was caught in the middle—the stuff holding fast to his body and oozing around his face.

He felt the air turning to stone in his lungs, but he couldn't gasp in oxygen past the layer of goop that glued itself to his nose and mouth.

It was like being caught in the middle of a pot of green-and-blue builder's caulk. But it felt like it was alive—deliberately fighting to hold him there until he died.

And he would die. He knew that now.

Would his own mother kill him? Or had she miscalculated the power needed to keep him away from Miranda?

He wanted to scream at her to let him go. But he couldn't waste the energy.

So he fought the sticky mass the only way he could, ordering his mind to slip and flow through the seams of the pattern, worming his way around the deadly obstruction.

He couldn't put into words what he was doing. But somehow he did it. Or maybe he was stronger than the force trying to annihilate him.

He dragged his way through the swirl of green and blue and fell gasping onto the riverbank where he had entered the scene before. For long moments, all he could do was lie there dragging in huge drafts of the clean forest air.

He stared up at the sky. It was afternoon at home. And here, too. Always late afternoon. Still, it felt as if he had been in that sticky mass for hours.

Maybe he had, for all he knew.

He was about to call Miranda's name when a blood-curdling scream cut through the silence of the forest.

Miranda. Oh, Lord, that was Miranda. In trouble.

Six

Caleb scrambled to his feet and dashed in the direction of the campsite. At least that was where it sounded like the scream had come from.

He broke through the trees and gasped. Miranda was struggling with someone.

A man—it looked like, but his outline was a blur. And the face . . .

At first he thought the face was covered by a hood. As he dashed forward, he saw that wasn't true. There was a head on the body, but it was blotted out by a dancing blob of shifting lights, like in a television picture where they wanted to hide someone's identity, so they covered the face on the video with a digital pattern.

On TV the dancing pattern was a bunch of colors. This one was black and shades of gray—matching the sweatshirt and sweatpants the guy was wearing.

No—now the head and clothing were blue and green, the colors shifting and wavering before Caleb's eyes.

It was like the pattern that he'd used to bring him into Miranda's dream. And that told him something important. This had as much to do with him as it did with Miranda.

He wanted to shout at the guy to leave her alone. But he couldn't risk the danger of distracting her.

When she'd tried to fight him off after he'd told her she was in a coma, her moves had been jerky and disorganized. Now she seemed to have remembered her martial-arts training.

Her total concentration was on the battle, her arms and legs moving like lethal weapons as she executed moves that took his breath away.

His own training was in street fighting—when kids had teased him about his mother and his aunt's profession. He'd taken plenty of flack as the son of a Gypsy fortune-teller.

He ached to jump into the fight. But he knew he'd do more harm than good. Frantically he looked around for a weapon. He needed a baseball bat or something. And one winked into existence on the ground near his feet. Score one for him.

Teeth clenched, he stepped behind the guy and wacked him smartly across the shoulder with the bat.

The headless man whirled, and Caleb couldn't hold back a gasp as he faced the featureless opponent. But he didn't let that stop him from swinging again. This time he cracked the opponent's raised arm.

The man made an angry, grunting sound as he leaped at Caleb—who kept swinging.

Maybe Miranda had taken a page from his book, because instead of keeping up with her martial-arts routine, she picked up a large rock and brought it down with a crack on what passed for the man's head.

He went down, sprawling on the ground. And while he was lying there, his body began to fade away.

Miranda screamed when he disappeared completely. As she wavered on her feet, Caleb surged forward and caught her in his arms.

She made a small sobbing sound, then seemed to get control of herself. "I was losing. Then you came—and saved me."

"Who was that? Your dad?"

She sucked in a sharp breath. "I hope not. . . . I don't think so."

"I think the colonel was in your room—doing something to you earlier. That's what yanked me out of here the first time."

"I . . . don't know who it was," she whispered. "Obviously, he didn't want me to see his face."

"Yeah, somebody hid it for him."

"Who?"

"My mother. My aunt," he suggested.

"That man came here to kill me," she said in a voice that she couldn't quite hold steady. "I hope it wasn't my father. You think *your* mother sent him?"

His own voice shook as he gripped her shoulders. "I don't know! Tell me what happened before I arrived."

She gulped. "I kept trying to get away from camp. And every direction I ran in, I ended up back here."

"Christ!"

"I saw shadows moving inside one of the tents."

"Which one?"

She pointed to a red-and-blue shelter, than took her lower lip between her teeth. "Before he came out, I couldn't tell if it was a man."

"Because you couldn't see clearly through the tent fabric?"

"No. He kept changing shape. I saw a man. I saw a bear. A tiger. A woman!"

Caleb's hands tightened on her shoulders, and he cursed again. "Who could manage that—besides my mother or Aunt Edith?"

"Someone my father hired?" she asked in a small voice.

"What's his motive?"

She took a step back and scuffed her foot against the dirt. "I can't tell you."

Anger boiled through him. "You have to! You have to stop playing games with me. It doesn't matter anymore. I know about the drugs."

The blood drained from her face. "You do?" she gasped out.

His eyes narrowed. "I know he and his partner were doing it eight years ago. You're saying it's still going on?"

Her face took on a look that mixed fear and anger. "I discovered my dad is back at it again," she whispered.

"How?"

She sighed, her hands fluttering as she struggled to find the right words. "I . . . he was acting strange, secretive. I . . . I . . . hired a private detective, and he gave me a report. As soon as I read it, I tried to talk to my father. But he wasn't home, so I left a message on his answering machine, but he didn't get back to me."

"You mentioned illegal drugs in a voice message?" he asked sharply.

"Not in those words." She sighed. "I didn't want to say anything . . . incriminating without talking to him face to face, so I said I wanted to discuss something important." She looked miserable. "Maybe the tone of my voice gave me away."

He shrugged, wondering if she'd said more to her father than she was telling him. "Let's get back to eight years ago when your mother disappeared. If your dad could smuggle drugs, maybe he could kill her."

"No."

"Then what?"

Again—her expression gave away strong emotions.

"Did he?" he asked. "Did you find that out?"

"No," she said sharply, then turned and began walking rapidly out of camp.

He caught up with her and grabbed her arm. "Wait a minute! You can't run away now."

"Why not?"

"Because it's too dangerous. Somebody besides me broke in here! That guy with the digitized face."

When her gaze darted around the clearing, he went on quickly. "We need to protect you. If Mr. Digital comes back, I want to make sure he can't get to you."

He strode to where cooking equipment was stacked beside the fire pit and picked up a pot. Squatting, he began scooping up ashes.

"What are you doing?" she asked from behind him.

"Practical magic."

When he had a potful, he turned.

"Which tent is yours?"

She pointed to a blue-and-yellow one.

He nodded, then looked inside, seeing a backpack and sleeping bag.

Starting just to the left of the entrance, he moved clockwise as he sprinkled a line of ashes in a circle around the tent, murmuring a chant that he'd read in a book long ago. She didn't interrupt until he had come almost full circle, leaving an opening at the tent entrance.

"You're making a protective circle?" she asked.

"Yes."

She tipped her head to one side. "You believe in magic?"

He looked at her and grinned. "I'm here, aren't I? What got me here if it wasn't magic?"

"Psychic powers you inherited from your mom."

"I think of magic and psychic powers as two sides of the same coin. You can't work magic without innate abilities."

"Whatever you want to call it. You've got it. Like that time I ran away from home, and I was sure nobody could find me. But somehow you knew I was hiding in the big drainage pipe."

"Yeah."

"You chewed me out for pulling that stunt."

He nodded.

"But really—you were worried."

"Yes," he whispered.

"I knew how you found me. And you did it another

time—when my truck battery went dead. It was just after I got my license, and I got stuck coming back from
the convenience store. You showed up at midnight to rescue me."

He nodded.

Her expression changed. "You have a way of turning
up when I'm in trouble. You're the one who called 911
after whoever it was forced my truck off the road,
aren't you?"

There was no point in denying it. Again he nodded.

"Am I the reason you tried to shut off your psychic
abilities?" she asked, her voice barely above a whisper.

His head jerked up. "How did you know that?"

"Because I would feel you reaching out to me, and I
would . . . I would clamp down. . . ." She gulped. "I
think I hurt you."

He swallowed. "You did. And now you're saying you
were doing that on purpose?"

"Yes," she whispered.

"Why?"

"So you would stop."

"Thanks for leveling with me," he bit out.

She winced.

He clamped his fingers on the pot handle. "But now
I'm using my powers again, whether you like it or not.
Get inside so I can finish the circle."

"What about you?"

He shifted his weight from one foot to the other. "I'm
going back to have a chat with your father."

Alarm bloomed on her face. "No!"

"I should have done it eight years ago."

"I'm not going in there—unless you come with me."

He knew from the tone of her voice and the fierce look in her eye that she was telling the truth. So he answered with a tight nod.

She studied his stony face, then ducked down and crawled inside.

He stood for several moments, staring at the opening. She had brought back all the old hurt with her admission. But he still felt compelled to help her. He was betting it took a lot of energy to send an enemy into her dream. And energy to get through his circle. Which gave him time to get out of here and make her father come clean with him. Or his aunt. Or the business partner. Or his mom, he thought with a pang. He didn't know which of them was involved. But he was going to find out.

For now he followed Miranda inside the tent, then turned quickly as he finished off the circle and said more magic words—words he hoped would keep any evil away from this fortress.

Despite his dark mood, he laughed.

"What could possibly be funny?" she asked, her voice jumping with nerves.

"This tent isn't very big. But I was thinking of it as a fortress."

"I hope it is."

She had switched on a camp lantern, creating a warm glow inside the confined space.

"You need somewhere to sit," she said, scooting to the side and unzipping the sleeping bag. Then, awkwardly, they spread it out so that it covered the floor of the tent.

They both sat, leaving as much space as possible sep-
arating them. When she saw him watching her, she
looked away. They had been talking about the colonel's
drug smuggling, and Caleb had let it go for the time being. But if she wouldn't let him leave, he would use the
time constructively.

He stared at the tense set of her jaw. "What aren't you
telling me?" he asked.

"About what?"

Maybe he should ask about the detective's report.
What he heard himself saying was, "About us . . . eight
years ago."

He saw her teeth clench, but she kept her eyes away
from him.

His anger flared. "Dammit, answer me. You came to
me and said we were finished. Then you put up mental
barriers against me. Were you afraid I'd find out that
your dad killed your mother? Was that it?"

When she sat without moving or speaking, he grabbed
her chin and turned her face toward him. "Okay, let's go
at it from a different angle. Look at me, and tell me again
that you walked away from me because I wasn't good
enough for you."

Her eyes were large and green in the warm light from
the lantern.

Maybe he could make confession easier for her.
"Were you acting on orders from your father?" he
pressed.

"Yes," she whispered.

He felt his throat clog. It was hard to speak, but he
managed to say, "I know he was pretty rough on you. I

guess that time he really scared you. He was going to punish you if you kept hanging out with me?"

She shook her head. "No."

"Just give me a straight answer, because I can't help you unless you do."

Seven

❖

Caleb watched Miranda's eyes turn fierce. "A straight answer? Okay, I'll give you a straight answer! My father told me he'd made a deal with my mom. She was his wife, so he gave her money, and he let her go—far, far away. But he didn't have to let the son of a Gypsy off the hook. He said you were dangerous. He said he'd kill you—unless I broke off with you. And he said he'd kill you, if I told you what he'd said. Or if I told anyone else."

He felt the air in his lungs solidify, leaving no room for another breath.

She was speaking again, and he struggled to hear the words above the buzzing in his brain.

"He wouldn't tell me why, but I knew. He was afraid you would pick up something incriminating from my mind. He was afraid your mother or your aunt would do the same thing. So he sent my mom away where she couldn't contact them." When he didn't speak, she went on quickly. "Of course, when my mom first started consulting them, he thought they were charlatans. He'd taunt my mother about how stupid she was going to 'those mediums.' But then they decided to tell her about his affairs, and she confronted him. He was mad at them. And mad at me for hanging out with you. But it wasn't until that drug deal that he came to the conclusion that you and your family were totally dangerous."

"That's why you were frightened the last time I was here—when we talked about my mother and my aunt?"

"Yes."

He was stunned by the information, but he managed to ask, "How does all this fit together?"

She sighed. "Dad promised he wouldn't do the drug stuff again. He said it was a one-time deal because he needed money. And I believed him, because I didn't have much choice when I was sixteen. But I don't have to live with his lies now. I was on my way to confront him when somebody ran me off the road."

She had finally put a lot of the pieces of the puzzle together for him.

He sat on the sleeping bag, trying to hang on to his sanity as all the assumptions he'd made about her— about the two of them—crashed and burned around him.

"I'm sorry," he heard himself say.

"For what?"

"For hating you."

"I tried to make sure you would! Because I was afraid for you."

"Oh, Lord, Miranda. All these years . . . I kept telling myself I never really knew you. All these years I was too wounded to think straight."

"I had to keep you safe."

"Thank you for telling me the truth."

"My father is still dangerous." Her breath caught as her gaze darted around the small tent. "Caleb, where are you—really. I mean in the real world. Are you safe?"

It was a strange question, but he answered it. "I'm in my car. With the sunscreen in the windshield. And tinted windows. I think I'm safe."

"Thank God."

"You're worried that your father could come looking for me?"

"Or Dustin. It could be Dustin."

"Is he about five ten? One seventy? A hard face? Salt-and-pepper hair in a buzz cut?"

"You saw him?"

"At the hospital."

"He and dad are close. Two peas in a pod. Stay away from him! He's violent."

"Did he ever hurt you?" Caleb asked sharply.

"No."

"Is he the guy who was fighting with you a few minutes ago."

"He could be. I can't tell without seeing his face. There are too many guys who work for my dad who look like him."

"Great."

She lifted her head. "I don't want to waste time talking about Dustin or my father." As she spoke, she scooted across the space between them and reached for him.

He caught her against his chest, his arms coming up to pull her close. Once she was in his embrace, all he could do was marvel at how wonderful it felt to hold her.

"I should have . . ."

"There was *nothing* you could do. You were just a kid. So was I."

"But . . ." he tried to argue.

Miranda pressed her hand against his mouth. "Do you really want to argue about it? Now?"

He closed his eyes, absorbing her question and the wonderful feeling of her fingers stroking his lips.

"No," he murmured, opening his mouth so he could play with her fingers.

Miranda closed her eyes, enjoying the sensation of Caleb nibbling at her fingers. His teeth on her flesh were tantalizing and arousing—and making her want more.

Moving her hand away, she pressed her lips to his. The shock of that contact was enough to make her pulse drum. With a moan she absorbed the wet heat of his mouth into herself.

She had denied herself this pleasure for years—because she had been afraid—for him.

Back then he'd been a boy. Now he was a man. A strong, sexy, talented man. The man she loved. And she understood what she had never been able to admit. She'd made a life for herself, but she'd only been half alive without him.

He angled his head, accepting what she offered and giving it back, kissing her with a desperation that awed her.

Her heart melted in the heat of that kiss. "Oh, Caleb. I missed you so much."

"God, yes."

She dared a glance into his eyes and saw a fierce, aching hunger that echoed her own.

They had shared almost everything lovers could share—except the ultimate joining. But she wasn't a shy, uncertain girl anymore. And now, in the confines of this tent, she was determined that they were going to express all the passion they had denied themselves for so long.

Quickly, before she could tell herself she was doing the wrong thing, she moved back against the tent wall, found the hem of her plaid shirt, and pulled it over her head without bothering to undo the buttons. After tossing it onto the sleeping bag, she unhooked the clasp of her bra and sent it to join the shirt.

She heard Caleb's indrawn breath, saw the fire leap in his eyes.

"You've hardly changed. You are as beautiful as the last time I saw you like this. So perfect," he whispered.

"You make me feel beautiful." She dared a wicked grin. "But one important thing *has* changed. I'm not afraid of going after what I want. Take off your shirt. It's been so long since I felt your chest against my breasts."

He scraped his sweatshirt over his head, then reached to pull her into his arms. The shock of his flesh against hers was almost too much to bear. A low sob welled in her throat, as her hands caressed his back, his shoulders.

His hands moved over her with the same frantic posses-siveness.

They rocked together, clinging, devouring each other's mouths in a kiss that was desperate and ruthless.

She felt her heart pounding in her chest, pumping the hot blood through her veins.

When his mouth lifted, his breath was ragged, and his eyes were fierce. "I want . . ."

"Yes. Everything. Everything I was afraid to give you before." As she spoke, she lifted her hand to stroke the harsh planes of his cheeks, then down to the crinkly hair that matted his chest. The last time she'd seen him, the hair on his chest had been sparse. Now it was thick and dark.

For heartbeats they stared into each other's eyes. Then his hands moved between them, cupping her breasts, his fingers stroking back and forth across the hardened tips.

Feelings welled inside her. Joy that he was with her again. Relief. Sorrow that they had missed so much time together.

And she saw her feelings echoed in his eyes.

She forgot where they were. Forgot everything but the taste of him, the feel of his hands and mouth on her hot flesh, the wonder of being with him again after so long.

"I want you naked," he growled.

"And you."

She raised up on her knees and unhooked the snap at the top of her jeans, then slicked them down her legs along with her panties, so that they pooled around her feet.

His strong artist's hand stroked the curve of her hip.

"So beautiful," he said again. "I was sculpting a statue of you. And I got it exactly right."

He dragged his fingers through the tight curls at the top of her legs before dipping lower to press over her clit.

Her breath caught.

"I missed that so much. I missed *you*," she whispered, desperate to make up for all the time they'd lost. While he stroked her, her hands went to the snap of his jeans, undoing, then lowering his zipper.

"My turn," she murmured, reaching inside and freeing his wonderfully hard penis. Years ago, she had felt tentative and embarrassed when she touched him. Now she boldly took him in her hand, enjoying the girth, the weight, the length of his erection.

"Lie down," she asked.

He did, and she leaned over him. Craving all the things she had never been bold enough to enjoy, she stroked her tongue up his length, smiling when she heard his indrawn breath.

Wanting more, she took him into her mouth, fueling her own arousal as she pleasured him.

He didn't give her much time to enjoy it.

"Sweetheart, stop," he begged. "Or this will be over before we get started." He reached for her shoulder, and she raised her head.

"Come here."

His gaze burned into hers, as she lay down beside him.

"Miranda." Her name sighed out of him as he gathered her into his embrace, raining kisses over her face, returning to her mouth over and over.

"Caleb. Oh, Caleb!" she cried out as he bent to suck

one tight nipple into his mouth, while his hand played with the other.

Slowly, then, he began to kiss his way down her body, pausing to lick a wet circle around her navel before delving into the hot, slick folds of her sex. He lapped at her, then swirled his tongue around her clit, sending heat spiraling through her body. As it had with him, the intensity built quickly—too quickly.

"Please," she gasped. "I want you inside me—finally."

He lifted his head, his gaze burning into hers.

"Lord, yes." He moved between her legs, and she reached for his penis, caressing him before guiding him home.

He made a hoarse sound as he plunged into her. And she wrapped her arms around him, holding tight. Finally. Finally. After so long, he was where he belonged.

They had both been frantic for contact. Suddenly he changed the rules, holding his hips very still as he dropped tiny kisses over her face and neck and shoulders before coming back to her mouth for a long, lingering kiss.

"I dreamed of this," he whispered.

"So did I."

"I was sculpting you because that was the only way I could get close to you."

"Oh, Caleb, I'm here now. Don't make me wait any longer for my fulfillment."

"No."

Her breath hitched as he began to move, sending a wave of ecstasy shimmering through her.

The ecstasy surged as he increased the pace. She matched his rhythm, her hips rising and falling as she reached for the ultimate pleasure, clinging to him, calling his name, lost to anything but the power of what was happening between them.

He lifted her up and up, into the clouds, and beyond. Her hands closed over his shoulders as she felt her inner muscles begin to quiver.

The explosion gathered. Then her whole body shattered in an orgasm that sent her rocketing beyond the universe.

She heard his shout of satisfaction as his climax followed hers, and she clung to him while they both returned to earth.

When he rolled to his side, he kept her in his arms, stroking her, kissing the side of her face, her hair.

She held on to him for long moments, drifting on a cloud of joy. Finally she raised her head and looked at him. "What we did together—before—that was so good. But never like that. This was everything I dreamed of."

"Yes."

He stroked a lock of damp hair off her forehead. "I'm not going to let you go," he said.

His words brought her back to earth. Well, not exactly to earth—to this strange place that she had created, and panic replaced the sense of security.

Outside the warm little world within their tent, she could hear the wind blowing now.

It wasn't a comforting sound. The nylon sides of the tent shook, and she moved closer to Caleb, putting the void beyond their fortress out of her mind. They had been apart for too long. Finally she was back in his arms.

But the doubtful expression on his face made her whisper, "What?"

She saw him swallow. "I brought something with me." Turning from her, he found his pants, then fumbled in the pocket. When he brought his hand out he had something in his fist. Slowly he opened it.

Her breath caught when she saw the opal ring.

"Oh, Caleb," she whispered. "My ring."

"You gave it back to me," he said in a gritty voice.

She felt her heart squeeze painfully. "I had to. But if you're willing to give me another chance, I'll wear it proudly."

His eyes met hers as he slipped the ring onto her finger. She was bursting with love for him. There was so much she wanted to say to him, but she couldn't do it yet. Not in this place.

Still, she felt a spurt of hope—for herself. She hadn't been able to break out of this trap on her own. But now that she felt the old bond with Caleb growing so strong, maybe he could help free her. That thought triggered another, and a wicked idea just leaped into her head.

Eight

❧

As Caleb looked down at Miranda, he saw a sassy smile flicker across her face.

"What are you thinking, you little witch?" he asked in a low, sultry voice, because just her expression made him suspect that he was going to like her answer. Hope bloomed inside him. By some miracle the girl who had stolen his heart so many years ago was back in his arms again—in his life. And now, she was a bold, sexy woman.

He trailed his hand over her shoulder, then down to her breast, cupping the soft mound. Her breasts were fuller than they had been when she'd been sixteen. But no less sensitive, and she reacted immediately to him with a small, indrawn breath.

It was tempting to keep caressing her. But he wanted

to hear what she had to say, so he lowered the questing hand to her ribs.

She flashed him the grin again. "You showed me some practical magic. What about the concept of . . . us . . . sex magic?"

He grinned back. "You mean use sex magic to help you get out of here?"

"Yes. A way to lend me your strength. Or maybe— combine our strength."

"I never tried sex magic before," he said.

"I hope not."

"But there's always a first time," he added as he pulled her close and lowered his mouth to hers for a long, arousing kiss.

They had just made love. But he felt his arousal surge back to life as his lips moved over hers.

Sex magic.

Yes, this was magic. Holding her in his arms again. Knowing she would let him do anything he wanted. Anything they both wanted.

His total focus was on her.

He smiled as her hand drifted down his body, finding his cock, her fingers playing over his descended flesh with a teasing stroke.

"You witch," he murmured.

"You like that?"

"You know I do."

Like an interfering ogre, a rumble of thunder shook the tent, breaking his concentration.

"What the hell?" he muttered.

Rain began to pelt the nylon, and an enormous gust

of wind made the canvas shudder. He wanted to ignore it, but the elements wouldn't leave them alone. In the next moment the tent gave a lurch, as though a cyclone were trying to pick it up.

Cold seeped through the thin walls. And into his veins.

When a frightening thought struck him, he opened the flap and looked at the protective ring of ashes he had poured onto the ground.

The wind had blown most of them away. And the rest were spreading in wet puddles.

"Shit!" he shouted into the wind and rain. While he'd been enjoying himself in here with Miranda, someone had been figuring out how to break into her refuge.

When he turned back, he saw a terrified expression on her face.

"What?" he shouted above the roaring outside.

"Someone . . ." She stopped and started again. "Someone . . . my . . . jaw . . ." Before she could finish, she began to cough.

"Oh, Lord, no!" He stared at her in horror. "No!" He wanted to pull her into his embrace, to hold her safe in his arms. But that would do her no good, because he knew what was happening. Someone had destroyed his magic circle, and now the same person was going after her in the real world. That was the only thing that made sense.

"Hang on. Just hang on," he ordered focusing on the panic in her eyes. "I can't help you from in here. I have to get back to your hospital room.

He saw her fear surge, and he almost lost his resolve. Instead, he jerked on his pants. Then he found his shirt.

The hardest thing he had ever done was climb out of the tent. But it was his only choice.

Freezing rain pelted him. Almost instantly he was soaked to the skin. He stood in the wind and rain, his hands outstretched as he called on all the power that he had used to bring him into her world. Only now he struggled to reverse the process.

He had two advantages this time. Overpowering fear gave him strength. And he had come this way twice before, so he had a better idea of what he was doing.

He conjured up a mental picture of the barrier that had kept him out. Then he started running, imagined himself charging toward the wall at full tilt, a massive log in his arms. He used the log like a battering ram, bashing a hole in the rubbery substance.

And as he broke through, he thought there might be another reason why he had done it so quickly. Somebody else had reversed the process—getting in to hurt Miranda. And he was using the energy that they had already supplied.

His eyes blinked open, and he found himself sitting in the front seat of his car, with his clothing soaking wet. Leaping out of the truck, he ran toward the hospital.

It was early morning in the real world. And someone was taking advantage of the short-staffed hours.

As a stone dug into his foot, he realized with a start that he was barefoot. But that didn't slow him as he crossed the mostly empty parking lot like an Olympic sprinter.

He pictured what he must look like—a wild man who'd just dashed out of the woods. He was pretty sure he'd be stopped if he tried to cross the lobby.

But he had to get to the intensive care unit. Fast.

"Hang on, Miranda. Hang on. Do that for me," he chanted as he headed for the side door where he'd gone out earlier. He knew it shouldn't be unlocked. But as he ran, he focused on the mechanism, telling himself that the door was open, that it wouldn't stop him at all.

And his need became truth. He didn't know if he'd unlocked the door with his mind, or if some negligent staffer had done his job. Frankly he didn't care. All that mattered was that he'd gotten into the building.

The tent blurred around Miranda. She had been desperate to leave this place. Now she tried to grab on to the scene. But it wavered, vanishing like mist evaporating in the heat of the sun.

Suddenly she couldn't see. Couldn't move. Couldn't hear. And cold terror squeezed her by the throat. She was between worlds. She was nowhere. And then something seemed to be pulling on her—pulling her back to earth. The old earth—where she had come from, she thought.

She should have felt relief. Instead, her heart pounded with tension. In the distance she could make out the voices of two people speaking. A man and a woman.

She caught snatches of their clipped conversation.

"Hurry. That bastard kicked me out of the dream. We have to do it this way."

"I don't like it," the woman said, her voice high and nervous. "I kept her from waking up. But I can't keep making things happen. I'm not that strong."

"Sure you are."

The man who had been in her dream! Who was he? Who was the woman? What were they doing?

Miranda stopped worrying about them when she felt water trickle down her throat, and another coughing spell took her. She was choking. She was going to die, and she was barely in her body. That wasn't fair, one part of her mind screamed. She hadn't come back to die. She had to fight them.

But she didn't know how. And to her relief, the torture stopped abruptly.

"The nurse is coming. Make us invisible," the man said.

"I . . . can only do so much. That's why we had to sneak in here when the staff was busy."

"Shut up and hide us."

Now Miranda recognized the man's voice. Dustin. Caleb had seen him at the hospital. What was he doing now? And how could he get invisible?

She heard scuffling noises. Then blessed quiet. Then someone rustling around the bed.

The nurse. Did she see the man and woman? If she did, why didn't she kick them out?

Desperately Miranda tried to open her eyes, tried to make her voice work. She had to tell the nurse that the two people were here. With her. But she had no control over her muscles. No control over her voice. She could only lie there like a limp rag doll.

A giant fist of terror pressed against her chest.

Help. You have to help me.

But the plea was only in her mind.

"I saw from the monitor that your blood pressure and heart rate are up," the woman said in a pleasant voice. "Is something worrying you? Or are you trying to come back to us?"

She wanted to shout "yes!" But the words wouldn't come.

She heard the nurse fussing around her. Then the woman departed. For long moments nobody spoke. Then she heard the two other people talking again. The woman. And Dustin.

She had been afraid of him for years. Now, as she listened to the conversation, it sounded like she had good reason.

He stood on one side of her bed. The woman was on the other. Her voice was familiar. Someone she had known a long time ago.

"This is all your fault," Dustin said again.

"How can you say that? You got yourself into hot water again."

"I'd like to kill you!"

"Of course. But my magic is too strong for that."

"Damn you!"

Her voice turned raspy. "If it weren't for me, you wouldn't know she hired a private detective."

If Miranda could have gasped, she would have. Suddenly she knew who it was—Caleb's aunt.

Dustin was speaking again, his voice hard edged. "Now get the rest of it right. Get rid of her."

"You were supposed to do that. And you botched it."

The conversation chilled Miranda to the bone. It was obvious Dustin and Caleb's aunt hated each other—but they were stuck together in some kind of devil's bargain.

She had to wake up. She had to stop them from killing her. But she couldn't claw her way back to consciousness. And now she thought she knew why. Edith had blocked her exit from the coma.

Without warning, water trickled into her throat, and she started to choke again.

Caleb's lungs burned as he dashed for the stairs, then pounded up to the second floor and down the hall.

Speeding to the intensive care unit, he pulled the door open and hurtled inside.

The nurse on duty looked up in surprise.

"Wait. Sir. You can't go in there, sir," she called out.

Ignoring her, he found Miranda's cubicle and dashed inside.

She was lying on the bed, coughing. At first it looked as if she was the only person in the room. But as he stared into the enclosed space, the air seemed to flicker like an image from a malfunctioning movie projector.

He blinked, then saw two people standing over her bed, his aunt and the man named Dustin Auger, Colonel Grove's business partner. Auger held Miranda's jaw open. His aunt was slowly pouring water into her mouth.

Nine

❧

"Stop!" he shouted as he leaped through the door and launched himself at Aunt Edith, knocking the water bottle out of her hand.

His aunt stepped back, pressing her shoulders against the wall.

"Do something," Auger ordered. "Hit him with a lightning bolt or something."

"I . . . can't. You've made me drain my power."

"Shit." Auger stepped around the bed, dropping into a martial-arts stance. The same pose that the man in Miranda's dream had used. And now he was in her room.

From the corner of his eye Caleb saw his aunt's image flicker. "No, you don't," he growled, using part of his mind to grab her by the scruff of the neck and force her to stay visible. But he kept his main focus on Auger.

"Come on Gypsy boy—just try it," the man taunted.

Caleb knew that the guy could take him apart. If he could have used his psychic powers to fight, he would have. But he was too inexperienced, and he might end up hurting Miranda.

Another figure distracted him for a split second. Colonel Grove—his eyes wide as he took in the scene.

"Get the cops," Caleb shouted. "Hurry."

As Auger lunged, Caleb danced back, then went into street fighting mode. He got in a couple of punches before Auger chopped at him. The blow was intended to break his neck, he was sure. But he managed to deflect it with his arm.

He held his own—more or less. But he had no illusions that he could win.

Auger bolted for the door. But Caleb caught him by the shoulders, just as two security guards charged into the room.

"Hold it right there," one of them ordered.

Auger immediately started talking—fast. "Thank God you're here. This guy and his aunt were trying to kill Miranda. They hatched a plot to get back at the family."

"You liar!" Aunt Edith shouted.

"They were pouring water down her throat," Auger continued, edging toward the door.

But Frederick came up and put a large hand on his shoulder. "I don't think so," he growled.

Miranda lay in the bed, unable to move. Unable to speak.

She wanted to scream, to flail. But she was trapped in her body. Then something was different. She could feel the bed under her, the sheet on top of her. And she could feel something else—the hard metal of Caleb's ring circling her finger. He had given it to her in the dream. And she still had it!

Making a tremendous effort, she closed her fist around the gold band—and broke through the barrier that had kept her away from the world.

A scream burst from her lips as her eyes snapped open. And she saw that everybody in the room had turned to stare at her.

"Dustin is lying," she gasped out, hearing the raspy sound of her own voice.

Her eyes met Caleb's. She knew from the mixture of raw emotions on his face that he wanted to leap to her side. "No! We have to sort this out."

He gave a small nod as she tried to gather her energy. She was pretty sure that most people who woke up from a coma didn't emerge in fully functioning shape. But she hadn't been in a normal coma. Aunt Edith had kept her there.

She pushed herself up against the pillows, her gaze swinging from her father to the guards. She was weak, but she had to make them understand that she was in control of her mind. "Dustin is lying," she said again, speaking slowly and clearly. "He and Aunt Edith were in here—pouring water down my throat—and cursing each other while they did it."

"No!" Dustin shot back. "She's wrong. She was unconscious."

She fixed him with a piercing look. "Don't you know that when a person is unconscious, the sense of hearing is the first to return?"

He blanched, but said nothing.

She swung her gaze toward her father. "I think Edith found out you'd started up your illegal business with Dustin again. I think she was blackmailing him for years. They were afraid I was going to call the cops, so he ran me off the road. Only I didn't die. So they had to try again."

Miranda looked toward the nearest security guard. "Dustin and Edith were the ones tying to kill me," she said again, wishing she was stronger. But she had used up all her energy, and she flopped back against the pillow, exhausted.

"Tell them, Aunt Edith," Caleb growled. "Tell them how Dustin forced her car off the road and you pushed her into a coma with your mental powers."

"Mental powers," the guard muttered.

"She made her living as a fortune-teller for years," Frederick growled. "And she was good at it. She knew people's secrets."

Caleb looked at his aunt. "Is my mother in on this?" he asked.

The blood drained from her face. "No! Don't blame her. She didn't know anything about my blackmailing Auger. I put a protective charm around her to keep Auger away. And Frederick, too." She sighed. "I thought you were safe, because you broke up with Miranda. So don't blame your mother for any of this. She just came along to the hospital to persuade you to mind your own business. She was afraid you'd get hurt."

Caleb breathed out a sigh, relief sweeping over his face when he realized his mother wasn't in on anything immoral or illegal.

His aunt's eyes filled with tears. "Caleb, I'm so sorry. But I knew for years that Miranda Grove was no good for you. I was glad when the colonel chased you away."

The lead guard had pulled out his walkie-talkie. "I have a situation in Intensive Care. I need police assistance," he said.

Uniformed officers arrived ten minutes later. After the guard related the past few minutes of conversation, the cops clicked handcuffs onto Dustin and Edith. But when they started hustling everyone away, Miranda roused herself again.

"No. Let Caleb stay with me," she pleaded.

Her father turned to the cops, his face a mixture of pain and resignation. He had always been strong and in charge. He looked like he'd aged ten years in the past few days.

His shoulders sagged in defeat. "Let Mancuso stay. He's the only one standing who doesn't deserve any blame. He was just trying to help my daughter." He dragged in a breath and let it out. "I was on my way down the hall when I saw him heading for the intensive care unit. I didn't see Dustin or Edith come in. There's only one entrance, so they had to be in Miranda's room when he arrived."

Miranda looked gratefully at her father. "Thank you," she whispered, fighting the tears that blurred her vision. Pulling herself together, she spoke to the cops. "I was in a coma. And my fiancé was worried about me. I hope you'll let him stay with me now, because, you know, I could have been separated from him forever."

"Fiancé. That's a lie!" Dustin shouted.

"I have his ring," she said, holding up her hand to

show the opal sparkling on her finger. "Our names are engraved inside."

She saw Caleb's eyes widen, saw her father press his lips together and the cops exchange glances.

"I guess we know where to find you if we have any questions," one of them said to Caleb in a gruff voice.

"Yes. Thank you. I'll be right here. With Miranda."

She thought she would be alone with Caleb now. But a doctor and nurse had been waiting outside the door. They spent twenty minutes asking questions and doing an examination before they told Caleb he could have ten minutes with her before he had to clear out.

When they finally had some privacy, the questioning look on his face made her breath catch.

"Your fiancé?" he asked.

"I . . . thought that would convince the cops to let you stay," she murmured.

"It did."

She caught her bottom lip between her teeth, then released it. "Maybe I spoke too quickly."

"I'm glad you did. That is—if it saves me from the hell of wondering whether you'll say yes when I ask you to marry me."

She gave him a tremulous look. "If you'll take me back, I'm yours."

He bent down and gathered her into his embrace, being careful not to disturb the IV drip that was still attached to her arm.

"Miranda, I never stopped loving you."

Tears glistened in her eyes. "Caleb, I love you so much. I've always loved you. Since we were kids."

He held her more tightly. "As soon as you get out of

here, I want to get a marriage license. We've wasted enough time."

"Yes," she answered, moving her lips against his shoulder. She was so happy to be back in the real world, so happy to be back with Caleb again. But worry marred her happiness, and she knew Caleb sensed it.

"You're thinking about your father, aren't you?" he asked in a low voice.

"Yes."

"He may do time for drug smuggling. But not for attempted murder."

"That's something."

"More than I can say about my aunt."

She nodded again. "Why did she do it?"

His voice turned hard. "She and my mom went through some hard times. I guess somewhere along the line, money became more important to her than anything else. The worst part is—I would have supported her, the way I support my mom, if I'd thought she needed me. But she told me she was fine. I guess she liked taking Dustin's money. Maybe she took other people's money, too."

Miranda squeezed his hand. "Yes. I'm sorry."

"I'm not going to let that spoil our reunion."

"Good."

He pressed his lips against her cheek, still marveling at the joy of knowing she was his again.

"Your psychic powers brought us back together," she whispered.

"Psychic powers. Yeah. I tried to push them aside."

"Because of me."

"I should have . . ."

"No. Stop. Eight years ago we were both too young to fight my father. Now we have to put all that behind us—and go on with our lives. Together."

He held her tighter, thinking he'd tried to run from his destiny. The irony was that the Iron Colonel had seen the psychic ability in him—and kept him away from Miranda because of it.

"Can your magic powers get me out of here faster?" she murmured.

"Maybe." He closed his eyes, focusing on healing and love, as he sent his strength to her.

"Um . . . I feel that. It's like a nice hot sun beating down on me."

"Good. Just wait until I get you home. I believe I can make you feel a good deal hotter," he said, then grinned as happiness surged inside him.

"Oh, I'm sure you can." She grinned back, then closed her eyes. "I'm tired."

"Rest. I'll be right here."

She relaxed against the pillow. Then her eyes snapped open again.

"Don't be afraid to sleep," he murmured. "You're safe now."

"Because of you," she answered. "Only because of you."

The Road of
Adventure

Robin D. Owens

One

He was the ugliest cat Jake had ever seen. The black-and-white tom had an aura of maleness surrounding him, even as he licked his paw and eyed Jake with disdain. One of Jake's ex-girlfriends had used that aura-of-maleness phrase to describe him, and he'd thought it was crap—now he knew what she'd meant.

The cat set down his paw and sniffed. "I knew you'd come here."

Jake must be dreaming. Cats sure as hell didn't talk. The surroundings hadn't tipped Jake off. He spent a lot of time in the gym locker room. He shifted. The bench seemed solid and hard for a dream.

He looked back at the cat and choked. Now it sat on what looked to be a small, ancient Greek pillar, like Jake had seen while watching the Olympics. Behind the cat wasn't the opposite wall of gym lockers, but a temple that showed bright blue sky between fluted pillars.

Jake swallowed. Definitely a dream, though since he'd never had a cat, he wondered what the thing was doing in his dream. He narrowed his eyes. That cat! The battered tom looked familiar. Didn't he have a run-in or two . . .

"I am not a thing or an it."

Great, now the cat was reading Jake's mind. He wouldn't let a cat correct him. "You got balls?" Pretty sure the tom didn't.

The cat lifted a pink nose with a black spot and sent Jake an icy stare. Jake's cop instincts rang loud and clear that something was very, very wrong. But what could be *too* wrong in a dream? He looked down. Yep, fully clothed. He wouldn't walk into the captain's office naked.

The cat hissed, "My name is Borisssssssss."

"Huh," said Jake. He stood and stretched; all his muscles worked fine. Some called him an endorphin-adrenaline junkie, but he just liked the way his body felt when he was in shape. Though he was thirty-two, he wasn't slowing down at all. Looking around his side of the room, everything was comfortingly familiar, the dull green lockers, the bench, the tile floor. But it changed in the middle of the room, becoming marble slabs.

"Boris, huh?" Jake tested reality by strolling over to the cat and looking down on him. This side of the room remained a Greek temple. Jake could sneer, too. "I think we've met."

He stepped back as the pillar grew until it loomed over him.

"You don't remember *Me*?" Boris hunkered down, his already horizontal ears flattened even more.

How the cat could speak and growl at the same time eluded Jake. He shrugged. He was dreaming.

Boris stretched out a paw and sharp, curved claws sprang out. Oh, yeah. Jake remembered those claws. He'd tangled with the tom on the front porch of a house and gotten scratched. Badly enough that he'd had to get a tetanus shot, and that made his arm ache so he couldn't work out for a day. Yeah, the cat had cost him. Hadn't it also pissed . . .

His stare latched on to the cat's paw where a bloody spot marked the side of the cat's white foreleg, like where a vein had been opened or a needle inserted. . . . Jake's heart started to pound in his ears.

"No," said the cat. "Your heart . . ." He sheathed his claws and tapped Jake's chest.

Jake saw it now, the big, dark stain on the chest of his uniform. Fear lanced through him. Woozy, he retreated to the locker room bench. He didn't want to think about stains. He wanted to wake up. *Now!*

Nothing happened except the cat lifted its leg to groom. Jake was right. Boris had been fixed.

Boris growled.

Jake couldn't help rubbing his hand up and down over a stiff, dark spot, hoping it would go away. If it didn't . . . *Out, out damned spot!* What was that from? Bugs Bunny?

"Shakespeare, his play *Macbeth*." The cat smirked.

Jake could really dislike this cat.

A door opened on his left. Jake blinked. There wasn't a door there in the locker room. Oh, yeah, he had a *really* bad feeling about this.

Boris jumped from his pillar and swaggered to the small, balding man in a gray rumpled suit who stepped through the door.

"Hello, Boris," the guy said. The cat rumbled a purr, then trotted into the next room.

The threshold looked ordinary. The man pinned Jake with eyes as gray as his clothing. Such colorless eyes shouldn't have had an effect on Jake but he couldn't move.

He'd faced down plenty of tough customers and won. His guts twisted. He should be the one in charge. He could lift this guy with one hand. He tried to speak and couldn't.

"Come in, Jake Forbes. You can call me Gray." The man turned and stepped across the threshold.

Finally Jake found his voice. "Whatever," he croaked. He wanted to swagger like Boris—Jake could swagger with the best of them—but his feet dragged until he reached the door and looked in.

The office had bare dingy white walls, utilitarian furniture, and gray linoleum. Hell, the captain had a nicer office than this.

Dull inside, but golden sunshine streamed through a window high in the opposite wall. Two doors in that wall framed a scarred wooden desk where Gray sat. Each of the other walls had two doors also. Jake didn't like the setup. Too many options and potential for danger coming through those doors—or going out through them. A chill feathered down his spine.

Gray raised a thin eyebrow. "Problem?" he asked with just enough patronization to challenge any guy.

Jake sucked in a breath and stepped into the room. Nothing earth-shaking happened.

With a pen the man pointed to a standard wooden office chair with arms. A couple of yellow aspen leaves were on the seat, and Jake brushed them off and sat. One of the chair legs wobbled. Jake cursed under his breath.

Boris sat four feet away, acting as if he were a king, but his seat was a raggedy carpeted post with long hanks of unwoven rug hanging around it. It was pink.

Jake grinned.

Boris looked supremely uncaring. Of course, cats couldn't see colors, probably not even in dreams. The cat batted a twig of yellow aspen leaves.

The man squared a stack of papers on his desk and placed his pen at an exact angle. He folded his hands and shot Jake another look. "This isn't a dream, Jake. Accept that and it will make all our decisions quicker and easier. You're dead. Boris is dead." He waved a boney hand around the room. "Consider this the atrium to a change, a new existence."

Breath whooshed from Jake's chest. He felt his heart beating, his lungs working—the guy couldn't be right. Jake hooked his thumbs into the loops of his jeans and angled his head. He wanted to tilt the chair back, but didn't trust the wobbly leg. "So, you're what? An angel?"

Gray pinched the skin above his nose. "A facilitator."

"Yeah, right." Jake curled one side of his mouth.

"Jake, you're a jerk. Look at yourself."

Gray's words punched Jake. *Jake the jerk. Jake the jerk.* More than one of his father's "ladies" had called him that—and more than one of his mother's men. Even his ma—he nipped the thought, as always. Heat rose from his feet to his face; a flush reddened his neck along the line of his T-shirt. He'd worked hard to make sure no one ever called him that again. Developed a smooth and charming manner. *Jake the jerk.*

T-shirt. Jeans. He looked down at himself. The police uniform he'd taken so much pride in had vanished. He was in his off-duty clothes of white T-shirt and jeans. The T-shirt had a hole over his heart and a red stain. Pure shock froze him.

"Boris," the facilitator said sharply. "You failed in your mission in this life. You were to bring Jake and Shauna together. The opportunities were there and you refused them."

A cat shrug rippled down Boris's back. "Not time yet," he said.

"Untrue. The truth is that you wanted no other male"—Gray glanced at Jake—"no male of superior strength in Shauna's life. You wanted to be the male of the house. You wanted to be the only male she loved. You knew she'd love and bond with Jake more than she could ever love and bond with you."

Boris sniffed. "He's human and ugly. I'm beautiful. I know this and Shauna said so. She is human and ugly, too, but she is Mine."

Boris had serious problems. He was ugly even for a cat.

"Jake's not good inside, either." Boris sounded triumphant.

Jake shifted. He was a good cop with plenty of friends.

"Men friends." Boris turned his head, his eyes like lambent jade. "You have men acquaintances. Only."

Jake shrugged, grinned. "Women aren't made for friendship."

"Wrong," both Boris and Gray said.

Gray tapped his pen on his desk, frowning. The hollowness Jake always tried to deny yawned wider inside him. He covered it with a flashing grin. "You want me to be friends with a woman, I'll give it a try." He winked. "But we won't be friends long."

"See!" Boris yowled. "I am better than he. He doesn't deserve to be in Shauna's life. He would not love her like I do, cherish her, *protect* her."

Jake snapped his teeth together, inhaled, and counted to ten. "That's enough. I'm a good cop. I serve and protect."

Gray's sigh seemed to shiver the room. "Jake, I'm afraid you didn't progress emotionally and spiritually in the manner anticipated. That's a concern."

Boris slurped as he washed his ear. "So I get My Crown, and My Temple, and when I am bored, My Road of Great Adventure."

The man frowned. "No. Your task was to introduce Jake and Shauna. You ignored the task."

The cat stopped washing and sat straight up, glaring. "He does not deserve—"

"That was not your judgment to make," Gray said.

"People can change, especially in a loving relationship."

Jake doubted that. He'd seen plenty of broken marriages, bad domestic crises, didn't even think there was such a thing as love between a woman and a man. Sex. Lust. Some tenderness, maybe. That was it.

"Boris, you didn't complete your task, so you don't get your Crown, Temple, or Road of Great Adventure. You don't even get wings to become a lower angel."

Boris hopped to his feet and arched his back. "No *wingssss*! I was good. I was the best. You know what I had to put up with from those other Cats! You know my bad life before Shauna! You know my sick-hurt and death! I should get wings."

Gray's face softened. Maybe the guy had some compassion and mercy after all. Jake began to think he'd need it.

"You're very close to wings, Boris, but haven't achieved them. We have several options available for you." Gray took a sheet of paper from the pile and Jake blinked. He couldn't read it, but there were bullet squares, most with checkmarks, and at the bottom some paragraphs in fancy lettering, each gleaming in a different color: red, blue, gold.

He narrowed his eyes at the rest of the stack. Cramped handwriting in dull brown. Sheets with empty squares and only a couple of checkmarks. Looked like a performance review. Were those about him? His gut tightened. He'd always done well in reviews. Before. What did the papers say about him, his life—hell, he started to think this whole crazy thing wasn't a dream.

Shaking his head, Gray stared at Jake. "You followed the path of least resistance. What happened to that ideal you had about a good family life? A loving wife, children?"

Jake scowled, trying to remember, but couldn't pinpoint when he'd lost that dream, abandoned the goal as unattainable.

"You could have had that ideal, Jake. If you wanted it enough to work for it and work at a relationship instead of using women and letting them use you. You had a destined mate in this lifetime. A woman who would have helped you grow as you would have helped her. You just didn't believe in yourself enough."

Fear spiked. "Bulls—" Jake shoved the chair back and stood—at least he meant to. Nothing happened. He was stuck sitting, couldn't move. Couldn't even speak.

Gray waved a hand. "You worked hard on honing your body, a charming manner, but you neglected your intellect, allowed your finer emotions to wither, ignored any spirituality that entered your life." He tapped his pen. "Didn't relate well to women. You would never have received that captaincy you wanted because you wouldn't have enough respect from others."

Jake's gut clenched. Respect from his peers was the most important thing in his life. "I was a good cop!" But his voice cracked. Jeez, he was talking in the past tense. A very bad sign. He gripped the arms of his chair until his knuckles whitened. Sweat gathered at the small of his back.

"Yes, you were a good cop."

Jake relaxed a little.

"Honorable, believing in the motto to serve and protect. But you substituted the general public for individuals. Easier than being intimate with someone, isn't it? You didn't even like being touched."

Smiling weakly with the most sincere smile he'd felt on his lips for a long time, Jake said, "A good cop should get wings?"

A flash of amusement showed on Gray's face. "I'm afraid the standards for human wings are higher than for cats."

Alarm jolted through Jake; his mouth dropped. "I can live without wings. I mean—uh, I don't have to be a cat, do I? I don't want to be a cat!"

Emerging from his sulk, Boris hissed.

Soft chimes wafted through the room. Gray tilted his head toward the room they'd come from. His expression folded into dismay and sadness. "I was afraid of this. Sometimes destiny can't be denied."

Jake didn't see Gray move, but the guy was at the door and through it before Jake could turn his head.

In the other room Gray said, "Come in, my dear Shauna. I'm sorry to see you. I'd hoped to avoid this." His mellifluous voice had the range and depth of an orchestra. "Welcome to the Atrium."

He drew a woman of about twenty-eight into the room, holding the tips of her fingers with exquisite gentleness, his manner one of old-fashioned respect and courtesy. With a gesture he indicated a deeply cushioned chair of green plush velvet patterned with golden aspen leaves that solidified between Boris and Jake.

"You're very beautiful," she said in awe, looking at Gray.

Jake frowned. The guy seemed to glow and was taller. Jake shook his head and the man appeared the same. Beautiful? Ha. If this was the Shauna woman Boris and Gray had talked about, she'd called Boris beautiful, too. Obviously she had no taste.

She looked at Jake and he was caught by her lovely eyes—a deep amber with gold and green flecks and a rim of brown around the irises. They were soft with emotion matching the sweet curve of her lips. She smiled at him with warmth and sympathy and— yearning?

Those eyes drew him to his feet. Words tore from him. "I know you. We met beyond those doors. Our last time together was far too short, mere days. . . ."

"I know you, too," Shauna said. The sun lit her blond hair.

Gray's voice came distantly. "Hmmmm. Recognition, rather easy here, harder during physical lifetimes. How- ever, probable that once both accept recognition, the knowledge will always be there, in every future life. In- teresting." His pen scritched.

Boris yowled. Shauna jerked. She hurried to Boris and picked him up as if he were delicate china, clasping him close.

Jake felt the loss of her attention like an absence of the sun's warmth. Stupid.

The sense of recognition faded. He'd never met her. She wore a floaty dress in blue that concealed her body, but he thought her breasts were nice handfuls and her hips good and round, even if she was a little plump.

Boris purred, opened one eye, and smirked at Jake.

When he heard her sniffling and saw tears rolling down her cheeks, he had an overwhelming urge to comfort her—but he'd have to brave the damn cat. He scowled and glanced at Gray, who smirked, too. Jake wished *he* could growl.

"Oh, Boris, it's so good to see you! It was so hard to put you to sleep, but I couldn't stand watching you die by inches. Say you forgive me."

Geeze, the dramatics. Jake sat down. Gray frowned.

"I am fine," Boris said. "Except I don't have My wings or My Crown or My Temple or My Road of Great Adventure." He sniffed. "Perhaps you can speak with—"

"That's not how things are done," Gray said.

Shauna glanced at the man behind the desk and blinked. Tears caught on her lashes, and Jake was transfixed at how pretty she looked.

"No intercession accepted?" She smiled.

Gray actually hesitated. Jake couldn't believe it.

She shrugged. "I don't have anyone to intervene for me, but if I can help Boris—" Her brow furrowed. "What about my other cats? Who'll take care of them? What of the feral ones I feed?" She whirled to face the door. "They won't be put to sleep and come here, too, will they?" Pain laced her voice.

As she turned, Jake got an eyeful of the deep, bloody indentation on the side of her skull, round and as big as his palm. He swallowed.

"Sit, Shauna, that tumble down the stairs was hard on you," Gray soothed. "There is no true security even in your home."

"I'm sorry." She sank into the soft chair. Jake became aware of the hard wood under his own ass. When she looked at him, he forgot discomfort. "Sorry to bore you with my tears."

He flushed, then shrugged. "No problem."

She smiled again, then set her shoulders and looked at Gray.

The guy tried to appear stern, but Jake could tell it was a facade. A paper edged with gold with a gold seal in the shape of an aspen leaf and gold ribbons floated to him. "We will review Shauna's life first."

Gray tensed.

"Shauna, you learned most of your life lessons."

Jake wondered if *she'd* get wings. He gritted his teeth and examined the doors again. Jake was sure he didn't want to open a couple of them.

Gray went on. "But you didn't take advantage of the greatest opportunity we sent you." One big checkbox was blank.

"I was considering it!" she shot back, then slumped in her chair, petting Boris. "No, you're right. I probably wouldn't have taken the chance. Too cautious." Her gaze slid Jake's way. "Too repressed." She sighed.

Oddly, Jake didn't believe that for a minute. He judged she was as intense and passionate about everything as she was about her damn cat. Ex-cat? Ghost cat? Geeze, his brain hurt.

As Gray gazed at them, the only sound was Boris's buzz-saw purr. Jake wanted to squirm, but sat at attention. Shauna leaned back, face composed, as if she didn't care which of the doors she'd leave by. His nerves jittered. Which door would be the worst?

Gray sighed. "We have a Situation here. Please put Boris on his stand," the facilitator said very gently. "He has his decision to make, as do you. You should not influence him."

Shauna rose and stood regally, with a straight spine— a pretty spine above a heart-shaped ass Jake would have recalled if they'd ever met. Thinking he knew her was another mind trick.

"Yes, Boris must be free to choose what's best for him," she said, setting the cat down. "Oh, Boris, that nasty tower." All she did was look at it and it became pristine quilted blue velveteen. Jake choked at the thought that Boris was now more comfortable than he. Shauna gazed at him with raised eyebrows.

Jake nodded at her and said to Gray, "What's the deal?" His voice came out rougher than expected.

"Had you, Jake Forbes, and she, Shauna Russell, met as was *intended*"—Gray looked at Boris, who lifted his nose—"you would not be here. Even if you hadn't stayed together as lovers or helpmeets, your lives would not have ended. As for Boris, he might or might not be here."

"So?" asked Jake.

"So, it's first up to Shauna to decide whether she wishes to go on or go back."

"*Go back?* We could go back?" Jake jumped from his chair and the longer leg clattered behind him.

"You want to go back?" Shauna stared at him with soft, luminous amber eyes.

"I sure as he— I sure don't want to pick Door Number One, Two, or Three," he said. "They can't all lead to good places."

"Why not?" she asked.

He just stared. An optimist. Geeze.

"You may have earned wings, but I didn't," he said.

She pinkened. "What are our options?" she asked Gray.

"Individually you may all decide whether to go back to your old life or go forward. If you go back you will have the chance to change vital decisions." He tapped the papers with a long index finger. "If you go forward, your new circumstances will be based upon what you accomplished in your shortened lives."

Her eyes widened and her breath became shallow. She licked her lips—signs of anxiety. Finally she got the picture that flower-filled meadows might not be in her future. Jake exhaled slowly.

"I didn't take the chance that was given to me. I could do it, now." She glanced at Jake. "Would we remember?"

"*After* you make certain decisions, you can remember if you try hard enough. But if you go back, there is no guarantee that you'll meet. If you do meet, you will be given the chance for a long lifetime of love."

"If we don't choose love, do we croak again?" Jake asked.

Shauna winced. She was prissy, too.

Papers shuffled. "No. You will live your allotted time, but you will have failed at one of your life goals."

Shauna looked Jake straight in the eyes, and he felt as if she saw into his mind and heart. He stiffened. Her lips firmed. "I want love. I want Jake."

A bolt of shock hit him. What had she seen in him?

How could she know that? How could she decide so quickly?

"Jake Forbes . . ." She frowned. "Sounds familiar. You died?"

"Yeah." Jake cleared his throat. He vaguely recalled his death now, and didn't like it.

Shauna said, "I'll take the risks. All of them. I'll work hard at our relationship." Her words echoed like vows in the room. Unease prickled Jake's skin. What was he getting into?

Gray stared at her. "You cherished security too much. You'll have to change, and you'll have to risk your heart. Even then, Jake has free will. He could walk away."

Her chin trembled, but she lifted it all the same. Jake felt a spurt of admiration.

"I'll take the chance," she said.

What about me? Jake wondered. Could he take the chance at love, with her? Or just a second chance at life? He eyed the doors and shuddered.

"Jake Forbes will have to grow, too. He will have to realize his core belief is that he is unlovable, then change."

"I'll love him more than enough!" The passion in her voice made Jake squirm.

"Jake must learn his own lesson. He'll have to know that he *is* worthy of being loved before he'll accept you," Gray said.

Boris snorted. "I do not want to go back, but I will help." He slid Gray a glance. "I will get My wings, then My Crown and My Temple and My Road of Great Adventure. I will be an Angel Cat."

"Done!" Gray's word roared like a whirlwind.

Shauna jumped on Jake and he caught her reflexively. She felt good and right and just plain incredible against him. Incandescent golden aspen leaves seared his eyes, then lightning-filled darkness descended.

Two

Earlier that August morning, Denver

In the police station locker room, Jake held his Kevlar vest at arm's length. "Phew, this *stinks*. They promised my new vest would be in today—that's why I let Roy use this one when he forgot his last night. It's still wet." He looked for Roy, but the man was long gone. Only Jake and Fred, his old friend and partner, were in the locker room.

Fred wrinkled his nose and patted his chest. "Yeah, and it isn't going to dry out. It's been over a hundred degrees for two weeks and I'm wet all day, every day. At least I can put up with my own smell. Yours doesn't look in good shape, and it's your last day as a patrolman. Maybe—"

Jake didn't think he could bear the hot vest or Roy's sweaty stench. "Maybe." He started to set it aside, then gritted his teeth and put it on, tightening the fraying tabs and donning his shirt. "There are times to break rules and take a chance. This isn't one of them. But I'll have something to say to Roy, you can bet on that." Something poked him. He pulled a yellow aspen leaf from where it had been stuck inside his vest. He stared at it.

"Let's roll," said Fred.

Jake dropped the leaf.

That afternoon Jake smoothed his police tunic again, wishing it didn't stink and he was better turned out on his last day in uniform. When he started his shift next Monday he'd be *Detective* Forbes. A promotion with more responsibility and more interesting work. He'd miss Fred, and working with a woman, Maggie, would be a challenge, but it was his first real step up to his goal of a captaincy.

He stood beside the cruiser and shook out his legs. Fred and he had been sitting for too long. He squinted at the neighborhood sandwich shop, almost able to taste ham slathered in cool mayonnaise, the bite of brown mustard on his tongue. He hoped Fred hurried up. The temp had reached 105.

A couple of pops down the street caught his attention. Backfires?

Screams. More gunshots. A child's hysterical voice, cut short.

Swearing, Jake banged on the sandwich shop's window, caught Fred's attention, and pointed down the street. Jake ran, pulling his gun from the holster. When he reached an alley entrance to his left, he stopped to glance down it. Nothing.

About twelve feet ahead of him a man ran from a liquor store, holding a young boy about four. And a gun.

The little boy opened his mouth and cried, "No, no, no, Daddy! Daddy bad." He started wailing again.

Jake's insides froze, but he kept running.

"Shut *up*, Mike," the man shouted in the kid's ear, then muttered, "I'm not bad. Just had bad luck. Shit happens and ya gotta deal with it." He saw Jake and snarled, "Get back. Get away from my truck."

Jake was next to the passenger side of a decrepit red truck; the keys were in the ignition. "Put the kid down!" Jake yelled above the child's cries. His heart pounded.

"No." Spittle flew from the man's mouth. He looked for a way out on the street full of shops and parked cars. People watched from windows. Sirens shrieked, coming closer.

The guy waved the gun. Put the barrel of the weapon near the boy's head—a head that flailed along with small arms and legs. "Holster your gun and get away from my truck!"

"Sure, man." Jake moved one step at a time, trying to keep the guy's focus on him. Fred had ducked down the alley and would be running around the half-block to come up behind the man.

Jake wanted the guy concentrating on him. Standing in the middle of the sidewalk, with a slow, broad gesture, Jake snicked the gun's safety on. One step back. He lowered his gun to his side. Step.

The child's screams seemed distant. Step.

Jake held his gun near his holster. Step. The man's bloodshot blue gaze followed Jake. The guy inched forward. Slow. One step.

Sweat pooled on Jake's body. Hell, it was hot. Step. The little boy sobbed and held out his arms to Jake. Hell.

Jake smiled and the kid started struggling and screaming again. Jake's gut tensed. He moved slow.

Fred moved fast. His weapon came up to the back of the guy's head. "Police. Drop your gun!"

The man jerked, dropped the kid, jerked again, and fired at Jake. The blow of the bullet to his chest knocked him down, head hitting concrete. Pain exploded in his chest and head, then blackness swallowed him.

The phone rang, snapping Shauna from her doze over a new landscaping plan. She blinked. The phone trilled again.

She knew who was phoning and had to pick up before voice mail did. She'd made her decision. Now she needed to confirm it. Where *was* the cordless? It rang downstairs. Hopping to her feet, she ran to the stairs and down, missed a step, and saw the banister knob coming straight at her head. At the last instant she grabbed the rail and ducked, taking a hard blow to her shoulder.

There was no time to stop and shake as she sped to the phone in the kitchen.

"It's Shauna. Sorry for the delay. I was upstairs working." She tried to steady her breathing, but there was no way she could hide that she'd run to the phone.

"Oh," her friend Phil Hassuk, a bank officer, said. "I hoped you'd thought better of this notion and were going to let us both off the hook."

"Put the loan papers through." The words coming from her lips shook her to the core.

"This isn't like you, Shauna; are you *really* sure? You could fail and lose your house. Starting up a little landscaping company in this economy is cra— imprudent, especially in mid-August instead of May or June. As your friend and financial adviser, I'm against it."

Shauna shut her eyes and fiddled with the phone's antenna. Her thoughts ping-ponged back and forth over the pros and cons of her action—her future. "I just won that city award for Best Landscaping." Her voice was high. If she hadn't been so terrified, she'd be filled with pride.

"For a cat sanctuary!" Phil sounded as incredulous as everyone else.

Steadying her breathing, Shauna said as firmly as she could, "It brought me several inquiries, potential customers. If I'm going to start my own business, now's the right time."

"Shauna—"

"Why shouldn't I step out on my own? Why shouldn't I have faith in my own talent and creativity and pure green thumb? So I'm petrified, but being a coward won't bring me what I want. Taking a risk might."

"I've never heard you talk like this," Phil said, disapproval lacing his voice. "You've always been cautious, wisely considered your future."

Despite the huge risk, she felt time slipping away from her, as if this was the last chance, perhaps the *only* chance for her to grab the dream she'd wanted for years.

"I have to do this. Now. Put the loan papers through.

Or don't you think I'm good enough to succeed?" Why did she ask? She trembled awaiting her friend's answer.

The pause lasted an eternity.

Phil said, "The chances of failure—"

"I can do it. Will you support me or not?"

"You sound odd. Have you been drinking?"

Shauna laughed. "Not yet." She rubbed her temple; hazy dream images appeared and voices whispered, trying to make themselves heard, but she didn't have time to focus on them. "Do I have to go to someone else, Phil?"

"You could lose your house. If you fail, I won't be able to bail you out."

"I've never asked you to help me and I won't." Shauna set her jaw. "Do I have to go somewhere else?"

"I'll put the papers through. At least you still have that lousy florist job with George."

She wouldn't tell Phil she was quitting. "Thanks, Phil."

"Do you want some company for that drink?"

"Not this evening. I want to contact my new clients." Mrs. Mally would be first. Shauna could be at the lovely home near Skyline Park with preliminary plans as soon as tomorrow evening. She did a little dance step; giddiness fizzed through her.

"Fine," Phil said. "As I explained earlier, the money from your mortgage should come through in about a week."

"Great." Shauna *would not* let fear close her throat. "I will have everything ready to ramp up by then."

"I've got to go. I have your business to transact."

Laughing, Shauna said, "I'm on the Road of Great Adventure." She blinked, wondering where the words came from.

"What? Never mind," Phil said, and rang off.

Shauna hung up. The room whirled around her. The air thickened until she had trouble breathing. Gasping, she let herself slide down the wall to the floor, not able to make it to a chair. Dizziness rushed through her. Jimbo, her fat gray cat, trotted through the cat door with a twig of yellow aspen leaves, out-of-season color. Something very, very strange was going on.

"Hello."

Jake jolted as the greeting echoed through his brain. Looking around, he saw an ugly black-and-white tomcat atop one of the stools in his curtained hospital space. A prickle slithered up his spine. The cat looked familiar.

He narrowed his eyes, then shook his head. For a minute he'd thought the cat had actually spoken. Geeze! Banging his head on concrete had made more of an impact than he'd thought.

"You're not dead," the cat said. "You were, but aren't now."

Jake ignored the whispery words. He finished tucking his shirt into his jeans, slipped his keys into his pocket, and strode to the tom. "Damn. What's a cat doing here?"

He'd liked the doc, wouldn't want her to get in trouble. He grabbed, but the cat leaped away and up to the hospital bed. Images of the cat and a pillar and temple flowed into Jake's brain, and he shook them impatiently away—fuzzy images of weird dreams when he'd been out. There'd been a woman—

"Sorry, Jake, I didn't hear you." Fred walked in.

Eyeing the cat, Jake saw bloody hands in his future, but guessed he was too macho a guy to ask for help in getting the animal out of the place. "Fred, hand me the towel, will you? I want to take care of the cat."

Fred picked up a damp towel the doc had used on Jake and tossed it to him. He grimaced, sure that trying to wrap a sodden towel around a cat would lead to injury. Huh. He'd faced down a gun and a bullet this morning, but hesitated at taking on a cat. Some hero he was.

"A cat? Since when did you get a cat? I thought you didn't like pets."

"That one there." Jake gestured to the tom.

Fred frowned. "What cat?"

Jake opened his mouth to say "Boris," and froze. Why would he call the cat Boris?

Fred looked at Jake strangely. The cat smirked.

"Your head hurting?" Fred asked.

Jake rubbed the bump on the back of his skull. "Yep."

"Seeing things?" asked Fred.

"Like cats?" Jake laughed. It came out strained. He pretended to scan the area. "You don't see any cats, do you?"

Eyebrows bobbing, Fred shook his head. "Nope. No cats. No dogs. No pink elephants in tutus."

Fred looked a little worse for wear, too. "What went down? You in any trouble?" Jake asked.

Hunching a shoulder, Fred said, "I didn't kill the guy, and Betty Pazinski from Social Services took the kid."

Jake nodded. "She's a good woman." He wished he'd known someone like her growing up. "She'll do right by him."

The cat sniffed. Fred stared at him.

Jake preferred direct action. He sauntered to the bed and started to sit down on the cat.

The tom hissed and hopped away. "You're not dead," the cat repeated. Then he lifted his nose and twitched his ears. "But I am. I am a Ghost Cat. Soon to be an Angel Cat. I will go home with you to help you meet Shauna. Then I will get wings. When you love her and marry her, I will get My Crown and Temple and Road of Great Adventure. And I *am* Borissssss."

"Are you okay, Jake? Hell, the blood drained right out of your face." Fred hurried to help Jake sit on the bed.

Jake dropped his head to his hands. "Geeze."

"You hallucinating, man? What kind of drugs did they give you?"

"Nothing," Jake mumbled. "It's nothing. Just a little dizzy," he lied. Summoning up a charming smile, he sent it to Fred. "I'll be fine."

Fred shook his head. "You're lucky." He grinned and Jake felt to his bones that Fred's lopsided smile was gold while his own was tinfoil. Jake didn't like his facade anymore.

Then Fred sobered. "I'd invite you home, but you know my sister is staying with us. We don't have room."

Now Fred was lying. He lived in an old sprawling farmhouse that had been surrounded by burbs. Jake rubbed his head again, glancing to his right from the corner of his eyes. Boris—no, he would *not* name the cat—was still there. Jake let his shoulders slump. "You don't have to say that, Fred. You just don't want me near your sister."

Fred's big feet shifted. "Sorry, no offense, but—" He stopped.

"Yeah, I know. I use women and let them use me." Jake didn't know where the phrase had come from and was appalled he'd said it. He scrubbed his face. "Don't know what's gotten into me. Tough day. I'd appreciate a ride home, though."

"Sure." Fred lightly punched his shoulder. For once, Jake didn't stiffen or flinch. Fred cocked his head.

The doctor, an older woman, came back in. Jake rose on unsteady feet and offered his hand. "Thank you, Doctor," he said sincerely. She shook his hand, then gave him a bottle with a couple of pills. "These will help you rest. Don't be as macho as you look. Take them."

"I will. Thanks again for all your help," Jake said.

Fred stared. The doctor nodded, then left. Studying Jake with cop's eyes, Fred said, "A close shave with death can shake up a man, make him rethink his priorities."

"Rethink his whole damn life," Jake said. Buzzing in his ears solidified into "Jake the Jerk." Had he been a jerk?

"Yesssssssss," hissed Boris. "Fred always thought you could be a better man, especially with women." Jake's gut twinged. *He'd* always thought Fred had respected him. Being respected by his buddies was the most important thing in the world.

Jake turned his head. The tom appeared as solid as ever. Ghost cat! "Geeze."

A short laugh came from Fred. "That's the old Jake, saying *geeze* instead of *damn* or *shit* or *f*—"

"Yep." Jake stood and struggled to find his balance. Flashing memories blew through his mind of slaps and backhanded blows accompanied by cursing from members of both sexes—his parents and their lovers that came and went. It was an old, sorry wind and brought the taste of blood in his mouth from a split lip.

He blinked, remembering for the first time in a long time the six-month stretch where an old neighbor guy gave him soda and corrected his swearing into the mild "geeze." It rocked him to realize that he'd used the word all this time out of simple respect for that man.

"Ready?" Jake asked Fred, glad nothing more revealing came out of his mouth.

"Sure."

"Yessss," said Boris, hopping down.

"I don't like cats," Jake mumbled.

Fred gripped Jake's upper arm. "I know, buddy, but you don't have to deal with any," he soothed.

That's what *he* thought. Boris marched, tail waving, in front of them. A ghost cat. Right.

"Jake?" Fred's voice pulled him from a light daze to find himself outside and next to a car, with Fred holding the door open. Jake slid into the front seat and fumbled with his seat belt, then grunted when Boris landed in his lap. For a ghost cat he was damn heavy.

"Yeah?" Jake pulled the door shut, trying to ignore the animal. Fred went to the driver's seat, slammed his door, hooked his seat belt, inserted his key, and took the wheel. His face set in impassive lines. His fingers flexed once, then curled around the steering wheel.

"Don't take this wrong, buddy, but it seems the hit you took is improving you. Keep it up."

"Up what?" Jake asked ironically.

Fred grinned and shrugged.

"Being honest," Boris said. "And not superficial, especially with women."

"Huh." Jake would have to think about all this. Boris kneaded his thighs and Jake tensed. "One last question, Fred."

"Yes?"

"Do you see any cats?"

Boris settled and lifted a paw to lick it, slurping loudly.

Fred peered out the windshield, checked the driver's and passenger's windows and mirrors. "Nope. Not a one."

"I may be turning over a new leaf, but I still won't like cats," Jake said, shutting his eyes and letting weariness take him. Boris grumbled. Not purred, grumbled. Jake sighed. "Geeze."

Jake crashed at his place—a rented condo near Skyline Park—for the rest of that day and the next. Strange dreams played through his mind. Mostly of a woman, but now and then there was a shadowy figure called Gray and an insistent cat. He liked the erotic ones about the woman the best, even though they stopped before he climaxed and left him aching.

Finally he awoke to a growl. He stared. There was the cat, sitting next to him on the bed, glaring at him.

"What's for dinner? It's four o'clock, time to eat," Boris said.

"You're a ghost cat. You don't eat," Jake said before he could stop himself. Hearing a cat and replying! He rolled over. "I'm asleep and dreaming."

"You always think that. We have *things to do*."

"We?" Jake asked. "You do them. You're the talking cat. You can do anything, right?"

"I'm hungry."

"Go catch ghost mice." Were there ghost mice? What was he thinking? How'd he get into this mess? If he got up and got his act together, he wouldn't be talking to an imaginary cat.

Boris moved in, glowering, until they were nose to nose. Jake sat up. Claws pierced his skin and scratched. He looked down. Where there should be red lines there was nothing. The stinging vanished as if it had all been an illusion. He narrowed his eyes at Boris and visualized sending the ghost cat through the wall.

The cat stepped out of reach, sat, and began to whine. Jake slid down and rolled over and put the pillow on his head. The yowl started low, then increased to pierce his ears.

"We need to go out to the park. Now," Boris said.

"This can't be happening," Jake mumbled. A heavy weight settled on the pillow over his head. The screech stopped. Jake sighed.

Something cold and damp touched his arm. Jake flinched, hoping it really wasn't a cat nose. Then the nose slid up his arm, leaving a wet trail. Jake couldn't stand it. He rolled from bed and stood, weaving a bit to get his balance and suppressing a groan at all the aches in his muscles. He opened one eye, then the other.

A scruffy black-and-white tomcat sat like a king in the middle of Jake's bed. He rubbed his face, shook his head. He turned and limbered up with stretches. When he glanced back at the bed, the cat had his back leg stuck in the air and was grooming. Jake stared. Boris was well equipped in the sex department. That didn't seem right.

"You have time to shower and dress before we go to the park. You should open a can of tuna so I can eat while you shower. You have slept very long and I am hungry."

Jake grunted. As far as he was concerned, the cat could scavenge in the garbage cans of the park. He wondered if he should bother talking to the tom. Maybe if he ignored it, it would go away.

"I am not an it—"

"Haven't we had this conversation?" asked Jake, then shook his head. "No."

Boris lifted a paw and licked it. "You can remember now, if you want."

Jake didn't. He stalked from the bedroom to the bathroom. The park might be a good idea. He could work the kinks from his muscles with a speed walk.

The park would also be crowded on a summer Saturday afternoon. Usually he'd think about picking up a woman, maybe near the tennis courts, but now the idea didn't appeal. Somehow he didn't think it would ever appeal to him again. His world had shifted—or maybe it was just his perspective—but he was going to try and figure out how to act without the shallow, joking mask he'd worn for so long. All his adult life. No more practiced and charming manner, just straight honesty.

A walk in a public park would settle him. The image of a golden aspen tree came, and he shook it away, though it made him smile.

When he finished cleaning up and went back to the bedroom to dress, he found a blue polo shirt and darker blue slacks laid out on the bed. The cat grinned. "Shauna likes blue."

Shauna. The name echoed in his head and to his amazement it also stirred his body with recollections of hot dreams.

He shrugged and dressed. If the tom wanted to visit the park so much, maybe Jake could ditch the cat there. Not much of a plan, but other than pretending Boris didn't exist, Jake didn't know how to deal with an alleged ghost cat.

Boris jumped from the bed and led the way to the front door—tail straight up and humming creakily.

Jake started out at a brisk walk along his sidewalk that led to the asphalt paths of the park. To his horror, several people jogged right through Boris. The cat grumbled and hissed and the runners stumbled a few steps later.

Others angled away from the tom, but didn't appear to see the cat.

Boris's head swiveled back and forth, his ears perked and rotated. He was obviously a cat with a mission. When they reached the tennis courts, Boris stopped. "This is a good spot. We will wait here."

"You can," Jake said, and got a couple of odd looks.

He snapped his mouth shut, took a stride away from the cat.

"If you continue on the path, I guar-an-tee you will step in dog shit and ruin your shoes." Boris grinned.

Jake liked him better when he scowled. Jake looked down at his new white leather, *expensive*, cross-trainers. "Geeze."

"Isn't it time you said *shit*?" asked Boris.

"Shit!" The word brought the image of the sad old man who'd corrected him and he felt bad. He could overcome that, but why? He scowled at Boris. "I'm going to stick with *geeze*."

The cat's smile was worse. "A mature decision."

"What are you going for, wings?"

The smile widened to Cheshire-cat proportions. If Boris disappeared and left the smile, Jake would check into the nearest mental health clinic.

But Boris remained, ugly smile and all. "Yesssss."

A cat's high meow distracted Shauna as she did a final tour with Mrs. Mally of her flower beds bordering Skyline Park. Since Mrs. Mally, also a cat lover, ignored the whine, Shauna did, too.

"I am *so* glad you've started your own business, dear. With the drought the last couple of years, I'm rethinking my lawns and gardens."

Shauna smiled briefly. "Very wise. Plants natural to the plains have their own beauty, and I'll ensure you'll have an arresting yard in all seasons."

"I'm very happy with our plans. The budget is

acceptable and so is the time frame. You can start on Monday?"

"Absolutely. You're my first priority." Shauna beamed back at the lady.

"How many clients do you have, my dear?"

"Five," Shauna said proudly.

Mrs. Mally nodded. "Off to a good start. We're finished?"

"Yes," Shauna said. The cat yowl was insistent. If it had been one of her cats, she'd have placated it five minutes ago.

"I'll see you Monday." With a wave Mrs. Mally entered her house.

As Shauna turned, she realized the cat sound wasn't coming from the Mally yard but from the park, near the tennis courts.

With a sigh she placed her plans and notebook in the car—she'd have to think about turning it in for a truck—locked up, and went to find the cat.

The howl rose and fell at irregular enough intervals to drive a sensitive person mad.

Then she saw the cat and stopped. He was black-and-white and hefty, like Boris, whom she'd had to put to sleep. She gulped. He seemed entangled in a swatch of old net hanging from a large trash can. She wondered if he was feral.

When she approached, he grinned a big, silly grin, a lot like Boris's. He looked incredibly like Boris, down to the black spot in the middle of his nose. She bit her lip. Boris had only been gone a couple of days. Seeing this cat hurt.

"Hi, guy," she said, advancing slowly, trying to figure

out how he was trapped. As she got closer, he rumbled a purr. She swallowed. So much like Boris!

Shauna looked down at the cat and frowned. He didn't appear caught in the netting, just sitting on it.

"Hey!" a man shouted.

She turned and stared. It was the man who'd haunted her dreams last night. All thoughts of cats vanished.

Three

❧❧❧

Her heart pounded. Her mouth went dry. She couldn't think of any reason for the trembling in her knees, or her breathless anticipation as he walked toward her. Except they'd been *very* intimate in her dreams. She remembered the feel of his body, his touch, and his eyes more than anything else. But she knew him now and would never forget.

He was slightly over medium height, well built, and muscular, obviously in fine shape. His blond hair, blue eyes, and ready smile made him the image of a mature all-American boy.

Very mature. His wide shoulders and the faint lines around his eyes showed he was in the prime of life. Vital. Virile.

Yet there was an air of darkness around him, painful

secrets behind those stunning blue eyes. Shauna didn't know *how* she knew, but she did. One look at him and she sensed he was the utmost danger to her. She could fall for him hard. If she let him into her heart, he could break it.

He was not a man she should ever consider being with. A woman who valued safety and security and a calm life would run from such a man. Screaming.

She wanted to fling herself in his arms and feel the hardness of his muscles pressing against her. She wanted to caress all of him, learning his shape and the texture of his skin and all his beauty. She wanted.

"Hey," he said again, more softly, and smiled.

"Hi," she managed, caught by the blue eyes with shadowy depths.

"Did you notice the cat? Want to take him off my hands?"

"What cat?"

He closed his eyes as if praying.

That lessened the spell on her. Enough for her to recall the cat and glance at the garbage can. The net was gone, and so was the cat.

"He *is* gone, finally!" The man grinned at her.

"Um, did he follow you home?" She hadn't heard that story in ages. She could understand why female gazes would follow him, why bolder women than she might literally follow him, but a cat?

The man scanned the park, shook his head, but his smile didn't dim—until he met her eyes again and they locked gazes.

She knew him. Didn't she? Even before recently in—

She felt light-headed, dizzy, and concentrated on her balance, the solid earth under her feet. Shauna could always count on the earth. Still, as she noticed the darker rim of blue-gray around his eyes, she felt as if he drew her very heart to him. To play with, put in his pocket, and forget? Could she even try to believe that he might cherish a woman's heart?

"Yeah. The cat has been a nuisance. You wouldn't believe . . ." He stared at her. "I know you. Haven't we met? Beyond—" He snapped his mouth shut, hunched his shoulders an instant, then straightened. "You saw the cat?" he asked in measured tones.

"Yes, he looks like one I used to have." Her smile wobbled a bit; she blinked. "Must be one of Boris's descendants."

"Boris," he said flatly.

Shauna frowned. "Is something wrong?" She touched his arm and sparks of desire zipped from his skin, through her fingers, to her core.

His gaze was cool, very observant. He held himself a little stiffly, and kept his emotions from his eyes and face. It was something he was used to doing, she realized.

"You're Shauna?" he asked.

"Yes, Shauna Russell." She took a step back from him.

His eyebrows raised, but he didn't follow. He held out a hand. "I'm Jake Forbes. I think we have a mutual— friend." Jake did a swift review of the garbage can, the tennis courts, the park. "The cat's gone."

The park was even more crowded than a few minutes before, but Shauna didn't see the tough, black-and-white cat. Jake Forbes. The name tingled at the back of her mind. She associated that name with—with what had happened to her yesterday. With Boris. Memory came. "Jake Forbes. You're the police officer who was shot."

He rubbed his chest and looked stoic. "Yeah." Then he held out his hand again.

She looked at his hand and the tingle increased. If she took his hand, everything would change.

She was turning over a new leaf. *Not* playing it safe anymore. There wasn't true security even in her own home. She put her fingers in his.

Everything changed. Her heart gave one hard *thump* as she recognized her man.

Jake started, dropped her hand. "Maybe we should do a lap on the path to make sure the cat's really gone. Would you take him if we found him?"

Shauna sighed. "I already have two cats. But, yes, I'd take him. No one could ever replace Boris, though; he was such a character." Jake walked rapidly and that was a blessing; it stopped the stupid tears behind her eyes.

"I haven't seen you around here before," he said.

And as a cop, he would have noticed her, she supposed.

"I'm a landscape designer." Saying it amazed and thrilled her. "I have a client." She waved a hand in the direction of Mrs. Mally's and tried not to pant. He sure was in good shape. She wasn't. Her breath escaped on a quick sigh. A man like him would want someone as buff as himself. She wouldn't qualify. Easy to dismiss the attraction. Not so easy to forget about him, but her new career would help.

"I live in Skyline Condos." He gestured.

Shauna knew them. They had no charm, either in the architecture or the landscaping. Another difference between them.

By the time they'd reached the path leading to the tennis courts, Shauna was sure she'd imagined her previous feelings and that stupid idea there was something important, *fateful,* between them. He couldn't have been her dream lover. That man had been sensitive to her needs, tender. She snorted, a dream lover for sure, nothing like a real man. Jake was a real man; his muscular body and the faint sweat of him told her that at every step.

Jake stopped when they reached the tennis courts again. She followed his glance to the garbage can. No net. No cat.

There'd been no cats at all in the park.

She summoned up a bright smile. "Nice meeting you." If she left fast, it would put an end to her indecision about him.

"Don't go," he said. By now he was sure this was the woman who'd starred in his dreams, doing wonderful things to him with her hands and mouth. That notion irritated and intrigued him, and being a cop, he had to solve the puzzle. Get his mind around it, his hands on it. His hands on *her.*

She was so pretty. So . . . different, like a fairy. No, that couldn't be it. Fairies were little and slender. She was little, but plump. Pleasingly plump. Nice round breasts his hands itched to touch. Nice round hips he wanted to squeeze. He'd copped a glance at her ass, too. Sweet. Very sweet. Yeah, that was it. She was sweet and had this distracted air—that's why he thought of fairies.

Her light golden blond hair was so fine that the breeze wisped it about her head in tendrils. He wanted to smooth and, in smoothing her hair, touch her skin, slip down her cheek, and tilt the small round chin up so he could gaze into her eyes for a long time. Eyes that were the color of an amber glass candy dish his mother once had, that he couldn't stay away from despite all warnings and slaps.

He'd loved picking up that dish and holding it to the window to watch sunlight stream through it and turn it into pure gold. But he'd touched it once too often, been caught, and in the jolting surprise and scuffle with his dad had dropped the dish and watched it shatter. More than a few slaps then. When he cleaned up the mess, he'd mourned. And inside her haze of drugs and liquor, his mother had never noticed the amber dish was gone.

So he wanted to touch Shauna, but kept his hands to himself and just stared. "Don't go."

She nibbled at her lip. "I should." She glanced to the west, where the sun was dipping behind the purple smudges that were the mountains.

"You like sunsets?" he asked. Fairies would like sunsets.

She stared. "Sure. What's not to like?"

The fact that it led to the dark, and in the dark a lot of crimes were committed.

"Skyline's the best place in Denver for sunsets," he said. He caught up her hand again, accepted—welcomed—the shock of attraction, of some sort of strange link between them, liked the feel of the sizzle along his nerves, the heating of his blood. He was throbbingly alive. "Walk with me," he said.

Her small, red, and tempting tongue came out and dabbed at her lips. "Yes."

They stopped at the west edge of the park, where it fell away to rocky hillside. "I want to kiss you," he said. He'd thought of other, more charming lines, but decided to go with honesty. Something about being with her demanded honesty from him. That was interesting and a little alarming, but part of the puzzle.

"I've dreamed of you," she whispered, and he got the idea that she hadn't wanted to say it and didn't want him to know.

"I've dreamed of you, too." He grinned wholeheartedly. "Excellent dreams."

She just looked up at him with wide eyes.

"Shall we see how they compare to reality?" He dropped her hand to slide his arm around her waist. He'd anticipated the move and figured it wouldn't be anywhere close to smooth. But his body, tight though it was with nerves, moved easily.

He drew her close to his side, and they fit as he'd never fit with any other woman—a fact his body celebrated but gave his scrambling mind pause. She pressed against him with muscles as quivering under her skin as his own. Her scent came to him, floral overlying the fragrance of her own womanliness.

He let his hand cup over the upper curve of her ass, and his heart picked up a beat. She didn't say anything, just kept a half smile on her face. He traced his finger up the indentation of her spine, spread his hand across the top of her back—she was small.

He paused a breath before his lips touched hers. That close, with eyes locked, tingles of sensation raced between them. Her body trembled.

Slowly he bent his head, brushed her lips with his own. No zipping sizzle like the shock when their hands first met, but the pulsing attraction between them was tangible, tantalizing. Her eyes darkened to deep amber flecked with gold, her breath sighed out between her open lips and into his own mouth, and a tremor rippled through him, sensitizing his skin until the air felt heavy like a coming storm. Thudding came to his ears—his pulse or hers?

Again. He pressed his lips against hers, accepting the shock of wonder, of desire. His tongue slid over her mouth to taste. Sweet. Almost too sweet to bear.

He couldn't keep his eyes open. Impossible, for the first time. But his body—demanded he learn her from her mouth, from the pliant arms around his neck.

Tentatively he sent the tip of his tongue past her lips. Her mouth opened wide to his foray, and he sensed her entire *self,* opened to him for his pleasure. For him to plunder and ravage if he wanted. He could only sigh.

She shuddered against him as she took his breath inside her, as if his breath alone would change her forever. Exultation surged within him. Triumph. He'd claimed her with his breath, with the lightest of kisses. Her. His woman.

He slipped his hand beneath the hair at the nape of her neck. Her head tilted back and her eyes looked at him, unfocused. "More," she said.

"Yes. More."

Jake angled his lips on hers. Her mouth opened and he swept his tongue inside to taste all. But taste was not enough; he pulled her against him. The feel of her body—that he wanted to savor, too, to stretch into as many moments of pleasurable tension as he could. She felt like no other, the plumpness of her belly cradling his hard erection in softness that teased him with how he'd feel inside her. Her breasts, with their hard little points against his chest, lured him to forget their surroundings so he could explore her curves. The silky fall of her hair over his hand at her nape made him think of all the other textures of her. All the tastes.

Passion roared through him. He lifted her and drew them together sex to sex. She moaned into his mouth.

Her tongue rubbed against his. He captured it and sucked it and brought the true taste of her deep within his memory so he'd never lose it.

She pushed against his shoulders, broke the kiss. Her panting breath sounded loud. As loud as his thundering heart.

"We were supposed to be out of the park by sunset. They'll be closing the roads." Her teeth flashed. "A cop will drive by to ensure only residents are here."

All his blood was pooled in his groin. He was in no shape to make love to a woman in short grass over earth baked hard from drought. Though he desperately wanted to.

"You'd better put me down before we do something that will humiliate us." She blushed.

He blinked. Even in the dim light of nightfall, he was sure. She had *blushed*.

He set her gently on her feet. "Shauna," he said, and watched his breath stir her hair.

"Hmmmm?"

He smiled. "Just trying your name out."

"Good. You'll remember it."

"No chance of forgetting."

"Not for an observant cop like you."

A chill made his toes curl. "Does that bother you? My job?"

She looked up at him, and her face, highlighted by the sun's dying radiance, was serene. Serenity wasn't something he'd often seen. He didn't know that serenity was an emotion many cops ever saw. He wondered how many cops would cherish it and only knew that he did.

"Being a police officer isn't just a job for you, is it, Jake? It *is* you."

How did she figure that out so fast? Was she learning things about him from the quiet between them? What things? How much was he unconsciously telling her?

"That's right," he said. The light was too dim to see the amber of her eyes and that hurt a little—how often would he see her eyes? How long would this strange interlude last?

"I've never had a friend who was a police officer. I don't know how I'll act when your profession affects me—us." She ended on a whisper. "Do you want there to be an 'us,' Jake?"

"Yes!" he answered without thought. "Want to get together tomorrow?" he asked gruffly and waited an eternity, staring into her eyes. Why was he letting her go now? He didn't want to. He wanted to take her home. To bed. And keep her there, preferably under him. He shifted at the thought and his bruises twinged. Well, maybe over him, then. *With* him, though, positively.

She tore her gaze from his. At least it seemed she was having problems not looking at him.

"Um," she said.

He thought that was a good sign. "Tomorrow." He ached with unfulfilled lust, but beneath that were the all too real aches from his recent bout with a concrete sidewalk and a bullet. A hot bath and as much sleep as possible would be best if he could talk her into bed tomorrow.

Clearing her throat, she said, "Sunday. Sunday is my Meditation Morning with Friends of the Forest."

He stared. She couldn't be serious.

She didn't meet his eyes, but her lips firmed. "I really need it this week. It's been a—very eventful week."

When she glanced at him again, he got the impression that he was one of the major events. His ego swelled, almost matching his body. His body that was getting tighter by the moment. His body that might start ruling his head any minute.

"Would you like to come with me?" Shauna asked.

To a Meditation Morning with some New-Age flakes called "Friends of the Forest"? More than anything else he wanted to be with her. Deep inside him a small, persistent need to please her started clamoring. "I've had a—uh—major week, too." Understatement.

Now she smiled up at him, trusting. An optimist. "We go to an old estate in Cherry Hills with huge trees. Very peaceful. You'll like it."

He wondered if they'd be back in time for the Broncos kickoff. Hell, it was only the second preseason football game and he could miss it if he was rolling around with her in another kind of sport. The *best* sport.

"Meditation Morning with Friends of the Forest. At an estate in Cherry Hills. Right," he said neutrally. Could have been worse. Could have been Catholic Mass in the Basilica all morning. But the guys would understand Mass better than a meeting of the Friends of the Forest. Maybe they would never hear. Yeah. Maybe he had pink hair.

Then he looked into Shauna's eyes and was caught. They told him he was valued and valuable. He couldn't recall the last time anyone looked at him like that.

And she—she was small and lovely with a childlike wonder encased in her very womanly body. He sensed an underlying delight and passion in everything she did, and he wanted that passion directed at him. Hell, he wanted her entire concentration on him.

"Yes," he said. "I'll go with you. We can spend the day together." To hell with the Bronco game. It was only preseason, after all. The way he and Shauna had connected earlier, it was a good bet he could talk her into bed tomorrow.

"I'll walk you to your car." He placed his fingertips at the small of her back and she trembled. He sucked in a deep breath and forced hot images from his brain.

She wanted him as much as he wanted her. He nearly staggered at the thought. This was more than lust. Just by looking at her, a person could tell she wouldn't hop into bed with a stranger.

But she didn't treat him like a stranger, and she didn't feel like a stranger to him. That was so odd that it might have scared Jake a little last week. Certainly, he'd have played this whole scene differently. But he was trying to be more up front and honest, and it wasn't as hard as he'd thought.

Just how noble he could be with her in his condo the next day was a whole different question.

four

The next morning Jake had second thoughts about the Friends of the Forest, but not about wanting Shauna, not after more hot dreams. They'd been even sexier since now he knew the scent of her arousal, the timbre of her voice, how her amber gaze seemed to melt after she kissed him.

Shauna was special, not like any other woman he'd ever met. Okay, her type hadn't attracted him before, women who wanted more than just a hot time between the sheets, some superficial dates. And how cold that all seemed now. How sterile.

He pulled up in front of her house and recalled he'd been there before—twice. Once during a winter day when a gang of teen burglars had struck the neighborhood. No one was home. The second instance had been the night two small planes had collided in midair and fallen, one crashing a half-block away.

The whole force had been called out that night, and he'd been part of a door-to-door giving residents correct information and looking for debris. Both times Boris had appeared on the front stoop before the porch, hissed, clawed, and pissed on his shoes—definitely making himself memorable. The house had been dark and he'd given a perfunctory knock and left as soon as possible. But the plane crash had been at the beginning of the year, just as night was falling.

Now it was the end of summer, before the cold nights and the first frost, and what a difference! Her front yard was terraced and showed a verdant tangle of blooming flowers.

He was halfway up the short sidewalk to her house when Shauna stepped from her enclosed front porch. "Jake." She smiled. He returned it and helped her into his SUV.

Jake was remembering Boris, and trying to remember Boris without thinking about how the ghost cat appeared in his life. As he drove, hazy visions of *someplace else* wisped into his mind. He wished he was at the gym where he could work out and think instead of on his way to a stupid New-Age thing. He answered Shauna's social questions distractedly.

"Please pull over, Jake," Shauna said coolly.

"What?"

"I asked you to pull over."

He slid a glance to her. Her profile was probably as stern as a pretty face like hers could get. He signaled and steered to the side.

When they were stopped, Shauna faced him. "Just what do you find objectionable about sitting in a peaceful natural setting for an hour and meditating?"

"Ah." He didn't want to offend her, but she just stared at him with serious amber eyes, eyes that didn't seem to indicate a mind that was the least flakey. He took his hands off the wheel and pushed his fingers through his hair.

"I'd imagine you aren't accustomed to meditation. Do you think it has no value?" she prompted.

"No. That is, I know some people find it—ah—soothing."

Shauna nodded. "That's right, I do. It settles me. And I find it even more useful when I'm surrounded by the beauty of nature. Do you have a problem with nature, Jake?"

"I like to fish and camp the same as any other guy," he said.

"So you probably are used to settling your mind while doing something else." She looked at him until a word was pulled from his lips.

"Exercise. I exercise a lot. I work on my body and let my mind rest then—let it take care of itself."

She flashed a smile. "It shows that you exercise. And it shows that I don't, a lot, but my new business will tone me up. Meanwhile, I find a need for meditation to let my mind rest. I don't like to drive to the mountains every weekend, and it's not easy meditating in Denver parks."

The thought of her sitting cross-legged with her eyes closed, completely defenseless, in a couple of the parks chilled him to the bone.

"That leaves personal property. My own yard isn't conducive to meditation, either."

She sounded way too logical.

They watched each other. Shauna tilted her head and a little frown line knitted between her brows. "Is it the name? I can see how the name might put some people off."

"How could a normal guy even want to meet a person who was a 'Friend of the Forest'?"

Shauna chuckled. "It is a little New Age."

"Why didn't you just call the group 'Tree Huggers'?" Jake muttered.

"Because we don't hug trees. We just sit under them and meditate."

He could deal with meditation. Maybe. "Like the Society of Friends, the Quakers?"

"I suppose so, though I've never been to a Quaker Meeting. The Friends of the Forest does have an activist branch, of course, and we have monthly meetings. But Sunday mornings are for meditation. You don't have to come if you don't want to. I'm sorry it makes you uncomfortable. The estate is only a couple of blocks away. I can walk. Someone will give me a ride home."

He didn't want her to spend any time in anyone else's company but his. "Seems a waste of time," he muttered.

"A waste of time?"

He waved to the city outside the window. "It's been hot all week. It'll be hot today."

"And you'd rather be doing something, anything, other than just thinking or stilling your thoughts and letting your mind rest." Shauna unfastened her seat belt. "This was a mistake. I'm sorry." She smiled at Jake, but he knew better than anyone else when a smile was false.

He narrowed his eyes. "I want to spend time with you, the day with you." He just plain wanted her.

Shauna inclined her head and a considering expression came to her eyes. "Don't the Broncos play today?"

"Second preseason game. In Texas," Jake said.

"You strike me as a sports fan."

"I like to watch. I work hard. I play hard. I relax watching sports."

"Sounds like you're a normal guy."

He hoped so. His hormones certainly were.

"I suppose you were going to invite me to watch the game with you out at some sports bar?" Shauna said.

Heat crept up the back of Jake's neck. "Actually I thought we could watch it on my big-screen TV. In."

Her eyebrows lifted.

His neck burned.

Her lips twitched, but her eyes gleamed. Good.

"I see."

"I have guacamole and chips," Jake offered, as if food would make the invitation more innocent.

"I don't often watch sports," Shauna said. "What with just starting my business, I have a lot of other things I should be doing."

Jake set his jaw.

"But I want to spend time with you, too, Jake. I sense a compromise." Shauna clicked her seat belt back into place.

A breath he hadn't been aware of holding released. "After the med—this thing, I could drop you off at your house and you could work a little. I'll stop by the grocery and pick up a pizza. Kickoff is at two p.m. If you got to my condo by one, we could talk before the game."

"Sounds like a plan." Shauna looked straight ahead. Serene, hands folded on her lap. A faint smile curved her lips, as if she was contemplating food. He hoped she was thinking about tasting him, too.

"About this upcoming hour. I can concentrate for an hour on my job," Jake said, checked the empty road behind him and pulled away from the curb.

"Or *guacamole and chips this afternoon*," Shauna said with a laugh in her voice.

So he was obvious. If it got her in his house, in his bed, he didn't care.

"Vanilla ice cream and hot fudge," Shauna murmured.

"What?" Jake said.

"I like vanilla ice cream and hot fudge. For dessert," Shauna said. "After the pizza. An all-American meal." She licked her lips. "Hot fudge. Yum."

Yeah, right, Jake thought as he drove into the circular entryway of the Cherry Hill address and parked. Like he was going to be able to meditate after *that* comment.

The owner of the large, old estate, Mrs. Freuhauff, was dressed in something gauzy and probably expensive. When introduced, she raised little painted-on eyebrows and showed even, white dentures in a smile. Her eyes were every bit as sharp as Shauna's. Canny old lady. Canny young one, too, he thought as he saw Shauna putting new business cards discreetly on a patio table beside the path that led to the garden.

They wended their way down the crushed red sandstone path until they reached a section of the estate that boasted towering trees.

"Geeze," Jake said. "These must be the oldest trees in Denver." They arched overhead like a natural chapel. About twenty padded chairs were set in the deep shade. It was almost cold, the space obviously rarely getting direct sun. In the distance a large fountain tumbled water, the sound adding to the ambience.

Shauna stopped suddenly and Jake ran into her. He reached out to steady her and felt a fine tremor go through her body. "What is it?"

She slid her hand down to twine her fingers in his. "A dream. I dreamt earlier this week I was in a place— almost like this—but more, better," she gasped.

Jake didn't know how it worked, but visuals flashed from her to him, and his own back. He tried to grasp them as they flitted. "No. It was an office. A shabby—" Their memories clashed in every way—an office/grove; a gray man/angel; ominous doors/windows of opportunity. Except they'd both seen the golden aspen leaf.

He felt dizzy. "I'll go save us some seats." He dropped her hand. He wanted a minute to compose himself. Too bad he had to sit instead of run.

Shauna looked up at him with eyes holding recollections of otherworldly experiences. "Sure, find seats for us, please. I want to talk to the facilitator a minute."

Facilitator. It echoed in his mind like an inward curse word.

The garden filled and Jake observed those who entered. Mostly women, some tweedy-looking men, and even a regular guy or two. They nodded at him like they accepted him right off. Odd, but nice.

People settled. Shauna stepped in front of the group, hands together and fingers twisting. She cleared her throat. "I asked Jennifer if I could provide the meditation topic for this morning and she graciously agreed."

Shauna's cheeks pinkened. "I thought we should consider risk. I am not a risk-taker." Her lips trembled. "But this week I quit my florist job and started my own business as a landscape designer."

There was a patter of applause and approving smiles. A lady in the row ahead of Jake murmured, "It's about time."

Shauna ducked her head, then looked at those in front of her with steady eyes. She was adorable.

"It was a very big risk for me, something I thought I'd never find the courage to do. I like security."

Jake shifted in his seat as dream-images flickered through his brain. Review sheets, his bad, hers good.

She inhaled, held her breath, then released it. Several others around him did the same.

"I brought a guest, Jake Forbes, a detective in the Denver Police Force. Police officers have inherently risky lives. They essentially put their lives on the line for society every day," Shauna said.

Jake recalled the sound and punch of the bullet that

had knocked him down and rolled his shoulders to release tension. He didn't think risk would be a good meditation topic. Who knew?

"So I thought we should all meditate on risk. The amount of risk we have in our lives and whether it is enough.

"My affirmation for the group is: 'I step out of my comfort zone and risk change so my life might be more fulfilling.'" She ducked her head again. "Thank you."

Then she walked with a steady step to take her place next to Jake. As she sat, he naturally reached for her hand.

The hour of thinking turned out to be too short. First he had to sort out the dream. His conclusion was that he'd screwed up before, and if he didn't shape up, he'd be going through one very bad door.

Then he thought of his promotion and his new woman partner, Maggie. He was determined to be straight with her at all times. His old manner toward all women had been one of superficial charm—that had worked on his ma best when she was clear of the drugs. But that was the old Jake. It was over.

Shauna shifted and her body brushed his. And she invaded his thoughts. He hoped she'd take a risk with him. He had a strong feeling in his gut that he'd be risking a lot with her. It wouldn't stop him.

In the supermarket Jake noticed the strange sound first. An odd *whooshing* intermixed with little cackles of glee. He let the heavy glass refrigerator door slam shut. He had a bad feeling about this. His life had been blessedly Boris-free since the evening before.

Sure enough, when he looked up, it was to see the ghost cat swooping down his aisle. Jake sighed.

Boris did a loop-de-loop, then whizzed past Jake like a rocket. The cat sure could move with those wings. Golden wings. Completely incongruous on a black-and-white cat.

"Got your wings, I see," Jake said.

"Yesssssss. I fulfilled my duty of ensuring you and Shauna met."

Jake grunted, eyed the wings closer as the cat hovered before him. "Gold, huh?"

"They wanted to give me *white*!" The cat wrinkled its nose.

"I thought all angel wings were white."

"*Ordinary* ones."

Well, that explained it.

The cat hunched a wing-curve forward so he could admire it. "I did not want white. Or black. Or gray. Or silver. Or—"

"I get it. Only gold."

"They will match My Crown," he said smugly. "I will be awesome."

"You'll be something."

"Open the seat of the basket so I can sit."

Rolling his eyes, Jake did so. Boris hovered, tottered, and landed in the seat with a lurch strong enough to rattle the beer bottles.

Boris turned his head and surveyed Jake's shopping

with disgust. "There is only frozen pizza and imported beer here."

"I'm buying guacamole and chips, too." And ice cream, hot fudge, and whipped cream.

The cat sent him a sly look. "Shauna makes excellent guacamole. I, of course, do not eat plant mush, but I have heard other humans comment upon it."

Jake grunted again. "Maybe you can point out a good brand for me to buy, then."

Boris abandoned his seat to press his nose against the freezer door. Then his whole head went through the glass. It gave Jake the creeps. Probably unsanitary, too.

When Boris's voice came, it was oddly muffled. "Shauna likes this stuff."

Jake jerked open the door. "What?"

Boris extended a paw to tap a frozen crust.

"Quiche," Jake grumbled. "Should have known. This will *never* work out." Not that any affair lasted longer than a couple of months after the sex got average, and a guy shouldn't really expect more. Hadn't wanted more. Now he did, with Shauna.

He recalled the look in Shauna's eyes when she stared at him, wide and soft and interested. He got the fancy quiche and studied it. It had eggs, cheese, and bacon. How bad could it be? Looking at the instructions, he realized all he had to do was heat the oven and put it in, just like pizza, only a little longer. He tossed it in the basket.

"Careful," said Boris. "The crust can crumble and break."

"Huh." Jake guessed so. He took the quiche out of the

cart, set it back on the shelf, and got a new one he placed carefully on the pizza.

Back on the seat, Boris scowled. "There is no Cat food in the basket."

"And there isn't going to be, either," Jake said, tooling the cart to the deli. Probably better if he got some store-made guac instead of frozen.

Boris's yowl went straight through Jake's head. He winced.

"You haven't fed me *at all.* I am starving."

"You can't starve. You're dead."

A pitiful cat face lifted to Jake. He shrugged.

"I need food," whined Boris.

"They should have fed you in, uh, well, before."

"I did not need food *there.* I only need food *here.*"

Jake wondered what had happened to his nice, steady, logical life. Nothing had been the same—since the bullet. He didn't want to take a leave of absence, not with the new job coming up.

"Okay, okay. I'll get cat food."

"Tuna fish would be all right. Fresh shrimp. Even sardines," Boris said.

"Sure they would. You get cat food, the store brand."

Jake glanced at the clock. The food was in his fridge, he'd changed the sheets, and dusted the TV and entertainment center. The rug had hardly any lint, so he didn't need to vacuum. Plenty of time to do a little home workout—no, cancel that, he might need all his energy later.

"I'm hungry and want food." Boris sat on the kitchen counter.

That looked unsanitary, too. Good thing he hardly ever used the counter. Jake considered Boris.

Boris smiled in a way Jake didn't like. The cat could screw up Jake's plans with Shauna. She could walk in, take one look at Boris, and shower him with all the affection Jake wanted.

Jake tapped a fork on a can of chicken and beef. Disgruntled, he opened it and spread it on a plate for Boris. The cat stuck his muzzle in the food and inhaled.

Jake waited. He wasn't sure what he expected, but shouldn't have been surprised when the food simply stayed on the plate. After a minute or two, Boris sat back on his haunches and grinned at Jake, then burped.

Waving the fork at the dish, Jake scowled. "The food is still there."

Boris lifted his nose. "I have absorbed its essence."

Jake wondered what sort of essence the bad parts of chicken and cow could give an angel cat. "It doesn't look any different."

"It's still good food. If you put it outside on your patio the feral Cat who lives under the bushes near the Dumpster will eat it."

That didn't sound like a good idea to Jake, but it irked him to wash the food down the garbage disposal.

"The Cat needs food," Boris pressed on. "Shauna feeds the feral Cats in *her* neighborhood. That's how she got Me."

"That's what I'm afraid of," Jake muttered.

His doorbell rang and Jake's insides tightened. The

stove buzzed that the quiche was done. He pushed aside the curtain of the sliding-glass door to the patio, opened the door, and stuck out the plate. "Beat it," he said to Boris.

"I will tell the Cat he has good food, and that you might be an acceptable human friend. We will both watch you in the future."

"I don't care if I fail probation," Jake said. Not with Boris. The doors were another matter. How much would he have to change? He thought he was well on the way.

His doorbell rang again. "Get out of here."

Boris zoomed through the glass.

Jake felt awkward as he opened the door. Usually he just had guys over, or women who'd spend the night and leave before dawn. "Hey," he said to Shauna.

"Hi." She smiled and nothing else mattered except that she was here.

Shauna walked in and her eyes went to the only greenery.

"That's my plant," Jake said unnecessarily. It was the only thing in the living room besides two leather recliners, a coffee table, a lamp, and a huge entertainment center.

"I can see that." Shauna walked around the rubber plant.

Jake was sure it looked okay. Its stalks were straight and strong, the leaves large and glossy.

"You take good care of this plant."

Simple pride flooded him. She made him feel good.

"You know, Jake, this plant has some bark, making it almost a tree." She slanted him a look. "I bet I could hug it."

"Aw, geeze," he said.

"You're cute. And you take care of your plant very well." She beamed, crossed to him, and stroked his cheek. "Does it have a name?"

"Of course not!" He was offended. He marched into the kitchen and got out the guacamole and chips, thought a little and dumped the chips into a big bowl and put the supermarket container and the bowl on a tray he'd gotten when he'd bought some Christmas cookies last year.

It looked fine to him.

After consuming the guacamole, they went into the kitchen and ate quiche and talked and laughed. It amazed Jake how good a time he had, especially when he tried to explain the rules of football to Shauna. She followed his gestures and explanations with a twinkle in her eye that told him she was humoring him. But he figured it was his turn, after spending an hour with the Friends of the Forest.

He lost track of time and it took the click of his recording equipment as it came on to alert him that it was game time.

They hadn't reached dessert and he grinned. Halftime, if he was unlucky, but he didn't think he would be.

Shauna eyed the far recliner, but he had other ideas.

"Com'ere," he said, and brought her down on his lap. He liked the weight of her, a lot. He even liked the idea of watching the game with her. He'd give her a little time to get used to him, settle in, and then . . .

The first quarter elapsed with undistinguished playing. Shauna couldn't get excited about the game. But getting excited about Jake was another matter. As each

minute went by, the atmosphere in the room thickened.
She was aware of Jake as she'd never been aware of anyone else. The air around her body seemed to crackle, and
she thought she could feel every inch of her skin and
wondered where he'd touch her first.

five

Shauna sat sideways across Jake's legs, her own dropping over the arm of the lounger.

Jake turned her toward him, widening her legs so the most needy part of her pressed against the hard length of him. Shauna bit her lip to keep a moan of delight from escaping. At the point of contact she could feel the throbbing beat of both their hearts. Her hands curled over his shoulders to anchor her—to keep her upright, though winding anticipation sizzled through her blood.

She met his eyes and fell into the deep blue. Connected. Though they hadn't physically joined yet, she knew they were connected. By the past. By dreams. By hopes for the future.

Jake wasn't watching the game, he was watching her. His face was tight, his eyes dilated; he radiated intensity.

He slipped his hands under her bottom and lifted. She

rose obediently. Locking his gaze with hers, he stripped her shorts and panties off. She adjusted her position so she knelt with her thighs on either side of his hips.

Vaguely Shauna could hear the wild cheers of the crowd on TV, the excitement in the announcers' voices. Jake unzipped his jeans and it was louder than anything in the room, even her panting breath, even the blood roaring in her ears.

He reached to the side table, a rip and a crackle, as he protected them. Then his hands curved around her waist, lowered her slowly down on him.

She gasped at the sensation of his hard erection penetrating her, slowly, totally. So *good.* Her eyes closed and her head fell back. Inch by inch he sheathed himself in her until the most important thing in her life was feeling him inside her, completing her. She didn't know how long she could bear the delicious passion rising in her without moving, without screaming her desire.

Shauna opened her eyelids and was caught again by his gaze. Blue eyes, boy-next-door features, blond hair. The leather recliner was one that could be bought in any outlet store. His condo walls were white, the room barely furnished, sports noise from the TV. Everything *ordinary.*

Jake was inside her. Pulsing. Watching her with shadowed blue eyes.

It was the most extraordinary event of her life.

He moved his hands under her loose T-shirt, unsnapped the front of her bra, and cupped her breasts. Instinctively she arched and he went deeper. A strangled whimper of pleasure escaped her. He filled her, caressing her inside. She rocked and neared the ultimate edge of passion.

"Don't," he said, and his jaw clenched. His nostrils flared and he inhaled. "Don't move. Let's just sit here. Enjoy ourselves. I want this to last."

His hands were on her breasts; her thighs and bottom rested on denim. His sex was inside her and *nothing* was casual. His forefingers and thumbs held the nubs of her nipples, pulled gently, exquisitely, sending a spear of passion clear through her.

"Don't move," he whispered.

She knew he was tempting her, goading her, pushing her limits to see how long she could just sit there with him inside her and not go mad with wild passion. She'd burn up from spontaneous combustion soon.

He tugged at her nipples. "Kiss me."

She leaned into him and slid along him and her inner muscles squeezed him and she thought she'd expire from the pure rapture of it. Somehow her lips found his and opened.

He plunged his tongue into her mouth.

Too much.

She clamped her thighs against him, rose until his arousal slid nearly out of her, pressed against the sensitive nerves of her entrance, then impaled herself on him with a cry of delight.

Up and down she pumped. He kept to her rhythm, his eyes going dark and glazed.

Faster.

Harder.

Now!

Shauna flung back her head and screamed her release.

Jake clamped his hands around her waist, raised her, lowered her, rocked his hips, and twisted.

She came again with a keening sob.

He pulled her bottom tight against himself, rotated, thrust upward until she thought she'd splinter from the pleasure of him, and pulsed into her.

Shauna fell against him, smelled the scent of man beneath his shirt, gloried at the pounding of his heart under her ear. Before she was ready to move, he lifted her from him, set her on the recliner.

"Jake?"

He stripped off her shirt, then shucked his own clothes. Never looking away from her, he picked up the remote, punched a button, and the TV died. He threw the remote on the chair and swung her up into his arms. His eyes blazed blue.

"Too restrictive, the chair," he growled.

"You—you didn't want to move. Wanted—"

"—it to last." He shut his eyes and she could swear he shuddered. When he opened his eyes his gaze was fiery with masculine need, male possession. "Slow first. Wild now. In bed."

She couldn't manage a reply.

He looked at her sprawled on his bed, ready for loving again. The dappled light accented different portions of her body—the top and nipple of one breast, one rounded thigh. He sensed her unease. He couldn't do anything but stare. Jake was accustomed to picking up hard-bodied lovers from a gym, or the tennis courts along the park. This woman, with all her lush curves, made him feel more of a man than any one of the muscle-toned ladies he'd had in bed.

She looked so . . . soft. Soft round breasts that fit in his hands, a slightly curved belly that had molded around his cock when they'd petted in the recliner. She was the epitome of woman for him.

"I'm not buff," she whispered. "I'll be doing hard physical labor soon and will tone up. But now . . ."

He couldn't get a coherent word out of his mouth. A growl emerged. He'd go mad if he couldn't feel her under him, all that comforting roundness telling him intimately, body to body, that she was woman and his. He swallowed, tried again. "Mine." And he pounced.

She felt better than he'd expected, better than he ever dreamed a woman could, soft and luscious, letting him sink into her.

He grasped her wrists in one of his hands and lifted her arms above her head so he could see how her breasts plumped. Tipped with tight rose nipples, her breasts were the most beautiful he'd seen in a long, long time.

Arching against him, her soft belly caressed him, and he lost all reason, consumed by hard, demanding desire. He slid into her and inside she was as lush and as welcoming as out. He flung his head back as a moan tore from his throat. He couldn't get enough of the sensation of sheathing and withdrawing; the warm, wet friction made him wild. He plunged and twisted and emptied himself in her, hearing her cry of release matching the ragged rasp of his breathing.

And was grateful for that female sound of pleasure. It

told him that while he'd completely lost control of himself, he had still brought her pleasure. He rolled to his back and took her with him.

Her limp body atop his felt incredible, womanly, right. Even the thought that sex had never been so unbelievably great before didn't bring a hint of wariness into his mind. Her charms were bountiful and he planned on sating himself with them—no matter how long it took.

The next two weeks were the busiest and the best of Shauna's life.

With her starting a new business and Jake beginning a new job, they spent more hours at work than together, and consequently she thought their affair was so much more intense.

They managed to spend some time out of bed, too. She took him to a play and went to a football game. Jake even attended two meditation sessions. They talked and laughed and ate and found they both had a passion for trying new restaurants.

Since his condo was close to her first job, they spent most of their time there and always made love there.

Jake dominated her thoughts and made her more physically aware of her body than she'd ever been—in a good way. As for her, she couldn't keep her hands off him, was total in her exploration of him.

She'd remembered the entire scene in the Atrium and had written it down. Jake was for her. But *he* had to decide and accept that, too. So right now she was enjoying the moment—a lesson that the angel hadn't told her she needed to learn, but a benefit nonetheless.

Finally it was time for the next step—time for her to invite him for dinner and overnight loving. When she'd confessed that she had two cats, Jake's face went odd and he said he fed two.

Shauna decided to keep the meal simple with salad, pot roast, and brownies for dessert.

She wondered what he'd think of her home.

Jake drove up to her house and sat outside a moment. The more he looked at the place, the more it looked just like it must belong to Shauna. From the landscaping she was putting in near Skyline Park and the plans he'd glimpsed on her laptop, she had a unique style that he'd always recognize.

Her own short front yard was a riot of late-blooming flowers. The casual-looking plantings were very deliberate—and they worked. Just looking at the flowers, he felt better. They reminded him that beauty lived in the world and could be seen in just one wild rose. He grimaced. Definitely hanging out with Shauna too much to be thinking that way, but he didn't have to tell anyone he had such thoughts. Jake stared at the flowers a moment longer and let the sight lift his spirits and bring him a measure of calm. Then he opened the door of his SUV and got out.

When he reached the steps, the scents of the flowers and plants came on a slight breeze that brought a hint of fall's chill and the contrast stopped him. In a couple of months the pretty blooms would be dead, the plants leafless and brown. The change of seasons was upon them, and it seemed as if his life was changing, too—but becoming more fulfilling rather than dying.

He snorted. The last thing he wanted to think about was dying. Been there, done that, returned—just as

Shauna had. He'd acknowledged the event, analyzed it a bit, but figured he was on his way to putting those checkmarks in the boxes. He'd changed and was up-front with everyone, now. But didn't want to talk about the experience.

Jake reached the front porch and rang the bell. No Boris "greeted" him this time. Jake grinned; the cat was an angel now and probably zooming around with those wings of his.

Shauna came to the door, and the sight of her took his breath away. She wore a loose-fitting dress of some filmy material and was barefoot. Definitely more summer than autumn. It suited her and started him thinking again about what her bed was like. And where it was. He hoped to find out soon.

She crossed to the front porch door and opened it to him. "Hi, Jake."

He smiled slowly, enjoying looking at her. She flushed a little and stepped back. He joined her and stared down. Here were more scents—flowers again, and woman. He liked woman better.

Her dress dipped into a V and he saw the upper curve of her breasts. Heated desire rose as he recalled how her breasts felt in his hands, the ripest and tastiest of fruits.

Since he felt like jumping her, he looked around the neighborhood again. "The last time I was here was after the plane crash."

Shauna paled. "The plane crash. I was on the street at the time."

"What!" His heart lurched. That was too damn close.

"I got off the bus early and bought some cat food at

the store and was walking home. If I'd gone up a block to walk . . ."

"Geeze." He glanced in the direction where one of the planes crashed, cleared his throat. "It took out three houses."

Her smile was tipped. "There's no security even in your own home. I haven't spoken about it much, but I heard the crash. I didn't know what it was, just felt this powerful, irrational fear and I hurried home. By the time I reached the back gate, there was this awful smell."

"I knocked on your door. Boris was guarding your place."

"I was next door. Chuck and Pete were solid as rocks. I'm so grateful. When I realized a lot of my friends would be calling, I went back home. Boris was on the front step."

"If Boris had yowled . . ." Jake said, getting mad at the angel cat.

Shauna nodded. "Yes, I'd have come running. It was a bad time. A bad time in the neighborhood for a couple of months." She looked across the street in the direction of the crash, then down at her flower beds.

"Come in, Jake," she said.

He had to kiss her.

Before she could move away, he placed his hand under her chin and tilted her face up to his. Keeping his gaze locked on hers, he brushed her soft mouth with his and welcomed the flash of arousal.

"Lovely Shauna," he breathed, and pulled her into his arms, glorying in the softness of her against him. Just holding her was a delight—and an exercise in control.

But he wanted to savor the anticipation. He didn't want to rush this time with Shauna. His tongue swept along her lips, asking for entrance; she opened her mouth on a sigh, then her tongue dueled with his and blood fled from his head straight to his groin. Maybe he was going to have more problems lasting through dinner than he'd thought. He broke the kiss and liked it when her hands clamped around his arms to steady herself. Her eyes were wide and dreamy, her lips ruddy from his kiss. He liked that she showed her reaction to him. She wasn't a lady to be casual about sex or light about emotions that tangled with passion. He hadn't experienced such emotions much with any woman before Shauna, but found his feelings growing. Sometimes it made him wary, but mostly he enjoyed how he felt when he thought about Shauna, or was with her, and most of all when he was with her in bed. In her.

"Jake, you are the best kisser," she said.

And the warmth that was different than passion, more than affection, suffused him, gathered around his heart. Yeah, he really liked being with Shauna.

She sniffed and her eyes cleared. "The brownies!" She pulled away from him and rushed back into the house.

Homemade brownies. Geeze, could a woman be so perfect?

The threshold to the house was dim and the entryway lit only indirectly from the porch. He stepped in and knew he was in trouble.

It was too perfect. Too comfortable. Too everything he'd always dreamed of as a child and his ma and dad never provided.

It was a home.

• • •

After the greatest sex of his life, Shauna drifted asleep beside him in the gentle rocking of the waterbed. The glow from the nightlight in the bathroom down the hall was faint, but comforting. Everything in the house was comforting, a home, just like he'd desperately wanted as a child. That concerned him. Her home attracted him just as much as her heart—welcoming strays open-handedly, her spirit—optimistic and completely honest and natural, not to mention her body. He curved his hand around her sweet ass. She twisted so sensually, shattering his control faster than he believed possible. He'd slaked a need he'd never known.

Yeah, he liked her body a lot. Liked that she was so unselfconscious in the act of love, so willing to do whatever pleased them both.

Nothing about this house was uncomfortable. He stilled. It wasn't just a home to him. It was a trap for Shauna.

It was *too* comfortable. She could withdraw from everything that was messy and *uncomfortable* in life here. Everything that didn't suit her. All the wild emotions that might make her live deeply. He could see her as the stereotypical old maid fifty years from now.

A *whuffle* and *thump* came from under the headboard, where her cat Jimbo slept. Geeze, Shauna already had a good start on the cat part of the old-maid scenario. She was twenty-eight and had two—three, counting Boris. By sixty she'd have six, and by ninety . . . Jake shuddered. It didn't bear thinking about.

He'd save her from that fate. Make sure she didn't

fade into this house and never come out, and only cared for by cats.

He frowned. Maybe he was wrong about the number of cats. How long did cats live, anyway? Boris sure hadn't looked too old. Beaten up and tough, but not old. How old was old for a cat? Surely one or two would kick the bucket along the way.

But she'd get more. She wouldn't be able to turn them away. Jake settled. He could rescue her. Make sure she lived life to the fullest. That was a quality most cops had. They didn't take life for granted, and they really *lived*. She would give him comfort and he'd give her excitement and they'd give each other great sex. That's how this relationship would work. Sounded good to him.

A faint *whish* of sound and his head rocked up and down on the bed from the addition of a new body. He stared up into the unblinking, gleaming eyes of Prima Donna, the little delicate Siamese. The snotty one. Boris had his faults, and they irritated the hell out of Jake, but Boris hadn't stared at him with the complete and utter disregard of the Queen of the Universe for a peasant too low to touch her dainty paws.

The cat walked over him with the deliberate prick of her claws, stopped near Shauna's head by his shoulder, then the thing scratched at the bedspread. Shauna mumbled and lifted the covers. Jake stared, appalled. The cat slept with Shauna? Under the covers? This was going too far.

He was under there, too, and he was naked. And he sure as hell didn't trust that cat and her beady eyes.

He picked her up. Her yowl woke Shauna. Prima twisted with a flexibility that amazed him. He dropped her fast over the side of the bed.

Shauna pushed hair out of her eyes. "Jake?"

"No cats in the bed under the covers," he said. "Especially when I'm naked."

She looked at him with sleepy eyes. "Oh. All right. We'll get used to it. I'll think of something Prima will like better."

Not possible. He watched warily as Prima Donna stalked away, tail high.

"No cats under the covers, eh?" Shauna purred. Her hand slid down his chest, over his thighs, between them. She found him and stroked, long and delicately.

He swallowed. "I could make an exception. *One* exception."

"And you're naked?" Her eyes were wide now, teasing. The tip of her tongue darted out to touch her lips, and she smiled. Once he would have said a catlike smile, but this was all woman.

"I think I'd better verify that you're naked," she purred. She ducked under the sheets. The purring stopped when her tongue took the place of her fingers, caressing the length of him exquisitely. She used her teeth, too, with just enough pressure and skill to shatter him.

Six

Shauna gripped the phone tightly. The mechanic continued to squawk in her ear, but she didn't hear him. Her car was dead. He paused and she said, "Thanks, don't work on it yet. I'll get back to you tomorrow morning."

Blindly she hung up the phone. Wrapping her arms around herself, she slid down the wall of the kitchen, waves of nausea washing through her. What was she going to do?

For a while she just sat there, sick, until Prima and Jimbo circled her, mewing in worry. Then she pushed to her feet and tottered out to the dining room and the business ledger. She didn't need to open the pages. If she poured money into her car, she couldn't make her first payment on her business loan—surely a big, red flag to the bankers who watched. If she didn't fix her car, she wouldn't have a business.

She propped her elbows on the table and put her face in her hands. Was life going to be like this every month? Full of worry as to whether she'd be able to make her business go, pay the loan? Full of moments of pure stomach-rolling nausea as she faced the future? She was doing what she always dreamed of, and this was the dark, nightmare side. She'd mortgaged her house and used all her savings for the start-up. Winter was near, along with an inevitable slowdown in projects. Money was coming in, just not soon enough to pay the loan. She should be all right through the winter unless there was a major disaster. . . .

After a few deep breaths, options marched through her head. She could set up payments with the mechanic; she'd been a good customer. She could rent out the spare bedroom and take on a roommate. She could find a part-time or a full-time job.

Or she could quit. Right now. Bury her dream. A last clenching of her stomach reminded her of the benefits of that. Less worries.

How much did she want this dream? Enough to pay the cost of moments of sick terror like this?

Another minute of deep breaths and visualizations— how she'd loved the designing and, most of all, the planting. How she'd anticipated going by her projects next spring and summer and seeing the fruition of her work. She set her shoulders and opened the ledger.

Jake banged the door as he came in. "I've got Chinese," he said. His footsteps stopped in the living room as he saw her. "What is it?"

She didn't want to look at him and let him see her failure or the tears in her eyes. Was torn for an instant as to whether she could share this with him. "Car is dead."

"Oh." He passed her on the way to the kitchen, and the smell of the Chinese food sent another rush of nausea through her. There was the crackle of bags as he set the food on the counter.

The next thing she knew, he was stroking her head. "Don't worry, Shauna."

She braced her shoulders so they wouldn't tremble. "I'll think of something. I'm not going to quit."

"Of course you won't," he said, but his soothing hand left her and she felt bereft.

Then he flipped open his cell phone and punched in a number. "Roy?" Jake said. "You still have that used truck that looks like hell but runs good in the back of your place? Can I borrow it for a friend?"

Jake looked at Shauna. She stared up at him, heart thumping hard. "How long?" he asked her.

Her brain scrambled, but she knew her finances and when more money was coming in. "Two weeks?"

"A coupla weeks," Jake said into the phone. He smiled at her. "Yeah, yeah, we'll get an oil change and a lube job. Promise." He glanced at his watch. "How about we pick it up at seven-thirty? Fine, see you then."

Shauna stared at him. Just like that. Jake, the man of action, had just given her two weeks of breathing room. With that she could look around for a truck of her own. She jumped up and her chair fell to the floor, and flinging her arms around his neck, she kissed him hard. "My hero."

"Oh, yeah!" He pulled her hard against him.

With the relief rolling through her body, she felt a little light-headed, but she knew what she wanted. "I feel like wild sex."

"Oh, *yeah.*"

Later that night Jake still felt like a hero. He'd had no doubt that Shauna could have fixed her problem on her own, but it was great to be able to help her. It was great to know that Roy trusted him—and Shauna—with his truck, too.

The world was fine, or would be after another bout of sex.

He pulled Shauna close, fitting her against him. Her smooth skin and soft body moved all along his own and he hardened, fast. But he fit his mouth on hers, slowly teasing her lips apart, probing with his tongue, and she gave the little moans that told him he was arousing her. He'd make her moan, then writhe, and then surrender.

He kept his thrusts slow and steady, bringing them both to the brink, then retreating, letting them calm a little before he began again. Her eyes glazed and her breaths became one long crescendo of whimpers for fulfillment. A fine sweat shone on her skin, accenting her breasts, dampening the hair along her brow—and lower. She was lost in the spell he wove for them, not thinking at all, only feeling what he was doing to her, and he was supremely pleased.

Finally the demands of his own body and the pressure

building in it snapped his control. He plunged and groaned and thrust until she shuddered and clamped around him and his mind exploded.

"I love you!" Shauna cried.

He froze, then realized she didn't really mean it. He could breathe again, though his heart hurt. A woman like Shauna would rationalize great sex with love. Her words had to be just bedroom words, like sex words. He'd heard them before without any meaning, and said them himself. But he wouldn't with Shauna.

All right, maybe they meant more than that to Shauna. She'd said the words because she'd been sleeping with him for more than a month now. She was a spiritual person and would need to justify the passion and hot sex and spending time with him as something more than . . . dating, a hot affair.

He shut his eyes and his mind and his heart and slipped into sleep.

Shauna bit her lip. Jake hadn't wanted to hear she loved him. Tough. She'd needed to say it. Difficult to believe she loved Jake so quickly, but they . . . connected. She admired him and his work.

She smiled in the darkness at his snoring. Jake was real and she'd needed a man in her life for a long time. He might not be a "good" man—she still knew he was dangerous to her heart if she got attached and they broke up—but he'd be worth the effort to forge the relationship between them. She didn't mind doing 75 percent— for a while. But only for a while.

She'd been set up by fate, and by the iridescent

Angel. She turned and rubbed her nose against Jake's shoulder, inhaling his scent and the fragrance of them together. Not to mention the sex was incredible. . . .

Her saying she loved him changed their relationship. They still dated, still spent a lot of time in bed and out of it, but Jake looked at her as if always measuring her words. She was sorry the phrase had slipped out, but she'd been biting her tongue for days and wasn't ashamed of her feelings—her love.

He just wasn't ready to hear it, though he hadn't said anything about her declaration. And he hadn't made one of his own, and for that lack her heart ached. She knew more of his background now; they talked in bed. Shauna learned that he would open up to her in the dark, whether or not they made love.

Another week passed and Indian summer slowly died. A couple of gray days brought rain and a spitting of snow, and when they were gone the days were noticeably cooler. Shauna worked from sunrise to sunset landscaping clients' yards and a couple more hours at her desk drawing plans. She'd been very lucky and was sure the business would survive the winter, though she might need a part-time job to keep her and the cats—and Jake—in food.

One late afternoon, as Jake and his partner Maggie were on their way back to the station, a report of shots fired and units responding came over the radio.

Jake was driving. "Sweet Motel, South Sheridan. We're closest." He glanced at Maggie from the corner of his eyes.

"Not our job," she said.

The dispatcher's tone rose slightly as she added that a child was involved. Maggie looked at Jake. "Let's do it."

"Right." He hit the radio and called it in. An image of the place formed in his mind's eye, and his gut tightened. It had a door—several doors that reminded him of doors he had not wanted to go through. "Put your vest on, Maggie."

"Huh?"

"Do it!" he said.

"Yeah, yeah. I'm senior here." She twisted and got it from the back. Slipped it over her head, and he felt her stare. "I've got to be sure of you, Forbes."

"I won't clutch 'cause I was shot earlier."

"Wasn't thinking of that." She cleared her throat and leaned into a turn Jake took fast. "You don't have a great rep for working with women. You've been fine with me, but I have to know you'll follow me into that motel room. I always go through the door high; you go in low so we'll cover the room."

"Yeah, well, I go in high, too, but for you, I'll go in low." He grinned, adrenaline rushing through him. "And I'll be right on that hard ass of yours." She was a good partner and a good woman. He reached out and yanked one of her vest tabs tighter.

She sucked in a breath. "Shit, Forbes, take it easy."

"Nope. That was the old me, pretending. I've got a bad feeling about this, about you." The car laid rubber as he stopped. Jake slid out, yanked on his vest, and pulled his gun.

Maggie kept up with his run to the front of the seedy motel. "Fasten your vest better!" she gestured with her free hand.

"Not my time to die," Jake said, thinking of Boris.

Maggie froze a second, hopped to keep up. "What, those trees you visit every Sunday told you so?"

He should have known that would get out. It couldn't bother him now. Wouldn't bother him, ever. What his buds thought of it didn't matter. "Yeah, they whisper to me. I'll know my time." He knew that with complete certainty.

People huddled in front of the motel on the cracked asphalt of the parking lot, fear mixed with fascination on their faces. Some looked at a broken second-floor window that had screams coming from it, some watched Jake and Maggie.

"Got news for you, Jake. There ain't no trees here," Maggie said. "What's going on?" she demanded of a potbellied guy who stepped forward.

He looked at Jake, but answered Maggie. "I'm the manager. I dunno. Guy just started shooting up the place."

"Is there a child in there?" asked Jake. "Who else is in there with him? What do you know about him?"

"A little girl may be in there. His wife, maybe. His name is Jones and he's paid through the end of the month."

Maggie jerked her head and they took off up the outside concrete stairs. "Police!" she yelled. "Put down your weapon and come out with your hands up!"

Shots peppered the window.

"Police!" Jake shouted, flicking off the safety of his gun.

They stopped short of the door. "Mr. Jones, this is the police. Put your gun down and come out with your hands raised."

"Davis—" A woman's cry cut short on a slap. Another shot zinged through the window.

"On three," Maggie said. "One. Two. Three."

They went in. A shot took Maggie high in the shoulder and she went down. Jake fired and killed a skinny man with wild red hair. A woman screamed and waved a knife she clutched. She stared at Jake, looked down at Maggie. Blood trickled from scratches on the woman's face next to her eye, her mouth. She gaped and Jake noted missing teeth.

"You killed my man. My Davis." She staggered toward Jake.

Taking a long stride, he twisted the knife from her hand, pushed her into a chair. "Sit. Stay." The situation reminded him of his childhood. Only worse. At least he'd been spared this ending. "You have a daughter?"

The woman burst into wild wailing. Keeping an eye on her, Jake went over and helped Maggie sit up. She rubbed her shoulder. "Shit." She struggled to stand. Jake set a hand under her elbow and boosted. Maggie nodded thanks and went over to the woman. "Ma'am, is your daughter here?"

No young girl peeked out at them from anywhere.

"His. The brat is his." The woman wiped her nose with her hand, then on the faded dress she wore. "She's in school." She stared at Davis's body with glazed eyes, lifted her head to glare at Jake. "We were just having a little argument." She said it as if their arguments generally included guns and knives. Just another loving relationship.

Jake remembered his own parents' "discussions." He'd hated the shouting voices, slamming doors, sizzling rage. But they'd never been as bad as this.

Maggie sighed, met Jake's eyes. "Thanks, partner." She cleared her throat. "Excellent job." She glanced around and shook her head. "Let's clean this up."

Shauna was waiting for him when he left the station. He spotted her leaning against the blue secondhand truck parked across the street. He hadn't taken her to the station, introduced her to his friends, hadn't been ready. Still wasn't.

He slipped his keys into his pocket, walked to her and straight into her arms. She felt so good. He closed his eyes and just savored the softness of her body pressing into him. The warmth of her, like the last warmth of Indian summer, steadied him, comforted him.

"I heard on the radio," she said.

"I'm glad you're here. I killed a man and I'm suspended while they investigate." He didn't open his eyes, just let her stroke his head and his back.

"I'm sorry."

"I am, too. It happened so fast. Maggie was down. I shot. He's dead."

"Is Maggie all right?" Shauna asked.

"Yeah. fine. But the guy's dead."

"Shhhhh." When was the last time someone held and comforted him? He hadn't ever wanted it, as an adult. But he needed her arms around him, her gentle touch. Too much had brought back his childhood today, and maybe it was the ghost of the old child that wanted her so. He breathed in her scent and the residual adrenaline transformed his need for comfort into something more basic. No, it was the man who wanted her. Now.

She shifted against him, hesitated, kissed the side of his jaw. "My place is closer."

"Yeah."

"Let's do it."

He seemed to have echoes in his head. Reluctantly he separated from her, glanced at his SUV in the station lot, and shrugged. He went to the passenger side of the truck, got in, and buckled up, then let his head fall back. He wanted Shauna's hand on his thigh, between them, but she was driving.

She gunned the motor and stamped on the gas, taking off faster and less cautiously than ever before. Jake smiled. She'd drive fast, but safe, and soon they'd be in her bed and it would be quick and hard and wild.

He reached out and put his hand above her knee. Her breath caught, but she didn't speed up. His smile widened. He hadn't fumbled, known exactly where her leg was, would always know.

They didn't make it to her waterbed. They didn't even make it to the living room couch. He took her on the floor with no finesse but all the need in the world.

The next morning Jake woke near dawn and stared at the pale green ceiling of Shauna's bedroom. "I've been suspended." It was standard after a killing, but nasty fear that he wasn't good enough nibbled at him.

She moved closer, pillowing her head on his shoulder, stroking his chest. The tightness around his heart eased.

"I'm sorry," she said. "I know how much your vocation means to you."

Vocation. Yeah. Trust Shauna to use the right word. Not a job. Not work. Not a career, though it was that, too. But most of all it was a vocation.

Of course she spoke of her own work as a "calling," or even worse, her "bliss." No one would ever say police work was "bliss," but he could agree that it was a calling, a vocation.

"So." Shauna ran her thumb along the side of his jaw, and he looked at her—pleasantly mussed from their loving, lips slightly puffy from his wild kisses. He rolled onto his side and caressed her smooth skin from her waist to the curve of her hip.

"So, what?"

"So, how would you like to help me plant four apple trees today and about three hundred bulbs the rest of this week?"

He thought of digging, of young trees that he could circle with his hand, of bulbs that would sit in his palm and, with their very being, show him promise of new life. "Yeah."

She sighed and snuggled closer. "It will be good for you to think of planting and growing and flowers in the spring."

Inside himself wonder bloomed. He was unable to express it, couldn't tell her how incredible he found her. So he slipped again into her body and showed her.

Jake weathered the hurt of suspension very well, with the support of Shauna, Maggie, his buddies in the force, Boris, and the Friends of the Forest at Sunday meditation. Even the feral cat crept nearer to take the food he offered every night.

The shooting was investigated and he was exonerated in record time. After the meeting, he was informed he was expected to be back at his desk the next day. On a bubble of happiness, Jake leaned against his SUV, pulled out his cell, and made enough indecent suggestions to have Shauna breathing heavily in his ear. She promised to meet him at her home.

This time they made it into her bed and bounced around it in cheerful passion.

After her pulse slowed and her breathing steadied, Shauna stroked his chest and looked into his fabulous blue eyes and said, "I love you."

"You don't mean it."

Shauna's temper broke. She jumped out of bed and stalked around the room. "At least you finally said it out loud. Every time I've said I loved you, you always changed the subject or started making love to me, or did anything except believe me."

Jake stared at her.

"What, you didn't think I had a temper? That I was too Goody Two-shoes and too Ms. New Age to think I couldn't get angry? Or is it that you think I'm just too much of a wimp?"

"No, I—"

"Too much of a wimp to get angry, then it would follow that I'm too mushy or whatever you'd call it in your macho-speak, to be in love with you. I'm just acting girly or have blinders on or think that since the sex is so great it has to mean I love you. Is that what you're telling yourself about me and my declarations of love?"

"Yes. No! Geeze." Jake rubbed his face.

She looked at him, lip curled. "You have a low opinion of me. Because I tend to think the best of people, because I try to be kind, because I experiment with different kinds of spirituality, you think I'm nuts, or stupid, or naive. That I don't know my mind." She thumped a fist on her heart. "I *love* you. I'm a mature woman. I've had other lovers, other men friends. I know what I've felt in other relationships, and I know what I feel now. I know how I love my friends and even my blessed cats! But you don't think I know my mind about you."

Now she stamped back close enough to drill a hole in his chest with her forefinger. "Just because you're too much of a coward to open your eyes and see I love you, to listen when I tell you, doesn't mean that it isn't true."

Jake shot out of bed and dressed. "I'm not the one in this relationship who's the coward. You made this house a home so comforting that you'd never have to leave it, risk yourself."

"Maybe I did, once, but not since I died and came

back. Not since we died and came back. I put this house on the line, mortgaged it to the hilt to found my new business—if that isn't risky, I don't know what is."

He could only shake his head. "You're making a go of the business; not a chance it will fail."

She was torn between pride and despair.

"You keep ignoring that we both died and came back for a second chance. It's a simple fact that you should deal with since you're a police officer."

"I haven't ignored it. I just don't want to talk about it. You think that just because some guy in a gray suit in a shabby office said we belonged together, that we do. That love is everything."

She straightened her back. "First of all, it was an angel in a magical grove. As for love being everything— yes, I do believe that. And I don't think that belief is anything anyone can call 'New Age.' It's been around for centuries."

"It's bullshit."

"Is it? Is that why we're arguing? If it were bullshit, if you didn't want to believe that I love you and I know the meaning of love, why are you so angry?"

"I don't want you falling for me. Getting expectations of being soulmates or something like the guy said."

It was true she had all the expectations of him in the world, but she wasn't going to say so. But she also knew that if he believed in their relationship, he'd work hard at it and they'd have a partnership that was loving and long-term and *special*. He obviously wasn't ready to hear that, either.

So she said, "My heart, my expectations, and my beliefs are mine. I can accept my feelings and the consequences that come with them."

He shifted. "Relationship-speak."

"And only women talk about relationships? You've been good with me, and Maggie, but I got the idea that you didn't always think much of women."

"Geeze, don't turn this back on me. Women can do as much as a man. They just tend to have screwy beliefs."

"Some women tend to have screwy beliefs." Tears clogged her throat, and her lips were pinching together as she tried to control her voice. "Namely me. You think I tend to have screwy beliefs and one of those screwy beliefs is that I love you. Well, *I* think that you can't accept you're lovable. We've circled around to the start of this argument and nothing's been resolved. Resolve it, Jake."

He stood straight and still and looked angry and absolutely beautiful and stared at her for a full minute. She was sick with an apprehension of doom.

"I'll resolve it. I'm outta here." He turned, grabbed his overnight bag—he'd never left anything of his in her house, as if her home would contaminate it—and marched out.

Out of her life. She sank down onto the bed and put her face in her hands. She'd done what was right, though. She'd never been dishonest, had told him she loved him when she needed to. Just now she'd confronted him. She hadn't waited and hoped. She hadn't manipulated.

She'd lost. She hurt like she'd been broken in two,

and all the glorious love and shining hope had trickled away like sand.

She sat there a long time, until Jimbo came and sat on her feet. Until Prima came and gave her cheek a lick, then whined for food.

When she rose, she moved like an old woman and envisioned a flashing image of herself alone forever in the house with cats. She straightened. She had her business. Keeping that going would work her hard and take her out of the house. She still had the same friends she'd had before Jake. With an awful feeling in her stomach that she would now always divide her life into "Before Jake" and "After Jake," she opened cans of food and dumped them on plates.

Jake worked out in the gym until exhaustion glazed his vision, then showered and went home to fall onto his bed in the twilight, one aching mass. The inner emptiness in his chest hurt the worst.

With a *whoosh,* Boris zoomed in, landing with a thump beside Jake. He didn't take the arm from his eyes. "Why are you here?" He heard Boris slurp. Probably licking his paw.

"It's dinnertime."

Jake grunted.

Boris started purring in his engine-like voice.

Lowering his arm, Jake looked at the cat. A golden outline surrounded him. One wing-tip was being studied in approval.

"If you are stupid enough to lose Shauna, then you need Me. I will stay with you and be your companion until you go back to Shauna."

"Doesn't Shauna need you, too?" Saying her name was hard.

"She hurts as much as you," Boris admitted.

Not possible.

"But she has the other Cats. You only have Me. What's for dinner?"

Jake sat up. "You're going to hang around and nag me to go back to Shauna. I get it."

"You are not too stupid. I think you will see things the right way soon."

When Jake stood his thighs protested. But he rubbed a hand over his chest where it hurt more.

He dumped out food for Boris. After the cat was done sniffing it, Jake put the plate outside. He saw the brindled, scraggly cat huddling behind the thorns of the overgrown rosebush, watching the food with lambent eyes. Maybe—

"It will take a long time for him to trust you; maybe he never will. He is old for a feral Cat. He is three."

Grief twisted in Jake and he shoved it aside. Stupid to grieve for a cat. For himself.

At work the next day Jake fiddled with his pen, until he realized that he was doing that bastard Gray's trick. Then Jake wondered how his score sheet looked now. How many little square boxes were checked. If suffering gave him brownie points, he should be damn near perfect. Yet he thought one big box might still be blank. The love and loving and lovableness thing.

He wondered about Shauna's. Were hers full now? Had he been good for her?

Boris glided through the window and lit on his desk, fluttering papers.

"Draft in here," said Maggie.

Boris grinned. "You were the best thing ever to happen to Shauna. She pines for you."

Jake ignored the cat, the twinge of hope that expanded his heart, picked up his notebook, and left to work a case.

Seven

❧

All that week and through the weekend, when he wasn't distracting himself with long hours at his job, he thought of Shauna's words. Her simple, incomprehensible words, which had been impossible for him to answer: "I love you."

How could she? How could she know after so short a time? How could anyone know, *ever*? And how could she love *him*? He'd been better with her than with any woman—any person—in all of his life, but that didn't mean he didn't know his own enormous flaws.

He was a good cop. Once—before—he would have said he was a good enough man. But ever since he'd escaped death, he'd been reconsidering what he'd thought was a good man, and he hadn't measured up. He was working on it, sort of like one of Shauna's brand-new gardens: He thought he had good seeds in him, and some strong roots, but he still was far too barren. A long time would pass until he could show a good crop of anything except weeds.

Boris gave a long slurp and burp. The food in the can on the floor had lost a little color and odor, but the feral cat would gulp it down. Jake shoved the plate outside, closed the door, grabbed a beer, and stumped back to his recliner.

Boris trotted into the living room, rose vertically to the arm of the recliner without even flapping his wings, and burped again.

"It's Monday night. Time for football!" Boris purred, eyes gleaming. "Turn on the TV!"

"The Broncos aren't playing," Jake said, taking a swallow of cold beer that seemed flat. Everything seemed flat since he'd broken up with Shauna.

The cat snorted. "Doesn't matter, I loooove football."

Jake usually liked to watch all the games, too. He had a problem with the recliner, though, recalling how wonderful Shauna had looked, how fabulous she'd felt raising and lowering herself on him.

With a flick of the remote, Jake turned the game on. The teams were running onto the field. He looked at Boris, whose gaze was glued to the tube. "What happened to your crown and temple and Road of Great Adventure?"

Boris's back moved in a cat shrug. "They wait."

Everything in Jake sharpened. "What do you mean, they wait? Did you earn them?"

Boris slid green cat eyes in Jake's direction. "Yesss."

"So why aren't you there!"

Turning his head, Boris leveled a gaze at Jake. "You need Me here."

"Not so much to make you stay with me when you could have what you really want."

"Verrrry good." Boris twitched his whiskers. "You *are* growing. You think of Me more than yourself."

Jake shifted in the recliner, shrugged. "Yeah, well, I know how much you loved the idea of your crown and temple and Road of Great Adventure."

With one of those uncannily wide grins, Boris said, "I grew, too, putting your needs before My own. Because I love you."

Beer spewed from Jake. He coughed. His eyes watered. "You—uh—love me?"

Boris wrinkled his nose at the pungent odor of beer coating Jake's shirt and droplets on the arm of the recliner. They both ignored cheers coming from the TV at a touchdown. Boris beamed, for the first time looking a little angelic. "Yesssss, I love you. You are a good man. You are worthy of love."

Jake's vision clouded. He couldn't explain the emotions flooding him. He barely understood them. He wiped his mouth on his shirtsleeve. "You—you—you *love* me?"

"Like Shauna does." Boris turned back to the TV. "Maybe not like Shauna. She loves you like a human. I love you like a Cat. I have grown, too, and you love Me. I have *always* been worthy of love, but it took you time to learn that."

Flopping back on the recliner, Jake guzzled some more beer. He had to really think about this.

The next couple of days he continued to wear himself

out exercising at the gym, but no answers came. Finally he picked up the telephone and called Mrs. Freuhauff, requesting some private thinking time in the Friends of the Forest glen the next evening.

Mrs. Freuhauff made some pointed comments about how both he and Shauna looked terrible lately, gestured to a stone chair that seemed more a piece of modern art to Jake, and left him in peace.

The seat was unexpectedly comfortable.

He surveyed the glen, truly appreciating the beauty of the surroundings. There was green, but also many layered colors of autumn that soothed his soul. Nature. Peace. Somehow one had become the equivalent of the other. To the old Jake, peace had meant a nice soft bed and pillows. Or the peace of unthinking exhaustion after a workout.

But he had felt uneasy in his bed since he'd broken off with Shauna, and the workouts hadn't helped.

Now he'd learned to still his mind. Meditate, he guessed. He closed his eyes and breathed deeply. Scents of fall, of leaves about to turn tickled his nose. Another long inhale—the only sound was his soft breathing.

His mind fell into calm rhythms. He opened his eyes and let them rest on the pretty scenery. A little path led away from the copse, overgrown with ferns. Not at all like the wide, golden Road of Adventure Boris had always projected. Jake smiled.

As his mind settled, he was able to separate his feelings from his thinking. He wasn't a loser like his parents—like the guy who'd shot him or the man he'd killed.

Looking at it logically, he'd made a great success of his life—especially lately. He'd had it all. A promotion, a rising career, the respect of others—

"A Cat," Boris said, appearing on a thick branch above him and to his right. "Two Cats, counting the feral."

Jake ignored him. Most of all, he'd had a loving woman.

Shauna loved him. She'd said it several times and he'd thrust it away, uncomfortable with the feelings that little phrase engendered. Gray had been right. Deep down he didn't think he could be loved, because the losers in his life hadn't loved him.

But he was a *success*. Shauna was a success. They were good people. Strong people, emotionally.

"And spiritually," Boris pointed out helpfully.

Jake winced.

"Of course you are human and not as superior as Cats, but you are good for humans."

"Thanks a lot," Jake panted.

They were loving people. Shauna loved him. If Shauna loved him, he must be lovable. A simple, logical syllogism that his feelings had stopped him from seeing before. His heart lightened.

"Not as lovable as Me," Boris said. "But you will do for her since I will be gone on My Road of Great Adventure."

"Will you shut up, Boris?" Jake asked. "You can't be seen. You don't exist."

Boris snorted. "Like love. Can't see it, so it doesn't exist."

"Wrong," Jake said and stood. Conversation with Boris wasn't conducive to good meditation. He needed to let the conclusions he'd come to simmer, make sure they were right. His mind said so, but he wanted them to feel good in his gut in the morning. If they did, he'd take the next irrevocable step that would change his life forever.

Shauna lay in bed, Prima on one side of her, Jimbo on the other. The nights were getting colder, and the cats liked the warmth of the bed and her.

She missed Jake's warmth. Her body was hot and throbbing and aching for Jake's hands and mouth. She wanted him with every fiber. Had she been stupid in thinking they were meant to be? She shook her head. She *knew* he was the only one for her. She was absolutely sure that she could fulfill him like no other woman in his life—if he ever let another woman into his life as much as he'd allowed her in.

Was she delusional, one of those poor, pitiful women who couldn't give up on a man? Couldn't see that the whole relationship was bad?

She thought and felt and moaned and thought some more until her brain ached. Finally it simply came down to the fact that she had died. She'd died and met Jake and Boris in the Atrium, and the luminescent angel had told her that they were mates.

The angel said Jake, that stubborn son-of-a-gun, had free will to break her heart and his own. She wondered if Jake suffered. She really hoped so.

The angel had also scolded her for not taking risks. Not accepting the greatest challenge life had given her. At the time she'd thought it was not believing in herself, not taking the chance on her business. That had been her greatest flaw, not taking risks, always following the secure path.

Since coming back, she'd tried to change. She'd started the business, put herself out to find clients, do advertising and promotion far outside her comfort zone. And the business had taken off, would show a profit this year, and she had a solid schedule set up all next spring. She'd won in that area of her life.

On a personal level she'd risked her heart with Jake. She swiped away tears. She'd been herself, not hiding her idiosyncrasies, and unwilling to accept less than she wanted, less than she was sure he could give her. She'd rushed him, but she had needed the commitment.

She'd lost.

Or had she given up? Was this one more challenge that she should rise above? One more life problem that she could face and solve? If she risked again.

She wanted Jake, the life they could have together, the children they could make. Was she going to let it go?

She would have if it hadn't been for that time in the Atrium. She believed in the angel, what he had said. She believed in herself and in Jake and her love for him. She believed Jake was close to loving her.

One more time. She'd try one last time to convince him that she loved him, then suck up the hurt and the rejection and get on with her life. In any event, she would have tried her hardest. Knowing that, she could find some measure of peace.

· · ·

After a night of tossing and turning, Jake rose and dressed carefully. He went to his bedroom closet and reached up to a shoebox he'd stashed on a shelf many years ago. The little, dark green velvet jewelry box that held the ring wasn't even dusty.

It had been his father's mother's engagement ring and had come to Jake on his dad's death. He'd heard his grandfather and grandmother had been very much in love. They certainly had died together, sailing on a small boat back East, when his dad had been a kid. Maybe there was some tradition of love in his family after all. He flipped it open and studied the square-cut emerald. The stone wasn't big, but it had a deep, rich color.

"Shauna will like that," Boris said in great satisfaction.

For Jake, holding the box in his hand was like holding his future. He wanted Shauna so much.

The doorbell rang and he stuffed the box in his jeans pocket.

"A present!" Boris called.

When Jake walked into the living room, the cat hovered near the door, wings quivering with excitement. Jake checked the peephole only to see a huge mass of flowers, then opened the door.

"Jake Forbes?" asked a man's voice.

"That's me."

With a grunt, the guy shoved the three-foot vase at Jake. "Flowers."

Jake stared.

"Take 'em, will ya?"

Jake grabbed the light green vase as it tilted. It was

heavy and he grunted himself as he balanced it on the way to the kitchen, where he set it on the table.

The florist guy, round face red, wrote up a slip. "Sign here."

Jake did, but the guy didn't move.

"You give him money!" Boris said.

Duh. Like pizza delivery. Jake felt stunned. He fumbled a couple of bills from his wallet and shoved them at the man. He couldn't wait to get back to the flowers and look at them. Flowers came with a dinky card, didn't they?

"Thanks," said the guy and left.

Jake slammed the door and hurried to the kitchen.

Flowers! It was such a *female* thing to do. Leave it to Shauna to do something like send him flowers. The bouquet included leaves and grasses, and the last summer blooming flowers.

His mouth dried. What if it wasn't from Shauna? Nonsense, it had to be. She worked with flowers, after all. And he hadn't been seeing anyone else.

No one had ever sent him flowers. It had to be Shauna.

Had to be. His heart started pounding.

The angel cat had already retrieved the card and circled the room with the little white square in his mouth.

"Give it to me, now!" Jake ordered.

A tiny envelope fell into his outstretched palm. Jake was glad angel cats didn't slobber. With trembling fingers he pulled out the little card. "I love you, Shauna." Her handwriting, big loops, slanted upward. His head went dizzy and he let the note fall to the table.

Shauna loved him. Still. She put it in writing. Somehow that made it all the more real. In writing.

He snatched up the card again and scrutinized it. Turquoise metallic ink. Only Shauna. He hadn't been able to forget her, probably never would. He'd had no wish to see any other woman.

He had to have her. But he also intended to do this scenario right. He picked up the phone and called Mrs. Freuhauff at her Cherry Hill estate.

An hour later, all his plans rolling along, he left his condo.

As he drove away, he was unsurprised when yellow aspen leaves whisked across his windshield, even though there were no aspen around. Some of the weight lifted from his heart.

Jake found Shauna sitting on the iron bench in the middle of the clearing. The whole place was beautiful, but it was Shauna who made his heart clutch. He touched the little box in his right trousers pocket, Shauna's little flower card in his left. Good-luck charms. Talismans, the dreamy-minded like Shauna would call them, and boy, did he feel better for having them.

She looked sad and he knew it was his doing and his breathing tightened. He hadn't ever wanted to cause her pain, but he had, maybe as much as the suffering he'd done himself, though he didn't think that was possible.

Just watching her was a pleasure. How he'd believed he could ever live without her, he didn't know. He'd lied to himself. But he'd lied to himself about a lot—that people wouldn't see through his charming mask, that his childhood hadn't mattered.

That Shauna didn't love him.

But she did, and he'd hold on to that truth forever.

"Shauna."

She jerked upright, stood, straightened her shoulders, and pasted a smile on her face. As she faced him, she gulped. When he walked closer, he saw behind the sadness in her gaze a desperate hope. Always hope. Yes, Shauna loved him and wanted him to love her in return.

He crowded her against the bench; he couldn't take the chance she'd run from him. He took her limp, cold hands in his. He wanted to remove the pain from her eyes, fast. "Shauna, I've been lost and lonely without you. Will you marry me? I'll work hard to make a good marriage with you."

Shauna could hardly believe Jake was standing here. Her ears rang. She thought she'd heard him propose. Marriage.

"What?" She tugged at her hands, but he didn't let them go. She couldn't think with him so close, could barely breathe.

His face tightened. He pressed his lips together, squeezed her hands until they hurt, and repeated: "Marry me, Shauna. I don't want to live without you." He thought back to their argument. "Believing in love isn't screwy. You don't have screwy beliefs, and I am l-lo—" He swallowed. "Loveable."

Shauna thought he sure had trouble with the L word. What he said wasn't quite enough, but it was a start, and the tenderness in his eyes took her breath. She'd never seen him so open, so vulnerable, so looking as if he might love her.

She licked her lips. "Yes."

When he put the emerald on her left hand, her mind went light and her knees weak. She plopped onto the iron bench.

Jake sat beside her, still enfolding her trembling fingers with his steady ones.

They sat a moment in silence, breathing together, holding hands, letting the sun filter through the trees, now bright with autumn color. Connected. She tried to think, but she could only feel an incredible, huge bubble of happiness.

He eyed the beautiful clearing around them. "This place would be perfect for a wedding."

"I think so, too. Mrs. Freuhauff would love to host it." Shauna laughed. "Denver's finest and the Friends of the Forest. What a mix."

He squeezed her hand and met her smile with a grin of his own. "Should be interesting to watch."

A shaft of light hit their feet and a triumphant growl followed. They both looked up.

"My God," Shauna gasped at the sight of a window opening in the clouds to a different place, with Boris.

"Don't give him delusions of grandeur," Jake said. "He already has enough."

The scene focused and magnified. Boris trotted through a marble temple of Greek columns, a small many-pointed gold crown on his head, tilted over one ear.

Jake gave a crack of laughter. "Must be a pretty light crown, maybe gold paper. Think they got it from a fast-food place?"

Now Shauna did the hand squeeze and leaned against him to whisper. "It's a *magic* crown."

Boris stopped. Sniffed. Looked down at them. Then he grinned. "You look good together. You love each other." He lifted his nose. "I have done very well."

Shauna coughed, covering a laugh. "I can see that."

"You will both do well, also." He scowled. "Jake, do not forget the feral Cat. Good-bye, Shauna. Good-bye, Jake."

Tears came to Shauna's eyes. She let them flow over and trickle down her cheeks. "Good-bye, Boris. Until we meet again."

"Oh, boy," Jake muttered.

Boris nodded, and his crown slipped from one ear to the other. "We will meet again someday, on this side of the doors." He smirked at Jake. "I have made sure they are good doors for you to go through here. Mostly. Now I must go on My Road of Great Adventure." With another nod, he trotted down stairs and onto a wide, dusty dirt track, on his cat business. The window closed.

"Looks like the temple got boring real quick," Jake said.

Shauna sniffled.

Jake raised their joined hands and kissed her fingers above the engagement ring. "You okay?"

"Yes. I love him. I love you."

Jake smiled one of the lopsided smiles that tugged at her heart. His eyes held only a few shadows. His vocation would bring more, some she and their love could vanquish, some that would stay, but they would face that together.

She pulled her hand from his to frame his face, stroke his beloved face. "But Boris is wrong, you know."

Jake pretended stunned amazement. "Boris wrong? How could that be?"

The last of her tears dried. "We're the ones on the Road of Great Adventure—love, marriage, children. It may get rocky, but we'll travel it together."

Jake's eyes softened. "You're right. I love you, Shauna, and always will." He stood and pulled her up, grabbing her hand.

A whirl of golden aspen leaves encircled them for a moment like a blessing, then blew away.

"I guess we made the grade," Jake said.

"I guess we did." Shauna smiled.

"Our road waits. Let's go!" Jake linked hands with her and they walked into their future together.

USA Today bestselling author

REBECCA YORK

Crimson Moon

Needing a fresh start, a young werewolf
heads west and changes his identity. As Sam
Morgan, he meets Olivia Woodlock, a woman
of many secrets, whose life is in jeopardy.
If he can't protect her, he'll never have a chance
to explore the passion that promises to bind
them together for eternity.

0-425-19995-9

"Rebecca York's writing is fast-paced,
suspensful, and loaded with tension."
—Jayne Ann Krentz

"A true master of intrigue."
—*Rave Reviews*

Available wherever books are sold or at
penguin.com